SONG

OF

BLOOD

AND

MIST

LORIN PETRAZILKA

FATEBOUND
BOOKS
A WOMEN-OWNED IMPRINT

Song of Blood and Mist
First Edition
Copyright 2024 Lorin Z Pillai

Published by Fatebound Books
For rights inquires, please contact rights@fateboundbooks.com

FATEBOUND�֍BOOKS

ISBN 979-8-9920575-1-5 (hardcover)
ISBN 979-8-9920575-0-8 (paperback)
Cover design by Lorin Z Pillai

*Dedicated to everyone like me,
who wants to swap out their high mental load,
bills, and taxes, for equal problems
of the magical sort instead.*

TABLE OF CONTENTS

PRONUNCIATION GUIDE

Sereia ser-EYE-ah

Brokk BROCK, Cymbrokk SIM-brock

Emblyn em-BLIN

Lily lil-EE

Neila NEEL-ah

Tyrus TIE-rus

Trachen TRAY-ken

Kerenza keh-ren-ZAH

Zia ZEE-ah

Deniza den-ih-ZAH

Rachael ray-CHEL

Maureen more-EEN

Zarneh zar-NAY

Prant PRANT

Rannoch ran-KNOCK

Syrenni sir-REN-ee

Umorfae -oo-MOR-fay

Ignisfae - Ig-NIS-fay

Petrafae - Pe-TRA-fay

Lacausia lah-COW-zee-ah

Adrilan add-RILL-an

TerraIgni tare-RAH-igg-nee

Capuli cah-pool-ee (coffee)

Bisporus bi-SPORE-us (mushroom)

Conniunx KONE-ee-uncks (spouse)

Filia fill-EE-ah (girl or daughter)

Filio fill-EE-oh (boy or son)

Linteum LIN-tee-um (wrap dress)

Magna MAG-na (great, excellent)

Mane Fare MAY-n FARE (breakfast)

Nocte Fare NOCK-tay FARE (dinner)

Bonum Mane BOH-num-MAY-n (Good Morning/Hello)

Dekkate DECK-kate (unit of measurement, inch)

Scolopendra sko-lo-PEN-drah

Bad words!

Stultus - stuhl-TUS meaning: dumbass, idiot

Faex - Fay meaning: shit

CHAPTER 1

"Sereia!" The sound of my name rippled through the air, carried on a wind I was determined to outrun.

I ignored it, picking up speed along the shore, my bare feet splashing in the ankle-deep edge of the greenish lake. I ached to run farther, to venture into the Praegra Forest, to escape the monotony and disappointment that waited for me back at the Syrenni commune on the shore of the south bank. Disappointment seemed to be the only common thread I shared with the Syrenni, aside from a few physical features. I dodged a small creature that jumped through the mud, realizing I nearly squished the poor thing out of existence. That was the last thing I wanted to do, the little ranas were my only friends that inhabited the lake. I slowed, coming to a stop as I looked to the east. I wasn't sure if there was anything for me *anywhere* in this world. Leaving the Syrenni might do me little good. I was an outcast no matter where I went. Lowering myself into the water, I let the ranas approach and held out my hand for them to jump onto my palm. I might have sobbed were I not so irritated with everything. Instead I sat and waited, trying to still myself and my raging emotions.

The water of Caer Lake lapped at the shoreline, murky silt

plumed up in small swirls around me as I adjusted my knees and pulled grasses out of the bank. Weaving the reeds always helped soothe me when I was upset. The iridescent scales of my dorsal fin shimmered, flowing with the slight tide, sometimes wrapping around my bent legs before being pulled back out to free float. Letting the to and fro of the current steady my nerves as I worked, my breathing finally leveled out. I finished weaving a tiny hat out of dried grasses, just the right size for one of the little amphibious ranas that hopped through the reeds. I dropped it onto the head of a green-and-yellow spotted one. Living at Caer Lake wasn't much of an existence, but it was peaceful for the most part. Located in the northern reaches of Alternis, our somewhat new colony was far from the Lacausia region where the Syrenni had spent nearly a millennium in unwilling servitude. But for me, the lake was all I had known. Having hatched in Lacausia, but being raised in the simple village made for the Syrenni by the Petrafae, I only knew the gentle currents that wove through the waters. My fins had never felt the tremendous rapids of Lacausia River, never jumped the falls into the churning depths near the great palace there, the pristine castle the Umorfae had previously claimed as their stronghold where they had enslaved us. I smiled in spite of that list of 'nevers' as another rana came closer. These were my friends, they didn't chastise me for being something other than a pureblood Syrenni, didn't fear me like the unmixed Syrenni did. I frowned, for as much as the Syrenni often hurt my feelings with their silent treatment, all I wanted was for them to accept me.

The sound of my caretaker, Neila, calling my name again off in the distance made my piked ears twitch. She became louder, more insistent as she approached. Neila continued calling to me until I saw her, still partially obscured by the foliage. She hadn't sighted me yet, I could make an effort to hide if I wanted. I didn't want to be found right now. I preferred to hold off returning to the common area for mane fare, I wasn't hungry anyway. But, hiding would only delay the inevitable, and I didn't want to punish Neila for the others' unkind demeanor toward me. Instead, I sat and waited as she approached.

"There you are, Sereia!" Neila tightened her shoulder wrap, the woven fabric nearly falling apart after so many cycles of use. I had offered to make her a new one, but she refused. Her shawl had been gifted to her by my maeder, who had been given it by their caretaker, Ondri. It was a prized possession of Neila's. The only other item we had inherited was the sigil of our ancient crest, the palm-sized metal disc that made shifting sounds when it was held. It was little better than a weight to keep items moored in my half-submerged room in the lake to the east. Any knowledge of what the sigil did was lost when the Taming happened, if the metal oval even did anything at all. But, with so few things passed on to us, I would always keep it, always treasure it. I imagined my maeder holding it, long before she had been killed. Holding the object my maeder once held was one anchor I could claim. I couldn't blame Neila for wanting to do the same with her shawl, besides we had no capabilities with fabric weaving. Any new fabric made its way to us from the Ignisfae, and that was only on their rare visits. Making Neila a new wrap would mean I would most likely have to weave it from the same reeds and grasses I used to make the ranas their little clothes.

"What are you doing all the way out here?" she asked as her quick glance darted around at my small friends, noting the hat that had just fallen off of the rana and rendered Neila's question unneeded.

"Waiting," I answered anyway.

"Waiting for what?"

"For *something* magna or interesting to happen in this place. I figured I would have a better chance of that away from the others."

She paused, her dark, large eyes poring over my face. "Did something happen again?"

I gave her an exasperated look. "Something *always* happens. It took all of two moments after I left my room. All I did was enter the common area. How dare I." I tossed a pebble into the water's edge.

She reached out and ran her thin webbed hand over my opal hair as I sat, caressing my head slowly. It was meant to be a comfort, but all it served to do was remind me of my physical differences from the Syrenni. My white-opal hair to their black, my piked ears to their finned, my towering height to their diminutive stature. Being the only known Syrenni mestisius, or half-breed, meant that I shared too many traits in common with the Umorfae half of my heritage. No one liked being reminded of the powerful, water-wielding race that used to lord over them, even though it had been over twenty cycles since we left Lacausia. I knew a little about the Umorfae, only what I had been told by Neila or Princess Lily of the Ignisfae, who sometimes visited the Syrenni commune.

Neila sighed. "I know it is hard, they do not yet understand what you may be capable of. I hope their fear and ignorance eventually turns to appreciation."

"Hard to imagine that happening, when they hate me even for something as small as my name." Named for their lost queen.

It was an insult to them. An affront. How could I be named after a queen when I was a filthy mestisius?

"Your name is an honor, and something they will come to respect eventually."

"My name is an abomination! I besmirch it, according to *them*. You have obligated me to something that I am only half part of. The other half a perpetrator of. Before I could swim or walk or speak, you obligated me."

Neila sighed heavily, her face looked careworn and tired.

"They do not all hate you," Neila offered. "What about Prant? You and he were together I thought?"

I groaned. "We *were*." I tossed another pebble in the lake. "It was after I pressed him for how he really felt that he admitted he didn't care for me, that it was because I had initiated the relationship that he felt compelled to be with me. It was not what he wanted. Damnatus Syrenni males and their spineless subservience." I threw yet another rock in the water, harder this time. It would have been nice to know the truth before going so far as to lie with him. And not just one time, either. The entire thing was a sham. I clenched my hands in anger, and the water responded in kind. A sudden wave lapped at the shoreline, crashing in around where I sat, coalescing in a semicircle.

I winced and looked at Neila. She pretended not to notice and looked away, though of course she had seen it. It was this exact reason the Syrenni feared me, or one of the reasons at least, whatever ability I might have had to summon water was the same as any Umorfae—although my ability was unknown and nearly dormant within me. It was an uncomfortable reminder to the Syrenni. I blew out a breath, letting go of the urge to unleash more. The truth was I rarely let my ability show, keeping it carefully tamped down to prevent what I had just done. I didn't even know how to use it with any manner of control, it only showed itself when I was upset. I *had* to leash it, keeping it in check might have been the only thing that kept the Syrenni from either killing me or ousting me.

"I am sorry about Prant, and sorry I brought it up."

"You didn't know." I thought about him again, even though I shouldn't. It had been some time since he made his feelings—or lack thereof—known. It hadn't been lies at least, it had been withheld truths, as if that were any better. He never gave any indication that it wasn't what he wanted at first, I had felt so stupid when he finally confessed he thought he had no choice. *No choice.* Syrenni males naturally bowed to their females, they would never go against what a female dictated, even if it was one they didn't actually want to mate with. What a stultus I was, so foolish. To think I had somehow bridged the gap and found a match that could see past my obvious split traits. I didn't miss him, but clearly the wounds were still there. I had avoided telling Neila when it happened, but I probably should have since I was still stewing about it however many rotations later. I hadn't counted. There was no reason to, it would only mark time since yet another poor outcome, rather than spending thought on looking toward something positive. And I was *positive* there was nothing good to come of me staying with the Syrenni any longer.

"Come, my filia, come back for mane fare."

"I'm not hungry."

"Please come, for me."

I sighed heavily. Looking up at the misty skies, their expanse of monochromatic nothingness beckoned me. I imagined free-falling through it, unencumbered by the meager existence we were scratching away at by the waterside. I ignored the call of it, the pull that offered empty promises within the formless sky. I blew out a breath, rooting myself back to the ground. Many had worked to save the Syrenni, to give them this home. Many had made the ultimate sacrifice. My maeder—Neila's sister—was one such casualty. For Neila, I would try.

The others averted their eyes as we fixed ourselves bowls of steaming food at the communal line. A thick, stew-like meal made from bisporus slid off the ladle and into my bowl. It was what we ate most often: stewed, grilled, or steamed mushroom. The Arbor Elves had helped propagate it here when we had first settled. I was only a youngling then, I didn't remember any of the passage away from the castle or the time spent acclimating to the new environment. Before they had moved here, the Syrenni never ate the meaty fungus that grew in the forest. Now, because the fish population was too easily thrown off balance by our growing numbers, it was what we ate every rotation. Fish were reserved for special occasions. I let a bite slop off my spoon, the chunks slipping with a slimy viscosity. I didn't want to eat, but I also wouldn't waste what I had been served. There was no way anyone would consider eating my leftovers, anything I touched was as good as cursed. It did mean I got to have my favorite bowl and spoon each time, even washed, the others refused to use them. I sat down next to Neila, not bothering to look at any of the Syrenni as I settled in to eat. An uncomfortable silence hung over the area. I brushed aside what I imagined their thoughts of me were as I forced down my food. The truth was, so many of them were still under the influence of the Taming, they probably didn't think as much as I worried they did. I finished my meal, then left the common area without telling Neila where I was going.

Walking always helped after a meal like that, and walking was something that wasn't as easy for the others—yet another thing that offset me from them. Though they had legs and spent a good deal of time on land, they were always stronger swimmers than they were runners. Their flowing dorsal fins, which could almost pass for diaphanous-looking dresses, were powerful once they were submerged in water. I had one as well, but it didn't reach down as far, and my lean legs had only grown longer through my formative cycles. Now, well past that growing period, I had developed strong muscles that carried me well.

I broke from a walk into a run. The trees rushed past me as I thought about all the hidden whispers, the wary glances, and the outright insults. I could keep running. I could let my legs work until I had reached another place. I desperately wanted to explore the world of Alternis and find what else might be out there. Neila had kept me sheltered all these cycles, kept me safe and loved me. But one being couldn't make up for how the rest of them were toward me. Lily had been kind to me, treated me well, and taught me sometimes, but her visits were infrequent at best. I couldn't blame her, she was a royal in the Ignisfae familia, she had responsibilities in TerraIgni and couldn't come running to me anytime I wanted. In truth I wasn't entirely ready to see her, she was who I had asked for advice about being with a male, I was too nervous to ask Neila. Lily had been open and easy about it, and had made it less uncomfortable. I wasn't ready to tell her I had completely misread his intentions. And the journey was long for her, so long that her visits were usually only twice a cycle. Three times on a rare occasion.

I stopped running, suddenly thinking over a new possibility. What if I could go there? To TerraIgni, where Lily lived. I knew I couldn't make the crossing into the Hinterdunes without the Ignisfae to ferry me, I knew that would mean instant death if I tried. Anyone without the gift of fire would perish at the boundary, crossing the expansive desert would be impossible. But if *she* were to take me there, I could survive the trek. Maybe they wouldn't accept me there either, but at least it would be different. At least I'd have a chance. There was no chance for me here, as much as Neila wished there was.

I counted on my webbed fingers the rotations since the last time I had seen her. With fourteen rotations of light, followed by fourteen of dark, it took me a few moments to figure out it had been a quarter of a cycle since Lily's last visit. It had been our time to join the circle and praise Goddess Tahia, who watches over our Faded sisters. My maeder was given a special remembrance, Lily had been invited to partake because she had known her, and because she had done so much for the Syrenni. Princess Lily had been a guest of honor. She hadn't brought the usual supplies for us back then, which would mean her visit may not be too far off, she might be due to deliver supplies soon. But, Neila hadn't wanted me to spend too much time with her previously, afraid of what I would learn about my powers, and already dismayed with how much Lily's way of speaking had impacted my own. She had let Lily teach me how to read and write, but Neila had been hesitant about Lily teaching me to wield my powers. Neila had thought it would only lessen my chances of fitting in with the Syrenni. And she was right, I wouldn't fit in if I unleashed what I might be capable of. But she wasn't right to block me from learning. If I wanted to make this work, I'd need to start subtly working on Maeder Neila.

I looked back in the direction of our settlement, and for the first time in as long as I could remember, I smiled at it. I had a plan, a possible course of action to get me away from this place. I was about to head back, when I heard the snap of a branch behind me.

CHAPTER 2

I whirled, facing the direction the sound had come from. There was no way it had been any of the Syrenni, I was too far from the lake. It could have been an Arbor Elf, but when they arrived they always appeared directly at the edge of our common area, and they always made their presence known. "Hello?" I called out. I honed my eyes to where I thought the sound came from, scanning the foliage. Though I had the same large, dark eyes as the Syrenni, mine were quick and clear. Not clouded from the Taming. I couldn't see a hint of a creature in the bramble or low-lying ferns. But I could feel them. I could somehow sense the mass of them. Different from the water in the plants, the water in their body was like a silent whisper. I couldn't tell their size or shape, though I knew someone was there.

No one answered, but my ears picked up another movement. So subtle, so quiet, but it was there. Just beyond sight and behind a tree. I tracked it for a pace, strafing and ready to run. "Who's out there?" I asked again. It was a short way off, probably far enough that I could outrun it, but I didn't know if what was there was a predator, if it was fast and ready to chase. Turning my back to it may be the last mistake I make. "Show yourself or I'll fucking come force you out!"

Another rustle. After a moment, a head emerged from behind a trunk. My breath stilled at the opal hair, just like mine. Shoulders came into view next, then the rest of a lanky body leapt into view. "Greetings!"

I lurched back at the sight of a male, now fully in front of me and a pace away from the tree he had been hiding behind.

"I did not mean to startle you," he said, reaching a hand toward me in a placating gesture. He looked me over with a wary glance, then a smile crept over his face. His eyes passed over me, taking in what he saw before him.

I had lifted my arms, prepared to fight if needed. One fist was balled and cocked back, ready to strike, the other held forward in case I had to block an attack. With a leg jutted out for balance, I stood poised for action should it come to that.

"I will not hurt you, I assure you," the male said as he lowered his hand.

"Yeah? And what are you doing creeping around this part of the Praegra Forest? No one comes here except the Arbor Elves." And he *clearly* wasn't one of them. With his hair, and gleaming, lustrous pale skin, he was undoubtedly an Umorfae. One of my faeder's kind, and though I had never known any of them, I knew them to be dangerous. Untrustworthy.

He took a step closer, at the same time I moved back an equal distance, shuffling my feet without tearing my eyes from him.

"I, ah, I realize this may seem strange, I suppose. I have traveled far and was merely looking for—can you lower your hands? I am unarmed and will not do anything." He spread his arms open then mocked a bow, perhaps intending to display that he had no visible weapons.

I still didn't lower my fists, not when someone potentially lethal was a mere stone's throw from me. He may have been acting with his seemingly cavalier, jovial performance. "And *why* have you traveled so far from Lacausia?" I demanded. "You have no business being in this territory."

"Ah so you know of Lacausia? My former home, as it were. I have been looking for a new residence. My last one became rather unbearable." He flourished a strange gesture, flicking his hand in a dismissive manner. He looked off toward the deeper forest, presumably in the direction he had come from.

"Keep looking, this one's taken," I said through gritted teeth.

"I see. May I ask who you are? How far does your region extend? That way I do not encroach into your area when I set up camp."

"Camp?" I blinked and dropped my hands. "You don't really mean to stay, do you?"

"For a little while at least, only to recover before I head to another territory. Surely there must be somewhere in this realm where I can go, some place that simply being who I was born as is not seen as inherently bad. I promise to stay out of the way until I depart. Do not worry, I do not intend to stay for long."

My membranes flashed over my eyes at his words, at the look in his eyes as he spoke. There was a familiarity in his glance, something unsettling. Being viewed as something negative, for having the audacity to exist. It was how I felt every rotation since I could remember. Something in me clicked, disarming my previous apprehension. I looked at him again, really looked. Though he came off as self-assured, and poised, his clothes were muddy and worn thin from travel. He appeared like he had been on his own for some time, with no access to things that made life easier. And no easy way to feed oneself. He was probably relegated to foraging in the forest, his lean musculature seemed to prove that he didn't have abundant food. Young for sure for a Fae, but also well past his growing cycles. Perhaps my age, even.

"No one ventures this far out," I blurted. "From my home, I mean. They keep to the lake. Stay away from the lake and you should be fine. There is a stream in that direction,"—I pointed behind him—"and stay hidden in the trees."

He sketched a bow as I started to walk backward away from him. "I shall endeavor to be a considerate temporary neighbor," he said with a charming smile.

"An *unseen* temporary neighbor," I amended. The last thing we needed was the Syrenni panicking at having an Umorfae in their midst.

An *Umorfae*. What the fuck was I thinking? This could be a disaster. He flashed one last grin before I moved out of his line of sight. I gave it another few paces, before I turned and ran back to the colony.

I laid in my bed, looking at the ceiling. Shimmering caustic patterns danced on the rough hewn rock. The small chamber—along with many others—had been formed when the Petrafae had helped the Syrenni transform the area twenty cycles prior. In spite of the tranquil, barely lit setting, sleep had yet to claim me.

I had spent the rest of the rotation trying to keep myself busy before heading to bed, but I couldn't stop thinking about that male. How close he had come to finding the others. How risky this whole situation was. Neila would have had a fit if she knew I had spoken with an Umorfae. It probably would have terrified her to no end. But, I was half Umorfae, and I knew very little about that side of myself. I flicked my fingers, feeling the shallow waters of my sleeping nook, trying to pull them gently to call them to me. As an Umorfae, he would know how to use his water ability, how to direct the water to his will. I had desperately wanted to learn, but never could explore that aspect. It would have scared the Syrenni too much, I was expected to keep it hidden. Even when Lily had asked to teach me what she knew, Neila had declined and said it had to wait until I was older. Well I was older now, and still it had yet to happen. If I wanted to know this side of me, maybe I had to take matters into my own hands. I had thought Lily might visit soon, but who knew for sure. Certainly I didn't know. And he was here now … Whoever *he* was.

Regardless of what his name was, he was an opportunity. I pushed my coverlet aside, then paddled quietly out of my room. Having the room that was furthest to the edge of our colony did have some benefits. I could slip in and out unseen. It was the least desirable location for a Syrenni, with not enough water in it to make for a proper Syran bedroom, but it was perfect for me. Being only half-blooded, I didn't need to be submerged as often as they did. They needed to return to the water every rotation, but with my physiology, I might be able to make it about ten. Though I had yet to test that theory, as I had never really left the lakeside community. It was a natural choice to designate it as my room, and probably a plus for them that it meant I was further away from the others. Yet another tick in the counter that measured the ways they pushed me away.

I slid silently out of my room, moving toward the bright diffuse light of the outside air. The light to dark cycle had still not reached its zenith, it would be another ten rotations of light before the dark phase. Plenty of time with the relative safety of light to seek out the Umorfae, at least to test the waters with him. To see if he could teach me. Or rather, if he *would* teach me. There was also the chance he'd do something nefarious instead, but so far I hadn't gleaned that he actually was as ruthless as rumor of his kind would have me believe. After all, how can we know someone in an instant? Anyone, of any race in Alternis, is complex. Many sides to make the whole. Sure, he *may* be bad, he was born into a notoriously problematic race. But was it fair to assume so much about him? I'd never know if I didn't try. And I might learn what I hoped in the process. Or, I might find a way out of here. Either chance was worth the risk to me.

I made it to the lakeshore, then looked over my shoulder to the wall within the lake which descended down into the lake floor, its serpentine shape mirroring the shoreline. Not one face peered out from the myriad of sleeping caverns that were carved out of the vertical space. Neila's room was near my own, one level down, and there was no sign of disturbance, not one ripple out of place. I crooked a small smile at the ease of my departure, then noted to myself how long I probably had before it would be noticed I was missing. With the Syrenni only having recently gone to sleep, I would have at least one-quarter rotation. Plenty of time to get there and back.

I turned to face the direction I had left the Umorfae, to the west, with the bright spot in the sky still to the east. I nodded to myself, ready to make this trek toward diverting my future, like water finding the path of least resistance.

20

CHAPTER 3

"What *is* all of this?" I demanded as I looked at the contraptions the Umorfae had built. "This doesn't look like a temporary stay at all." It hadn't taken much wandering to find his camp in the forest near where I had last seen him, he had selected a location right next to the stream I had mentioned to him. Then he had apparently decided to begin construction on a homestead.

"Oh come now, it is not *that* much! It all has a purpose, look here," he said, pointing to a rope system that threaded up into the trees, "this can help you ascend to the platform easily." He cranked the rope, lowering a narrow plank to the ground. "You step on it, then raise yourself with ease. And this,"—he motioned to another mess of ropes that went into the stream—"catches fish."

I frowned. "We have to be careful with how much fish we eat in the area, my people only eat the ones from the lake on rare occasions because of it."

"Well they are plentiful here! I have only caught a few, but I can tell you there are a great many. It is the best I have eaten in some time. Come, I will show you."

He opened an arm, guiding me toward a spot nearby that had what looked like a place to sit down. I held back, unsure that I should be following him into his camp further. He noticed my hesitation, then encouraged me with another wave of his arm. I sighed and relented at last. "I promise, you will like this," he said with a smile.

I glanced around again, noting what he had set up as a makeshift culina area, where he could cook meals. A low fire pit had been dug into the ground and steadily burned with a soft crackle. "Seriously though, how did you put this whole camp together so quickly? I was only gone for less than a half-rotation."

He arranged a log for me to sit on, then motioned to it as he said, "I had all of the rope, I have built and rebuilt this camp in every place I have stopped. So, I have gotten faster at it." He settled himself on the other log, then reached over to one of the steaming, wrapped bundles that had been placed on a flat rock near the center of the flame. He passed it back and forth between his hands quickly, trying to avoid being burned by it. Unfolding the packet, I saw he had taken a large leaf, then bound up the fish to cook it over the fire.

He glanced up at me, still hovering at the edge of the culina. I rolled my eyes and sat down at last, while he reached for the other wrapped fish still in the fire. "I took rope and nets when I left Lacausia, and figured I would find what else I needed when I stopped for rest. Sometimes I would not go through the trouble of building the whole camp, and other times I would. I also brought a good blade that is fast at cutting branches. So really, it is about doing things in the right order. Set up the nets to catch something, then build the fire ring and fire, then the rest of the culina around the fire pit. If I caught anything, then I would prepare the meal to cook, once in the fire, I would work on the sleeping area. I found it too uncomfortable to sleep on the ground, so I devised ways to elevate myself into the trees." He pointed up to the platform anchored into the crook of a large tree.

With both packets unfolded, he handed one to me. I sniffed it uncertainly, though I had to admit my mouth was already watering at the sight of it. White and flaky, with something sprinkled on top that smelled spicy, I had a hard time not outright gobbling it down. It had been so long since I had any fish, and we didn't prepare it this way. Our way wasn't bad, but it *was* bland. It didn't have nearly the same rich smell that wafted out of these filets.

He took a bite, using the leaf as a plate held below. "Try it," he encouraged.

Oh, fine. If he wanted to kill me he could have easily done it already. There was probably only a small chance it was poisoned. Probably.

I took a bite, and it tasted even better than it smelled. I closed my eyes, focusing on it, savoring it. I opened my eyes, realizing that he was staring at me. "It's really good," I managed to get out. "I haven't had anything like it. Are you always able to catch something in your nets?"

He huffed a laugh. "Sadly, no. I am not the best hunter. I have caught some things here and there, but never enough to keep me fed often."

"I figured as much," I said after I finished another bite.

He laughed and slapped his leg, almost losing the bite he had just taken. "Is that so?" He chuckled again, managing to get the food in his mouth down at last. "You are not afraid to say whatever crosses your mind, are you?"

My skin went cold as I dropped my jaw. "I didn't think about what I was saying, I just meant I thought you looked … lean. I had thought you might not get to eat often."

"Perceptive then, too." He winked, then waved a hand to dismiss my worried expression. "I am not offended, I thought it was funny. Where I lived no one would say that to me. There was always too much preening and posturing. No one ever says what they actually think there."

"Is that why you left?"

He stilled as he held his leaf, the fish cradled carefully inside it. Everything seemed to stop as he looked at me. Even the air. Nothing moved as he peered at me. "I had a lot of reasons for leaving. I was in search of something. A different life. Just, searching for something different."

The corner of my mouth turned down at his vague answer, and yet it felt all too familiar. *Looking for a different life.* He set his leaf-plate down, then picked up a cup that fit easily into one hand. Reaching out his other hand toward the river, he opened his palm, then with a quick motion he curled his fingers toward himself. A narrow bead of water funneled out of the stream, coursing through the air in a thin line, which he directed into the cup. I watched intently as he finished filling his glass, then he cut the stream off and let the remainder return to the source. It was such an easy, natural motion, like he barely thought about it.

"I want to make a deal with you," I said, causing him to pause before he took a drink from his now-filled cup.

"Oh? This sounds interesting already." He motioned for me to proceed.

"I have been wanting to learn to use my ability, but I have no one to teach me how to use it, not here at least. I want you to show me."

"I only know how to manipulate water, that is the limit of my skill."

I nodded once and didn't elaborate, letting it silently settle that water was the skill I was referring to. His eyes rounded.

"So you are an Umorfae?" His eyes sparkled as he asked. "I thought that might be the case, but I was not sure, you look … different."

"I am half Syrenni," I said as I sat up a little taller.

He rubbed his jaw. "Yes, I see it now. This is surprising, to say the least. I did not know what one would look like, I have never seen a mestisius like you."

"Like it's a bad thing?" I lowered my brows and folded my arms.

"No, I did not mean that. Just unknown to me. I have not even seen a Syrenni since I was six cycles old, so I barely remember what they look like. I remember black hair, and they were not very tall."

"So you're twenty-six cycles old."

"Twenty-seven."

"Then you must remember the forced Syrenni servitude."

"Not really. I mean, yes, a little. We had one caretaker whom I was very fond of. She was kind, and then she was gone. I knew only that … they left. Do you remember it?"

"I was there, just a babe, hatched shortly before the end of the enslavement. I don't remember anything."

He gazed at me, silent and unreadable. Finally he said, "For what was done to the Syrenni, I am sorry."

I frowned. Such a weight we carried. The choices of our

ancestors had been forced upon each of us. Were we responsible to carry on our predecessors inflicted trauma? To breed that hate for generations? I could hate him simply for being an Umorfae, for being one of *them*. After all, my maeder was killed by one of them. But I was half them, did that make me half responsible for what they had done to the Syrenni? I said nothing in response, but nodded my acknowledgement. I couldn't brush aside what had transpired, couldn't accept his apology and then forgive. I could no more forgive an entire race than he could give a proper apology for them. I decided we were best off to leave those issues where we had left them for now: in the past, in Lacausia.

His expression lightened entirely. "So, about your deal. What were you intending?"

"What?"

"You mentioned a deal if I taught you, what did you mean by that?"

"Right. I will help you stay hidden here, for as long as you want to stay."

"I see. So you would overlook your discomfort and disdain of my proximity in order to learn to wield your supposed water ability," he supplied.

I rolled my eyes. "It wasn't so much my discomfort, my concerns were for the Syrenni in general and how they would feel at having an Umorfae close by. But, then I decided if they didn't know, they would be fine, they'd be none the wiser. And there is the issue of me being half Umorfae, and having no one in my colony to guide me in that respect. It seemed like a logical fit. You were looking for a place to stay, I am looking to learn my limits."

"Magna, discomfort handled, but disdain, that is another

issue." His eyes dance at me as a smile curled up at the corners of his mouth.

I crinkled my nose at him, taking a moment to process what he said. "Was that a joke?"

He grinned and nodded.

I laughed and shook my head. "And here I was thinking most Fae didn't understand humor."

"I am not like most Fae, well, most Umorfae at least."

Different, I said to myself. I brushed that thought aside and kept a placid look on my face. "We'll see about that. What do I call you then, Umorfae who is not like most Umorfae?"

"Cymbrokk."

"Sim-brock," I repeated slowly. "Unusual name for an Umorfae."

"As I said, I am not like most. You can call me Brokk, I prefer it. And what shall I call you, fair Syrenni-Umorfae?"

I had always heard to be careful giving your name to a Fae. Them knowing your name could give them power over you. But, I had known other Fae who knew me, Kerenza and Rannoch of the Ignisfae were two such individuals. They had never made me worry or question. Cymbrokk was taking a small leap to trust me, I would do the same. "Sereia," I said without deliberating further.

28

CHAPTER 4

Finally back in my bed, I smiled to myself as I nestled into my woven coverlet a little further. I had set a plan with Brokk, every rotation we would meet. He would teach me to expand and control my abilities, and I would help keep him hidden there, as well as bring him bisporus. I had made him promise that he wouldn't eat too much fish, and would add the meaty mushroom to his diet. The bisporus grew fast, it wouldn't be noticed if I portioned some off for him after each mane fare. But, I'd have to collect fresh ones on my way to see him, then teach him how to cook it. Taking it from the already cooked stock *would* be noticed, and I had to be careful not to do anything that would raise suspicions. I needed to keep it hidden long enough for me to learn what I needed. Once I had developed some skill, I could consider leaving, then make my way to finding a place where I belonged. Where I wouldn't be constantly frowned upon.

"Why are you grunting like that?"

"Because I'm trying!" I shouted at Cymbrokk. We had been training for what felt like a full rotation, though I knew it hadn't been *that* long. I would have had to head back already if that were the case. The lack of progress definitely made it feel like it was taking ages. We stood by the waterside of the gentle stream near his camp. I had been trying to pull up a small amount of water, just enough to form a sphere with my hands. I had only been able to get the surface wobbling. I hadn't been able to get even a single drop to release off the surface.

He studied me for a moment, with a calm, appraising demeanor. "We should take a break."

"I want to keep trying," I insisted. His relaxed attitude made me even more annoyed.

"You have been trying too hard, I think that is the problem. Come, I will make you something to drink."

"*Fine.*" I motioned with an abrupt chop of my hand to lead the way.

He gave me that obnoxious, charming smile again before he turned to head toward the makeshift culina. "Some capuli will do wonders, I think."

"What is that?" I asked as I picked a path through the sticks and brambles.

"You mean to tell me you have never had capuli?" He looked over his shoulder at me, and I shook my head "no". Brokk smiled again before turning back to face where he was walking, and damn if I wasn't ready to smack him for that dumb grin.

"Is that funny or something? Maybe capuli is only found in Lacausia."

He stopped walking and turned to me again with his jaw

dropped. "Could that be true? I hope not! I have never left Lacausia before, so I do not know. I had never even considered it!" He rubbed his chin. "I would hate to return to Lacausia just for capuli."

"You'd go all the way back there just for that? It's that good?"

"Well, I enjoy it." He shrugged as he turned back toward camp.

It wasn't too long until he was pouring me a steaming cup of a rich, deep brown brew. I sniffed it carefully. "It almost smells like our hot drink we make from dried bisporus. We drink it with mane fare."

Brokk gagged and looked horrified. "Made from those mushrooms?" He wrinkled his nose.

"It's actually pretty good, it doesn't sound like it would be, but it is. Maybe it could be a fair alternative if you can't find more of this capuli," I said as I swirled my cup, watching the contents spin. I took a sip at last, which he watched with interest.

"Well?"

"I'm still tasting it!" I exclaimed, but I couldn't hide my smile. "Okay, it is really magna."

"See. Capuli is the *best*. Some like to drink vinirubrum or vocafortis, but not me. Those make you too soft, or even inebriated. They make you feel off. Capuli makes you *sharp*. It is made from small red beans that grow on dense bushes, they are roasted, then ground down."

"Oh! Red beans! I think I know what those are. They do grow here."

"Thank the gods! I was carefully portioning to make mine last."

I took another sip, mulling over things he had mentioned before about the supplies that he brought. "So wait, let me get this straight. You left Lacausia with rope, a sword, and capuli? Kind of a strange selection, don't you think?"

"I also brought some food—which of course did not last long—and some other items. These cups, for example. The pot to boil water. A bed roll. And I could not go anywhere without parchment and charcoal."

That piqued my interest. "What is that?"

He gave me a lazy half-smile, then took a sip from his cup. "Keep coming back for training and I will show you. Now, time to finish our capuli and get back to work."

I awoke groggy, but motivated to return to Brokk as soon as I could. Training had not resulted in anything worth noting, but I was excited to try again. I pushed myself out of bed, then set about helping Neila with the early rotation chores.

It took longer than I would have liked to leave the lake, but I needed to make my exit seem natural to keep Neila's suspicions at bay. By the time I reached Brokk, he was pacing by the waterside. His concerned glance quickly vanished as he greeted me, then he motioned to his two cups he had set by the shore.

"We're to have more capuli?" I asked.

"No, we are going to try something different. The volume of water may feel too big, perhaps starting smaller would be better." He sat down, then picked up one of the cups which was full of water. He tipped it over the empty one, a stream spilled out which would have missed the lip of the cup on the ground. Using his free hand, Brokk held his palm toward the rivulet and pushed with an invisible force to redirect the stream into the cup, filling the one below. "Now you try."

I let out a breath and tried to center myself, hoping that maybe this time I would find some success. I sat down across from him, then picked up the cup that had water in it. I poured slowly, holding my other hand in near where the water passed by. *Move, move, move.* I pushed at the water, but I had a hard time narrowing down to the source. I clenched my eyes shut, giving one more nudge to it. I heard the tone of the spill change, the water striking the inside of the empty cup that sat waiting.

I opened my eyes, looking down to see the partially filled volume. "I did it!" Some had not made it in, it had not been redirected in time to catch most of it. I looked up at Brokk with a triumphant grin.

He looked stunned. "You pushed me."

I glanced around, then noticed the short path etched in the ground from where he had been forcibly scooted back. It was only a few deccates, half a hand-length at most. But he had been moved away. I looked over his shoulder to the brambles that edged the stream, they had been forced out and away, now curving over in a semicircle.

"How did you do that?" he asked.

"I just pushed. I couldn't feel the thin stream so I pushed at everything."

"At everything," he repeated. "You ... you feel everything?"

I stared at him. "You mean you don't?"

"No," he shook his head slowly, "a body of water will be all I feel when I am near one. A lake, a stream, a river, they all have their own song but there is none other that adds to the chorus."

"But what is it like?"

He held his hands up, looking at them cupped out in front, like they were holding invisible water. "The lake becomes a drop, the drop becomes power. Everything else shuts out as my sight narrows to the flow of the fluid. It is a song and a dance."

I frowned. "Pretty words, but it doesn't really tell me much.

Brokk lowered his hands, resting them on his knees, his shins crossed beneath him. "What do you feel then? When you feel everything, have you tried to describe it before?"

I closed my eyes, reaching out again for the water around us. At first very little registered, just a general sense that water was near. I had spent so long trying to hide that I had any skill that it had possibly atrophied within me, withered before it even bloomed. A seedling that failed to sprout. Instead of pushing out, I pulled in, trying to evoke more of a response. I took stock of what I sensed, and I could tell where things were even without opening my eyes. Much like when I had first sensed Brokk just before I met him, when I knew he was nearby. Not only the sounds of twigs but also the water in his body had given him away. "It's like little points in space, like dots suspended everywhere. The stream is solid, too many dots to separate, but the air, the leaves, you, the trunks of the trees … I can feel where it all is because of the water they hold."

"You can even feel it in the air?"

I nodded. "Especially up there," I said, pointing to the mist. To the shroud that covered our entire world.

He looked in awe. "This does present an interesting problem. But, perhaps this makes sense."

"How?"

"One thing I spent much of my time doing in Lacausia was studying. Our world, the nature of it, how our world exists essentially overlaid on another world, but offset because we exist on a different frequency. Our shifted frequency means we have a full twenty-eight rotations to complete a light-to-dark cycle, whereas the human world only has one. Day to night in just one rotation, could you imagine? It is also our shifted frequency that gives us power over elements. Umorfae have the skill of water because of our connection to a certain frequency that resonates with water. Ignisfae have a different frequency, their state of being seems practically ready to combust, and they connect to fire. And so on for the other types of Fae."

"I fail to see how that makes sense for me," I said, my voice more than a little tinged with exasperation. Lily had taught me most of this long ago, as she was originally from the human realm, but I didn't bother telling him anything about that.

"You are a mestisius. You are of a mixed heritage. That would naturally change your frequency, alter what you connect with, and how. You are half Umorfae, that connects you to water, but your Syrenni half shifts you. Once we figure that out, unlock that, who knows what you can do."

I twisted my mouth half down in a frown. Brokk seemed to be even more excited by the prospect than if I were simply able to connect, my potential might be far greater. But I only heard that he felt water one way, and I felt it another. Which might mean, he wouldn't be able to teach me after all. I dropped my gaze to my hands which rested in my lap. The thin webbing that reached halfway up my fingers glimmered with an iridescent shimmer. The webbing which was one of the markers of my Syrenni half. The

Syrenni had no influence over water, over any element. Perhaps it meant mine was dulled enough to not be controllable.

A hand to my chin startled me out of my thoughts, Brokk's cool touch so unexpected, so gentle. I looked up at him, surprised by the contact. He looked at me for a long moment, his fingertips still resting under my jaw. No one ever touched me, no one ever reached out except Neila. But Brokk looked at me in earnest, with what I could only describe as a hopeful, encouraging gaze. His bright, aqua blue eyes connected with mine in a way that made my breath pause. It was a look I had never seen on a male. I nearly recoiled, as I started to wonder what it was that he wanted. And why. Why would he want to help me discover this skill?

Sure, we had our deal, I would keep him hidden. But how much was that worth on my end really? Was that enough motivation for him to make so much effort? "Why do you care if I connect to my skill? Why try?" I asked.

He lowered his hand. "I did not leave Lacausia just to find something different, I left to find a way to make a *difference*, too. Maybe helping you will do that."

CHAPTER 5

I dropped my hands, utterly spent after my last attempt. I had been focusing so much I had developed an ache between my brows, and a dull-throbbing sensation at the base of my skull. The trees surrounding Brokk and I slanted suddenly, and the ground rushed up to meet me.

Brokk caught me before I hit the ground, and I blinked back into the moment. My eyes had played a trick on me, I hadn't even processed that I was falling.

"Here, rest a moment, you may be overusing your skill," he said as he lifted me up, his arm supporting my bent legs, his other cradling my back. "You could be approaching burnout."

"Burnout?" I mumbled. I was having a hard time keeping everything in sight from wobbling. I cringed and shut my eyes. He walked a few paces away from the river's edge, holding me tight to his body to keep from jostling me.

I cracked an eyelid open after he settled me gently on the ground, next to his culina. He stoked the small fire, making it flare to life, then swung the pot he used to boil water over the top of it. The light seared into my sight, so I clenched my eyes closed once again.

"Burnout happens when you use too much magic. You will need to stop and let it refill. You have a well within you, when it runs out it is called reaching burnout. You will feel disoriented and exhausted. But it will refill after some time."

I groaned. I was getting close to connecting with my skill, it was *working*, I could feel it. It was nearly tangible, but having to wait for this was a detour I didn't want to deal with. I moved to try and get up, but his hand to my shoulder stopped me.

"Rest, please. Give yourself the time your body needs. Here, as promised."

I glanced up and saw he held something out to me, a bundle of square, pale tan leaves with black marks on them.

"Parchment with my studies on them," he answered my unasked question. "I draw things I find and write observations about them. Studying our world is something I enjoy."

I took it, looking at each one while he served us capuli. The pages were filled with detailed drawings of leaves and various plants, strange animals, with notes scribbled alongside each one. He settled down across from me, holding out my steaming beverage for me to take. I took a few sips as I thumbed through the rest of the sketches. Whether it was the capuli, or simply sitting with him on the ground to rest, I started to feel a little better.

"These are magna, Brokk. I've never seen anything like them." I looked at the words he had written, recognizing some of the letters Lily had taught me. His handwriting was scraggly enough that it was only partially legible.

He shrugged, suddenly looking far less suave. "They could be improved upon."

I smiled and shook my head. "I don't see how." I noticed that he wasn't comfortable showing someone his work by the way he shifted his shoulders and fidgeted.

I handed back his drawings, which he looked at for a moment before he said, "You have a funny way of speaking. I wanted to ask about it. I do not remember how the Syrenni spoke."

I quirked a sideways smile at his obvious subject change, but decided against ribbing him about it. "The Syrenni speak a little differently from me, I learned mostly from Princess Lily. She has a way of talking that I gravitated to naturally."

He visibly stiffened, his face practically turned to stone at the mention of her name.

I pulled back my head, motioning to his sudden change in demeanor. "What's wrong? You seem upset."

"You mean you do not know?"

I looked around. "Know what? I don't know what you're referring to."

"Princess Lily is an enemy of the Umorfae. She was tried for treason and she killed many of us."

"What! When? I've never heard about this." I was absolutely shocked. I knew Lily was a formidable fighter, and powerful with her skills, but I had never heard that she *killed* anyone. Frankly I had seen her do very little, I had only heard rumors about what she was capable of. Clearly I hadn't heard it all.

"When I was a young filio. She felled a great many and destroyed our castle. Everything changed because of her." His hands were balled into fists, and a vein throbbed in his neck.

Something clicked into place, stories of our history, of how we came to our new life at the lake, how we escaped the grip of the Umorfae oppression. "Probably when she freed us," I whispered.

Of course there would have been casualties. I had never thought about the other side, the losses they likely incurred. The things she must have done to make that escape possible. She was exalted in my eyes, she could do no wrong. I suddenly felt so young and foolish, what else did I not know? What other terrible histories might my elders be hiding? I looked back to Brokk, who sat stock still. I wasn't sure what to do, so I reached toward him and touched his wrist. "I didn't know about that, what the past might have been between her and the Umorfae. That isn't the person that I know. You and I both have darkness surrounding our people from when we were younglings. Please don't let that past ruin who we are trying to become now."

He blinked, and his face lightened. His *everything* lightened. "I think that is the wisest comment I have heard you make."

I lifted the corner of my mouth and flipped my hair off of my shoulder. "I'm pretty fucking brilliant."

He laughed and shook his head. His eyes twinkled and that curve returned to his brow that I sometimes saw when he looked at me. I blew out a relieved breath, glad to have side-stepped the momentary discomfort, and glad that the darkening I had sensed from Brokk had vanished.

We were well into the dark rotations when I finally started getting some results, finally seeing the progress of all of my meetups with Brokk. He never once lost his patience with me, even though I regularly did with myself. Learning to focus my skill onto one thing turned out to be so much harder than I anticipated. I eventually was able to cast my invisible, magical net out and push, pull, or even halt movement by holding the water within something. But narrowing it down to affecting one while not affecting another was extremely difficult. Now that we were nearing the bright and early light rotations, we were at the point of fine tuning my abilities.

I walked through the forest to meet up with Brokk again, bearing a gift I had foraged for him in the forest. I found him cooking fish in the culina, carefully wrapping leaves around the prepared filets as I approached.

His smile lit up as he saw me, Brokk's eyes nearly glowed with joy as he greeted me. He motioned to the food. "It's a special occasion, I thought fish would be all right to have, to celebrate all that you have learned."

I grinned and nodded. He had been learning how to speak more like me. I had given him lessons here and there to understand which words could be combined. I hadn't told him, but I liked it. It made me feel less alone. "You've been very tolerant of me making you eat so much bisporus when there are technically fish nearby. I think you've earned it."

"Especially when I've had to drink it, too," he added. "Let's not forget that all we've had to drink lately is the bisporus capuli since our capuli ran out." He frowned in a pouty, comical way that made me laugh. A sliver of his chest peeked through his shirt as he shifted, now looking far more chiseled than when I had first met him. Though he would have preferred to eat fish exclusively, the bisporus had done wonders for him. He had filled out and packed on muscle quickly with the regular meals. Something about that narrow view of his broad chest made me feel like I should look away, but I couldn't help eyeing the bare skin. I shifted my eyes further down his arms, I liked seeing the corded muscles of his forearms work as he prepared food, the way his rolled-up sleeves showed off his strength.

I smiled to myself as I watched him cook. He had shared all of his capuli with me, every time we met until it was gone. It became our tradition, sharing capuli before training. In spite of it clearly being his favorite thing, he was gracious and generous with it. It had become my treasured time, those quiet moments before we would exert so much effort to hone my skill. It had already been six rotations of the bisporus brew, so I was looking forward to surprising him with my gift. "Here," I said, lifting the bag I had hidden behind my back. "A gesture of my appreciation."

He tried to clean his hands off on his pants. "What is this?" he asked, reaching for the bag. He grabbed the handles, his hands brushing mine. My heart leapt at the touch, at that momentary pause where he didn't seem to try and take the bag, his eyes searching my face before he glanced at the contents. "Capuli beans! You really found some!" He danced a little jig that I chuckled at, as he carried the beans over to the fire.

"You were kind enough to share all you had with me, I went looking to replace your supply."

He was giddy as he started sifting through them, removing twigs and cleaning them off. He made some space by the fire, then spread them on a slanted rock which was close enough to the heat to roast them. "You collected a lot! I hope you got some rest, this must have taken you most of the time since you left after training."

"It wasn't that long," I lied. He was right, it had taken quite a while to pick the best ones from the small grove I had found them in. I had the small pricks dotted on my fingers to prove it.

He smiled up at me, that left eyebrow arching in a way that set my stomach tumbling.

"So, you have nearly mastered your skill. Is the gift of capuli beans a sign that you have no more need of me and I should be on my way? A parting gift?" He said it jokingly, but there was something more in that question. Something layered within as another, deeper question. "We did agree my stay here would be temporary, after all. I should move on before the night rotations set in again."

I opened my mouth, trying to get words to form. "No!" I said at last. "I don't want you to go, I mean …" I searched for the right thing to say, unsure of how to express everything.

Brokk noticed my hesitation, then left the capuli beans forgotten on the stone as he stood to walk back over to me. His gaze pierced mine, as he strode with such surety and intent toward me. My breath caught at the way he looked at me. The air felt charged with something intangible, like a force snapping alive every point in my body.

"Sereia!"

My blood went cold at the sound of my name being called off in the distance.

"Shit!" I hissed. "I have to go!"

44

CHAPTER 6

I attempted to head Neila off, making sure she wasn't anywhere close to Brokk's camp. I ran at a diagonal clip, coming into her line of sight from a different direction than I had actually been. I had looked back at Brokk only briefly before he disappeared from view. His face looked pained, worried. Or maybe disappointed. It was hard to tell. I didn't even have the chance to tell him that I would come back when I could.

I slowed my pace as I neared Neila, sucking in breaths to slow down my system, trying to make it seem like I hadn't been running.

"I'm here, Maeder Neila, I—what's wrong?" I abandoned the story I had been cooking up when I saw her face and the concern that furrowed her brows.

"I have been looking everywhere for you. Princess Lily is here. And she has brought others."

My head spun with the information. I had previously hoped that she was coming soon, and then forgot about it once I started working with Brokk. *Oh no, Brokk!* With Lily so close to his camp, I would have to make sure she stayed by the lake and didn't go into the forest.

"I had thought you would be happy to hear she had come,"

Neila said, eyeing my expression.

My eyebrows shot up in surprise, realizing my face had betrayed my emotions. I quickly gave her a demure smile. "I am just surprised! This is magna news. Let's go greet her! Who else did she bring?" I started walking toward the lake, looping my arm through Neila's to encourage her to walk with me.

"Quite a few! Her maeder and her maeder's sister, Kerenza, Kerenza's conniunx Zia, Queen Deniza, and someone else I think you will be excited to meet."

I saw the circle of females standing at the center of the common area as Neila and I approached. Lily was hard to miss with her bright, gold-yellow hair. I remembered meeting her maeder, Rachael, and Maureen, her maeder's sister. Queen Deniza stood with Kerenza and Zia, but then a face I didn't recognize turned toward me. Her black hair—with wisps of ruby highlights framing her cheeks—shifted as she spun to look at me, and her face lit up with a vivid, warm smile.

Kerenza was saying something to her, but the unknown Ignisfae broke out in a run, rushing to meet me and completely ignoring whatever Kerenza was trying to say to her.

Her arms wrapped around me the moment she reached me. "Sereia! I've been so excited to meet you!"

I dropped my jaw as she squeezed me. I looked over to Lily and Kerenza, who both chuckled and shook their heads. The female released me and pulled her head back to look at me. "Hello!" I said, still in shock over the exuberant greeting.

She laughed. "I'm Emblyn, Kerenza's filia. I've been asking to come here for *so long*. Like seriously, *cycles*. They finally said yes!"

I laughed, too. She was almost a little unhinged, but her excitement was infectious. Her eyes were positively electric, their color a bright, honeyed amber that seemed to have their own light. And her beautiful linteum matched them, a gorgeous shade that had a subtle shimmer. She threaded her fingers through mine and squealed with glee. In a way she was so over the top, so intense, but at the same time I clung to the way she fearlessly connected with me. How she looked at my face with a curiosity that told me she *liked* what she saw, that she was looking forward to this moment for a long time and she was not let down. It was immediate acceptance, instantaneous friendship.

I was still stunned, but I managed to speak more coherently than my first greeting. "I'm excited to meet you, too! I didn't know you all would be coming." If I was being honest with myself, I was trying to work myself up to her level while trying to not be awkward. Not an easy task for me.

"Yes, well, it was all a big surprise. They didn't tell me until it was happening, it was my gift for turning twenty-five cycles. Lily calls it a "birthday present," whatever that means. She has lots of human customs like that which she likes to observe." Emblyn pulled my hand and started walking us over to the others. "My maeder *never* lets me leave TerraIgni, even though I am plenty old enough to go. But, here we are, twenty-five cycles and it's my first real trip. I figured I'd make an effort to show her I can go somewhere and *not* be a maniac."

I giggled. "And how's that going?"

"Not magna!" she said with a huge grin.

We were both laughing as we arrived at the waiting group. Lily stepped forward to greet me.

"Princess Lily," I said, bowing my head to her.

She smiled and reached out to grab me for a big hug. "So formal! You know I prefer just Lily."

I melted into the embrace. I had missed her so much. But then I stiffened, what Brokk said flashed in my mind. What had happened all those cycles ago? I wanted to hear it firsthand from her, but how could I even ask without raising suspicion? After all, how would I know anything about that unless an Umorfae had told me? I brushed the thoughts away. Lily was perceptive, and if I wanted to keep Brokk a secret, I had to avoid thinking about him. My wandering thoughts had already snagged Neila's attention, I didn't want to unintentionally alert Lily to something amiss as well.

I backed up, breaking off the hug. "I'm so glad you're here! How long will you be with us?" I tried to keep the question as natural as I could, but I couldn't help myself, I knew exactly why I wanted to know. And it wasn't just for casual conversation.

"Well, that's something I wanted to talk to Neila about," Lily said. "But, we've just arrived so I'd like to settle in and rest a bit."

After the newcomers had built their tent and then taken a rest, we all gathered out in front of it as she showed all the supplies she had brought for the Syrenni. Grains to make bread, dried meat and fruits, and swaths of fabric for new clothes to be made were the main things she brought, along with some other gifts of metal. Her mate, Rannoch, had smithed a new set of pots for cooking, cutting implements, as well as drinkware and bowls.

"How did you carry all of this?" I asked, stunned at the amount the somewhat small group of females had managed to pack in from wherever they had hiked. Their tent alone seemed unwieldy, it was large enough to sleep all of them and had at least minimal bedding for each one.

"My teacher, Yantzen J'Dun, designed a special cart that carries what twenty males can. I told him stories about the arthropods, the huge creatures with tons of legs that live in the ore mountain at the center of this lake. Have you ever been there and seen them?"

"No!" I blurted. "We don't ever go there."

She nodded. "The passage is pretty scary. But really the creatures aren't bad. Anyway, my stories gave him an idea to build one out of metal, its legs scuttle over things easily and the large shell stores tons of stuff. It works better in the forest than anything with wheels because things with wheels always need a path. These don't. They can follow along and not damage the forest as they go. We even take turns riding it when we need a break."

I nodded, feigning interest in the story, but really I wanted to know juicier details. Such as why did they travel without any males this time? What was the true history between her and the Umorfae? If she had killed so many Umorfae, had she been the one to kill my faeder? To that point, did she know who he was? Questions swirled in my head as I realized she was still talking.

"That is why we wanted to take her with us," Lily had just

finished saying to Neila.

"What?" I asked. *Oh my gods, was she talking about me?*

"I do not like the idea of you bringing her to TerraIgni," Neila said. "She is all I have left of my sister. She entrusted me with Sereia's care and I will only do what is safe for her."

I breathed heavy and fast, something rose below the surface of my skin that caused my heart to beat loudly. I felt helpless as Lily and Neila started debating over what they thought would be best for me.

"She may be safe in TerraIgni, but crossing the Hinterdunes is anything but safe," Neila stated. "Plus I would not be able to cross without an Ignisfae. As I cannot make the crossing myself, the answer is no."

I could tell Lily was a little frustrated, but she tapped her chin as she pondered aloud. "What about Adrilan? It's to the west of here and only a little north, not nearly as far as TerraIgni. I had promised Rannoch I would return home soon, but as I am due for a visit in Adrilan with the Petrafae, I could request we train there instead. It's a beautiful city and she would be safe there."

"Train?" I spoke up finally.

Neila touched my arm. "I sent word to Lily. It is not a coincidence that she came for a visit. Your abilities were starting to manifest more and more, and I thought it would be wise for you to learn how to control them finally. However, I had thought you could simply train here."

Lily shook her head. "I do understand, but it would be difficult for me to stay here for the length of time she would need. And she will receive far better training without the distractions of Syrenni watching on, I imagine they would feel uncomfortable at inevitably seeing Sereia learn how to wield water. We won't leave for a few rotations at least, so there is some time before we plan on departing."

Neila's face was hard as she looked back and forth from Lily to me. Finally she relented. "All right. Sereia will accompany you to Adrilan."

52

CHAPTER 7

My blood rushed, I was actually leaving Caer Lake, leaving the Syrenni to go on an adventure. I had excused myself from the group to go to the lakeside alone. I needed some time to process everything that had just shifted. Had this news come a quarter cycle earlier, *before* I had stumbled upon Brokk, I would have jumped at the chance. Now, I was conflicted. Not to mention not a single one of them had asked *me* what I wanted to do, what my choice was. I was nearly twenty-one cycles, why wouldn't they ask me?

The unknown logistics started to pile questions in my head in a disorganized list. How long I would be gone, whether I would come back here when I was done, who I would stay with while I was there … and how soon I was leaving. Things were happening fast, too fast for comfort. It was almost unfair in a way, that this would happen now and not earlier. But, the chance to travel with Lily, with Emblyn. With a whole group of powerful females that were not afraid of my gift. And Lily was the one who had once told me that change *is* uncomfortable. I had known I wanted change, but now that it was upon me …

"This must seem like a lot," a voice said from behind. I spun, and found Emblyn standing there. "The idea of leaving the home you knew, when it comes down to it, it's pretty daunting. Even though I wanted to go, when it was finally happening I had my moment of worry. So, I understand, if you're nervous."

I looked at her for a moment before answering. "Yeah, I guess that's it. And it's not like I don't want to go, but nobody asked me what I want to do."

"Ugh, welcome to my *life*," Emblyn sighed dramatically, then she reached forward to grab my hand. "But, they mean well, and it's also because they are experienced in this world. Lily has been a protector watching over me since I was a young filia, she has a hard time letting that go. And my maeder even more so. I think the same extends to you. I get it, though, it's frustrating. It's hard to feel like I've grown when I barely have autonomy. I imagine you feel something similar."

"That's exactly it. I have no choices of my own to make."

Emblyn grinned. That huge, beautiful smile that made me mirror the expression. "Then let's go on this trip, and start finding how to make our own way." She motioned with a wide sweep of her arm while taking an exaggerated step along the shoreline, tugging me with her. "Clear the path! Sereia is coming through!"

I laughed, a real laugh that made my cheeks hurt. "More like clear the path, Emblyn is coming through!"

She leaned in closer with a conspiratorial smirk. "You better believe it."

I waited in my room for as long as I could, until I was sure everyone else had fallen asleep. As tired as I was, I couldn't sleep. There was too much excitement buzzing through me. I snuck out, making sure to steer clear of Lily's tent on the northern edge of the Syrenni encampment. I closed my eyes, gently casting out my senses, seeing if I could count everyone that should have been in there. I felt all seven of them, though I couldn't tell them apart, I could at least tell they were all about the right size. With more training maybe I could refine that aspect, home in on it a little better. For now it would have to do. I only needed to ensure they didn't see me. I listened for a moment, making sure none of them stirred.

Smiling to myself as I hurried away, I pulled up the hem of my sleeping gown. I didn't want it to drag through the dirt, leaving a trail of strewn sticks and debris showing exactly where I had gone. I slipped through the ferns that marked the edge of our home, then made my way through the forest to the west.

I nearly ran the whole way to Brokk's camp, anxious to see him and tell him the news. I found him pacing by the waterside, muttering to himself. It seemed like he was having an imaginary argument with someone, in some sort of heated mental debate that distracted him from my approach.

"Brokk?"

His eyes flung wide as he turned to me. "Are you all right? I have been worried sick!" He raced forward, clutching my hands within his. The warmth of them was surprising, the feel of his calluses against my palms ... It was like coming back to something I didn't know I was missing. Like coming back home, it instantly centered me and rooted me in the moment.

I suddenly remembered my hasty departure the last time I had seen him. So much had happened since then. "I'm fine! Everything is fine." My excitement ebbed. Telling him I was leaving now felt off, and terrible. And what would happen if I told him not only was I going to Adrilan, but also that I was going with Lily? He had reacted badly the last time I mentioned her. Now telling him the news sounded like the worst idea possible.

"Sereia, what's wrong? What happened before?"

I faked a smile, washing any concern from my face. "It was just Neila, she got too close so I walked with her back home. All is well." I squeezed his hands for emphasis.

That one eyebrow of his twitched down at an angle, the subtle movement I had come to learn of his that showed itself when he gave pause to something. I nodded again with a smile, willing away his doubt. A sour feeling crept into the pit of my stomach, something unsettling and foul. For as much as I had tried to put on a pleasant face for him, I could no longer hide it. I pulled my hands away from him, then rubbed my abdomen.

"Are you sure you are well?" The concerned expression reappeared, gone was the look of disbelief. Now he focused intently on me, seeming to appraise my health. "Perhaps we should sit down. No training this time. Let's just sit and rest."

I didn't argue. In a way I was relieved for the diversion. What was this strange sensation coursing through me that turned my stomach? I let him lead me to the sitting area he had near the culina, then sat down on the log as he set out a pot to boil water. Brokk busied himself while the water heated up, leaving me to my thoughts for the moment. As I mulled it over, I felt sick at my dishonesty to him. I had lied by omission before to Neila, and perhaps that's what I was doing now; I was lying by omission. But this time Brokk has specifically asked me what happened, and I didn't tell him the truth. It was true that it had been Neila that came to find me, but I hadn't told him about Lily. I had hid it from him because I thought he wouldn't react well. Maybe that wasn't fair. Perhaps I should tell him, some of it at least.

"Princess Lily showed up at our camp," I said suddenly, as he reached to pick up the pot before tossing in the ground beans.

Brokk stopped making capuli, then swung his body to me, the pot still clutched in his rigid hand. "What? What does ... What is she doing here?"

"She came to train me. They finally decided to deal with my unruly abilities and teach me."

He looked petrified. "And, did you tell her you already have been? Did you tell her about me?"

"No!"

He sagged. "Thank the gods! But—damnatus!" He dropped the pot back onto the fire, it clattered on the rock but didn't tip over as he shook out his burnt hand. He cringed, looking at his reddened palm. The heat must have finally made its way up the handle.

"I'm sorry, I didn't mean to distract you," I said and reached forward to take his hand. Peering at it, I domed my other hand over the wound, wishing I could take away the injury.

"It's not your fault, I forgot what I was doing. Usually I only hold it for a moment while I toss in the capuli." He paused, then added quietly, "I suppose you will have no need to visit me further."

I looked up at him, keenly aware of our hands gently clasped together. "No need? I don't think that's true." I searched his face, not sure what to say, but I knew I didn't want to stop learning from him. I didn't want to stop seeing those expressions on his face that I had come to adore. How the subtlest changes in the narrowness of his eyes or slight tug upward of his lips could indicate a myriad of moods. I wanted to learn them all. "I still have so much to learn from you."

He nodded and sighed, but it wasn't a content one. I had trouble reading his expression and tone as he said, "Of course. Then we shall continue." He slid his hands from mine. "But not this time. For now, we will share capuli and relax."

After I had two cups and listened to him chatter on about his latest endeavor to unravel the science of the mist, I left to head back home. I hadn't mentioned anything yet about leaving for Adrilan, but since it wasn't for a few rotations at least, I had time before I really needed to tell him.

I snuck back into the common area, as Syrenni were just starting to set up the mane fare meal.

CHAPTER 8

Emblyn lounged and sipped capuli as I approached. "Bonum mane," she said with a knowing smirk.

I slowed, taking in her expression. Pretending to be nonchalant, I took a seat next to her. "Bonum mane," I said as I yawned. "Have an extra cup?"

She swiped one from the table near her, then held it out and nodded with her chin to the carafe nearby. "We brought it from TerraIgni. Give it a try. It's got some zing to it!"

"Zing?"

"Honestly, I don't know. That's what Lily's maeder, Rachael, always says. I think you'll like traveling with her, and her sister, Maureen. They always make me laugh. They'll be fun on the trail to Adrilan."

I nodded as I poured. As soon as she mentioned traveling, I thought of Brokk.

"I imagine you could use a hefty cup, you probably didn't get any rest, did you?" she said over the rim of her mug.

I shot a glance at her and she waggled her eyebrows. "What do you mean? I just went for a quick walk after I got up. I got plenty of rest." *Lies, lies, lies.*

She made a show of giving me a flat, disbelieving look before she laughed and rolled her eyes. "Oh *come on*, at least give me the details! Who, where, how, how long did it last?"

"Emblyn!" No way was I telling her anything, besides it wasn't like that. Brokk and I, we just weren't like that.

"*Sereia*, with a maeder like I have, you had better believe I'm the master at this. And I can spot a fellow sneaker from a hectate away."

"Sneaker," I repeated, scoffing. I was doing my best to put on an air of indifference, but my heart was absolutely pounding inside my chest. How could she have known?

"Bonum mane, filias!" Kerenza's sing-song voice filled the area.

I turned to see her arriving at the common area, with Zia in tow and Lily walking with them. I twisted back to Emblyn, giving her my best *kindly shut the fuck up* face that I could quickly muster. She laughed and waved me off.

"Bonum mane, Maeder!" Emblyn returned the greeting in the same lilting manner. She lifted her eyebrows at me one last time for good measure, before standing to welcome them. "I was just telling Sereia about our capuli we brought from TerraIgni, it is fresh and hot! Come join us for some."

Before long we were all laughing over hot mugs of capuli, my alarm at Emblyn's guess had subsided. Because really that was all it could have been: a guess. She didn't *know* anything.

I was practically buzzing with energy once I finished my second cup, which would actually make that my fourth.

"Sereia?"

I nearly jumped out of my skin when Lily said my name. I nodded to her, wordlessly telling her to go ahead with whatever she wanted to tell me.

"You seem on edge. Why don't we go for a walk?"

I nodded again, then motioned for her to lead the way. In the past I would have been desperate for any time with her, any chance to talk with her. Now, being alone sounded daunting somehow. I wasn't even sure what made me nervous about it. Maybe it was the excessive amount of capuli. After all, they didn't know I had snuck off and had two cups with Brokk when I should have been sleeping. Lack of actual rest and then an additional spike to my system was probably not the best idea. *Sneaker.* Emblyn's description of me echoed in my mind. I had done exactly that. Snuck out, then lied about it.

Lily cleared her throat as she walked with her hands clasped behind her back. "I noticed you didn't seem entirely happy about the idea of leaving. I was wondering, is it perhaps that male you were seeing?"

I just about tripped over my sleeping gown, fumbling my steps at her comment. "What? No!"

"Oh, I had thought that since you asked for advice regarding him last time I visited, that maybe things had ... progressed. That maybe you didn't want to leave him behind for this trip and weren't looking forward to it because of him."

I almost facepalmed myself. She wasn't talking about Brokk. "No," I repeated with a relieved sigh. Thank the gods she didn't somehow know about my liaison, too. "We are no longer together. We were, but it didn't work out." Truth be told, I had entirely forgotten about Prant. Funny how that happened. I shrugged to myself, enough time must have passed that I didn't care any more about the failed relationship attempt. "It's over and I let it go," I summed up. I didn't want to discuss what went wrong and how. "I apologize if I seemed unhappy about the idea of leaving, it's not that I don't like the plan."

"Then what is it?"

I paused. In the past I would have been too nervous to tell Lily how I felt about anything she did. I always held her in such high regard, saying anything even remotely negative about something she had done felt abhorrent. But, even she had told me change was uncomfortable. And nothing was more true lately than the fact that I was changing. "It's that I wasn't asked to make decisions about myself, about my future. You and Neila decided it for me."

"I see. I only intended to give you the best chance at learning, I didn't think that would be possible here."

I nodded, giving her a look like I understood, but really, I didn't. I started walking again, thinking over her words, and her lack of apology. It was just like Emblyn had said, Lily is a protector that has a hard time letting go. She saw a particular path to help me achieve my training, and didn't consider it necessary to ask me. I walked back with her to the common area in silence. In a way I was dismayed with the situation, it was what I had previously wanted, but not in the way I wanted it. It felt bitter, like I was compromising on something that gave up too much. What made it worse was that she didn't seem to realize how it bothered me.

Emblyn spotted us, catching up to me as Lily peeled off to speak with Kerenza.

"What was that all about?" Emblyn asked quietly, walking with me toward the lakeside Syrenni dwelling.

I smirked, giving her a sideways glance. "Just figuring out that you were right."

"Of *course* I'm right! … Right about what?"

"That we need to clear the path. We need to make our own way if we want to have a chance in this world of living our own lives." I blew out a breath. I was simultaneously excited and exhausted. I probably needed some sleep to order my thoughts. "I think I need some rest, can you cover for me for awhile?"

She grinned. "Absolutely."

I hugged her. Somehow, she had immediately become the one I could trust the most. I wasn't sure how, but I knew we'd be able to work together to find our path to freedom. We'd clear the path ourselves, we didn't need anyone to do it for us.

64

CHAPTER 9

I slipped out of my room, having slept far longer than I intended. Everyone was making food, preparing for nocte fare before sleeping again. I couldn't imagine going back to sleep again so soon, I had startled awake with worry and was instantly on my feet. We would be leaving on the next rotation. This meal, then sleep, then leave. That was it, I was out of time to tell Brokk about it all.

I made an effort to sit with Neila, to enjoy her company before I wouldn't see her for who knew how long. It was precious little time before everything would change, I hung onto those moments with her. Lily and her companions kept to themselves for the meal, eating around a small fire she had built next to their tent. I sometimes forgot how easy fire was for her, for most of them I supposed. All she had to do was muster up a small amount of will, and flame would burst forth from her. My skill with water had grown to nearly that level, springing from me with ease. Little did Lily know, of course. Yet another secret I had tucked away. There had been so many secrets, lies upon lies. Maybe leaving would give me the chance to clear them away, to stop making a habit of it. I frowned, it *was* a habit. An easy one, it came naturally to me, and I was getting more adept at it. It wasn't something that I *wanted* to be good at.

Everyone shuffled off to bed. I went back to my room as well, to do my usual exit after I had waited long enough.

My stomach tumbled as I left the lake, dreading telling Brokk the truth. I stopped walking. Why was I so nervous to tell him? After all, he had said he intended on leaving, what difference would it make if I left too? It's not like he wanted to stay for me, he was set on finding a place where he could live, and it wasn't going to be in the forest where he had built a *temporary* camp. I straightened up, then started jogging. Maybe this would actually be a relief for him, he could excuse himself from having to teach me. Our agreement had run its course, and I should accept that.

Even as I rationalized everything, I still had a leaden pit gnawing at my insides. There was a very real chance that this could be the last time I saw Brokk, or the last time for a long time at least. My swirling thoughts abated as I saw him at his camp, drawing on his parchment. He didn't notice me right away, and I took my time approaching so I could absorb the image. So I could watch how his gaze softened at whatever he sketched. His drawings had such a certain unique quality, I felt like I would never see them elsewhere. My heart sank, the drawings were so *him*, such an endearing aspect that I would also miss.

Brokk looked in my direction, and his smile lit up his face as he jumped to his feet to greet me. Seeming to remember that he had been drawing, he pocketed the paper, then checked his hands and clothes for smudges of charcoal. The corners of my mouth turned up at the bit of black I noticed on his jaw as I came to a stop in front of him.

"Here for some more training?" he asked. He had a pensive

glance that made me think he hoped I was there for something more.

"Well, no, not really. Here to talk."

At first he looked happy, then his smile faded and his expression turned wary. "Is this about Lily visiting you?"

I gulped. "Yes, in a way. I have something to tell you." I looked down, not wanting to gaze into those crystal blue eyes while I unloaded the news on him. "I'm leaving for Adrilan after mane fare, I'm being sent there to train with Lily for awhile. I'm not sure for how long." I looked up at him finally, then took his hands with mine. They felt cold, and rigid as I grasped them, like he made no effort to hold my hands in return.

His face darkened. "So that's it. She swoops in and whisks you away. I was right, I suppose. You have no need for me anymore."

"That isn't it! And what could I do? I couldn't tell her about you, tell her what I've been learning with you. What if her vendetta against Umorfae still persists? I've never known her to be violent, but you said she killed tons of your people. How could I be sure? And ... well maybe the trip would be good for me. Maybe I'll learn something I don't expect. Besides, you had said you were leaving."

"You could go with me! We could leave this place together! You don't have to go to Adrilan."

"If I went anywhere besides Adrilan, it would be against Neila's wishes. I don't have my maeder, but I have Neila, and she agreed with Lily that I would go to Adrilan."

He scoffed, pulling his hands away. "Don't you see? Lily has taken nearly everything from my familia, and now she's taking you too!" He turned away, his anger palpable. Everything felt heightened, on alert as his gaze swung toward the river.

A curse erupted from him as he threw his arms forcefully in the air. Twin whirlpools of water shot out of the river. Brokk raked his hands to the side, his fingers bent in a claw-like grip as he directed the churning force. The two walls of water smashed into his camp, obliterating everything in their path. I instinctively held up my hands, shielding myself as the torrent pummeled around us. The culina where we had spent so many rotations having capuli, the net contraption he made to catch fish, the platform where he slept, it was all blasted away in an instant.

The water didn't touch us though, as my hands held steady and created an invisible shield around us both. I lowered them at last, the remaining currents sloshed around our feet, before retreating back to the river.

"So," he said in an icy tone, "looks like the student has surpassed the teacher. Like I said, you have no need for me anymore."

"Brokk, I'm sorry. I didn't mean to do that, I was just … reacting."

"It was good," he said simply and shrugged. "You've grown. Or rather, you've *out*grown me. You should go where you can learn more. You are obviously beyond my capabilities now." His voice was too calm, too distant. Like whatever care he had for me before had retreated with the water, it had washed away his feelings along with it. He looked at me with a bland, disinterested expression. "I shall take my leave now. Best of luck to you, Sereia."

I gaped at him, at how quickly he could dismiss me. I almost preferred him being mad over this, whatever this was. The way he acted now was like none of it had ever mattered. "That's it?" I said through clenched teeth.

"You have told me you're leaving, and I'm now doing my best

to part graciously. I shouldn't have had any hopes for anything, you made no promises beyond what we agreed upon. You are doing what's best for you."

"You call destroying your camp with us standing in it gracious?"

"That was a mistake and I'm sorry for it, I was reacting as well. But I then quickly reminded myself of what you had told me you wanted when we first met. I shouldn't be disappointed that you're keeping true to your word."

"And what word is that?" I demanded.

He cocked his head to the side. "That you were looking to learn your limits. I shouldn't be mad that your plans don't include me. I can no longer help you on that quest for power. I can't disagree with the logic, though I was initially upset. And so," Brokk sketched an overly dramatic bow, "I will be on my way. Truly, I wish you the best."

He turned, then quickly collected pieces of rope which had been blasted loose from their previous uses. Picking up his other items, then finally his sword, he arranged them for easier carrying before he left, giving me one last gesture to say goodbye. It was only a flick of his two fingers motioned away from his temple, and it felt so cold, sterile. Like a forced, formal farewell that blocked any emotion behind it.

I stared at him, wounded and appalled, as he disappeared to the east.

CHAPTER 10

Mad. *Fuming* mad was the best way to describe me as my feet pounded the forest floor. I stomped my way back to the Syrenni lakeside. When Brokk had first left I had wanted to cry, to lament how we had ended things. Then I felt my blood practically boil as I thought about how he had worded things. Talking about my quest for power and making it sound like I was just discarding him because his usefulness had run out. *Quest for power,* what a crock of faex. He villainized me, making me sound like I used him while it was advantageous.

I couldn't get out of this place fast enough. Adrilan was now *exactly* what I needed. I burst through the ferns close to the side of Lily's tent. Emblyn shot up from where she had been sitting.

"Oh! I didn't mean to startle you," I said. "I was just—"

"—Going for a walk again? Relax, I have your back. I won't say anything about it. But, are you okay? You seem upset."

I released a frustrated sound. "Upset doesn't nearly cover it. Let's just say I'm ready to get this fucking trip started."

She walked over to me, then gave me an understanding rub on my shoulder. "Then let's get to it. Clear the path, right?"

I shook out my body, trying to release the irritation. I finally gave her a nod of agreement.

Leaving was a blur, and it wasn't much of a send off aside from Neila's goodbyes. The other Syrenni made no effort to wish me well. And so, before long, Lily's group and I had made considerable progress through the forest. We had long passed Brokk's former camp, no one seemed to notice the disarray of the foliage from where he had washed away proof of his stay. Anger bubbled up again at seeing it, and I spent a solid half rotation stewing over our parting as my group made our way to Adrilan.

Emblyn dropped back with me, letting the others pull ahead. "Why don't we talk about it?" she suggested. "I can tell you're still upset."

I debated for a moment, but then decided as he had now moved on, there was little chance of putting him in any danger if I told her. The thought alone surprised me, that even after how I had felt about what transpired, I still worried for his safety. I told Emblyn nearly everything, but I left out one critical detail. Well, two, actually: The fact that he was teaching me to wield my water ability, which would shine a light on the fact that he was an Umorfae. But then, I made one mistake, and mentioned the way he demolished his camp.

She stared at me open-mouthed. "He's an Umorfae," she whispered.

I cringed at my error. I had thought ahead to not tell her what he was teaching me, but clearly didn't think quite far enough ahead for her to not figure it out. "Yeah, and? I'm half Umorfae, remember? Does that make me bad, too?"

She was quiet for awhile, seeming to chew on her words before saying anything. "My first thought was that you were lucky to escape, things happened to me when I was a young filia because of a bad one. Or, several bad Umorfae, I suppose. But then I thought about how a lot of what I know of the Umorfae is from others and what they've told me, and from those long ago experiences. I made a snap judgment as soon as I realized he is an Umorfae, but you clearly cared about him. For that reason alone I should have been more mindful. I was wrong. I apologize."

I stopped walking and my eyes rounded. There was no fight in her voice, no taunt, and there didn't seem to be any sort of hidden agenda. I didn't know what I expected, but it wasn't that. My lip wobbled as I looked at her, utterly appreciative of everything that she was. In the span of several heartbeats she had put aside her preconceived notions about Umorfae because of her trust in me. Or at least that was the reason I had gleaned. She had immediately pivoted her thinking *and* apologized.

Emblyn faced me and put a hand to her heart. Saying nothing further, she simply looked back at me in earnest. I threw my arms around her and held back tears. I rarely cried, but right then, I nearly did. The others turned and glanced at us finally, seeing that we had fallen behind. I wiped my eyes, then smiled at Emblyn. She returned the soft expression and nodded, a hidden, silent accord that she would keep my secret. At least there was one person I didn't have to lie to.

Once we settled down after a long rotation of hiking through the forest, Emblyn wanted to know all about Brokk. I had to break it to her that in fact there was nothing physical going on, a detail that she couldn't believe.

"So, not even once?"

I shook my head as I cradled a warm cup of tea which Lily's maeder had poured for me. "I don't think he was interested in me like that." I took a sip after sniffing the herbal scent.

"That can't be true. Look at you! Unless he doesn't like females, or he has no pulse."

I almost spit out my drink. Instead I huffed a garbled laugh through my nose, trying to keep everything from sputtering out of my mouth. "Timing, Emblyn!" I managed to say after I swallowed my tea.

She giggled. "Well then, since there was nothing between you two, as you say, we'll have to find a hot Petrafae for you in Adrilan. And while we're at it, one for me, too." She wriggled with glee and laughed maniacally.

I smiled and nodded, though I was anything but enthusiastic. Finding someone like that did not sound even the slightest bit enticing. However, Emblyn was excited about it, so I would play along. Emblyn and I may have wanted different things, but I did want to spend time with her, and this was something she was clearly focused on. The trip for her was, in part, to seek out males. And so far there had been zero chance for that. Syrenni males didn't exactly qualify, and the rest of the time for her had been traveling with a group of females. I couldn't really blame her for being interested in romantic pursuits.

Emblyn excused herself to get ready for bed.

As I finished my tea, I thought about what I wanted, what motivated me. Learning to wield water had been high on my list for some time. Brokk had helped me level up very quickly. Even if I was still mad at the way we had ended things, I appreciated what he had done for me. I cast out my senses, closing my eyes and feeling the water around me. We weren't near any main water sources, but the trees, the plants, our companions' bodies, all of them responded to me. Like beacons suspended in the environment. But most of all I felt the mist. It was an ever-present barrier hanging over us all, watching. It was formless, while at the same time being composed of millions of points. I could feel all of those points, like fine threads tethering me to them. I was tempted to tug at those threads, to feel how taut they could get.

Brokk had been borderline obsessed with the mist, seeking out the science behind it, the how and why of it. It had persisted for an eon, I had wondered at first if the why mattered. It was a part of our world now, it had been since long before I had hatched, long before any currently living Syrenni swam the river or any living Fae walked the land. As I thought about it, the why was exactly what drove Brokk to learn more. His thirst for knowledge and understanding made me smile, it was endearing the way he tried to unravel the mysteries of our world. In truth I had taken them for granted, they were as they are, and it was as simple as that to me. It wasn't until I met Brokk that my eyes started to open to what truths might be out there, what more there was to learn. And how we should always question what we're told.

He had mentioned one time during a rest between training sessions that he had read every book he could find in Lacausia. I wondered if Adrilan might have a collection of different volumes. Perhaps that could be part of my quest, not just training for my skill, but learning as much as I could. Brokk had definitely rubbed off on me. I now questioned the world and the things in it. I wanted to seek out answers. The why *did* matter. The why and how our world came to be had shaped all living things within it.

The thought excited me for a half a moment, the idea that I could learn new things to possibly share with Brokk. My face fell with realization. The reality was I probably would not get such an opportunity, and would need to seek knowledge for my own growth. He had gone one way and I had gone another, both literally and figuratively. It was most likely for the best, how long would it have been before I did something that would truly change his opinion of me? Emblyn saw me as this beautiful thing, this pretty creature that any male would like. She didn't yet know how I would deceive to protect whatever it was that I wanted. I sensed Brokk was starting to see me for what I really was, so in a way it was better that it did end. Let him take the memory of me that was more forgiving, the more appealing version of me.

CHAPTER 11

My whole body ached, and I decided I did *not* like long distance hiking. Lily kept saying things like it was "good for the spirit" and other such faex. It had gone on for far too long. Even with the breaks I would take to ride the strange metal arthropod, it was becoming too much for me to handle. Though, riding the eight-legged mechanical creature wasn't much of a rest, as it clicked and clinked its way through the forest. With each rotation that passed I became a little crankier. I was beginning to think we'd never reach Adrilan, when it finally came into view through the trees.

Emblyn spotted it before I did, hooting as the tops of some sort of structure peeked through in small slivers. It wasn't until we came to the edge of a clearing when I saw it in all its overwhelming glory.

I craned my neck trying to see the tallest building. I gulped, forgetting to breathe as I stared.

Maureen nudged me with an elbow. "Pretty impressive, huh?"

"It's … it's … it's fucking huge!" I gasped finally. More eloquent words eluded me as I gaped. I had never imagined such a place, never thought that something so large could be built. The city rose from a wide column of sheer polished rock, its smooth sides appeared to have no entrances at the base. The column splayed out high above us, even if all of us climbed one atop the other, we wouldn't reach nearly a quarter of the way up to where the massive platform swung out into an enormous disc. The city was then built vertically from there, small structures sprouting upwards, all made from hewn stone. "How do we even get up there?" I wondered aloud, scanning the area for how we could enter it.

"We call," Lily answered, "only a Petrafae can let us in, they open the stone and a staircase descends."

"What's a stare-case? As in … stares… right?" I bulged my eyes dramatically to illustrate my point.

Lily cringed. "Oh, geez, no. I should have told you more about this place. Or about architecture in general. Stairs are short platforms linked together that rise slowly up, allowing us to climb levels."

"Like a ladder," I supplied.

"Yes! Sort of. But meant to be more permanent and they stretch out at an upward angle, allowing you to walk up rather than climb vertically."

I nodded like I understood, but I definitely didn't. I knew I had a lot to learn, but this felt like the first in a long line of lessons that could be titled "Things I Should Already Know." Lily called Livi, her bonded Faerie, to take the message up to the Petrafae. I wanted to know how others who didn't have a Faerie friend would get the Petrafae's attention, but I didn't especially want another explanation that would end up making me feel unaware and inexperienced. It was probably as simple as shouting until someone peeked their head over the side high above.

The rock opened at the edge of the disc, the wide sliver that shrunk in was not directly overhead, sliding back until it locked in place. Then the entire outer disc started to rotate, I hadn't noticed that there were concentric rings etched into the underside of the stone, allowing the outer ring to move independently from the inner. It continued along its curved path, the sound of stone against stone grated at my ears until it came to a rest, the opening now directly above us.

"They can turn the pieces of their city?" Emblyn exclaimed, then laughed. "I bet that makes for some pretty good pranks! Younglings turning the whole city when they're not supposed to, or turning it too fast."

Lily smiled. "I asked them about that possibility once, because I thought the same thing. They told me there are very few authorized and capable to move the pieces into place. You can't see it from here, but there are additional blocks which have to be moved first, like a puzzle lock, and the puzzle is changed every so often so that only the magistrates know the combination."

I made an effort to pick up my jaw to keep it from hanging. I had never felt so small before, and so uneducated about the world. Brokk had made a comment once about how when he learned things, it opened his eyes to how much more there was to learn. How he didn't know what he didn't know. The phrase at the time had been confusing, but something about it now clicked. That the breadth of knowledge probably couldn't even be measured, or with each new understanding that unlocked, another ten levels or more lay beyond. I had never imagined that something like the city of Adrilan could exist. I had been raised in the mud by a lake, that was the totality of my world. Lily brought her influence from the outside, funneling in bits and pieces to add some understanding about other places. But I now knew it was distilled down to short explanations and reduced to a glossing over of what the rest of the world was like. If this was Adrilan, what was TerraIgni like, or Lacausia where my faeder's kind were from? My head buzzed with the expansion of curiosity, when Lily's description of the locks sunk in. "So, to turn the city to get it to open again, only the approved few Petrafae can do it. They could keep us here, if they wanted to."

Lily appraised me for a moment. "Yes, I suppose that is true. But the Petrafae are allies with the Ignisfae, and I'm an appointed dignitary. We're welcome here, and will not be trapped by any means. I've visited many times and have always been able to come and go easily. Really the only ones who would have an issue are the Umorfae."

Emblyn raised her hand to her mouth, seemingly the only one who noticed Lily's comment aside from me. I stepped back a pace, away from the great rotating city. "As I keep having to remind everyone, I'm half Umorfae."

Lily started to approach me, but Emblyn held up her hand to her, stopping her. Emblyn moved closer to me, linking her arm through mine and tugging us away from the others.

I almost smiled at the brazen move, it was so Emblyn. Lily was a princess and Embyln's elder, yet Emblyn stepped up to be the one to speak with me. What I then did smile at—after I managed to shake off the unsettling feeling of what the Petrafae might think of me when they saw me—was that Emblyn had recognized what Lily had said. She could understand me in a way that no one else could. She knew how I might worry about the implications of me entering the Petrafae stronghold. Honestly, shame on Lily for *not* telling me more about it. Was it information intentionally left out?

Or was it a simple slip of the mind? It almost didn't matter because if I asked Lily, she would of course say it was the latter. And yet, how many opportunities did she have to tell me on our way here? To use one of Lily's favorite phrases, a fuck ton.

"I know how you might be feeling," Emblyn said once we were well away from the others. "I don't think she hears herself or understands your trepidation, but I do. I'm not a mestisius, like you, so I know it's a limited understanding of mine. But, I think I get it more than most. It's hard being half of a race that everyone else hates. But all of us here love *you*. And really, it's been a long time since anything negative happened with any Umorfae anywhere, that I know of. I think that hatred has simmered a lot. And, you are here as Lily's special guest. What I mean is, I think given the situation, you are safe."

"And what if Lily wasn't here to vouch for me?"

She didn't answer right away. "I think your hesitation would be warranted then, because you're right, they'd see you're half Umorfae, and not trust you."

"See," I retorted. But then I went quiet as I thought. Emblyn *did* see, she saw me. Around her, I *felt* seen. The parts I was willing to allow to be seen, that is. And she never disregarded my feelings, however she was adept at getting me to look at my feelings from a different perspective. I sighed. "All right, Emblyn."

"All right what? I didn't ask anything of you."

"Yeah, but, I know you are. You're asking me to get past my feelings and go with you all up to the city."

"Well when you put it like that! So will you?" She batted her eyelashes at me.

I groaned, then laughed. "You can be so insufferable. Yes, let's go."

Emblyn danced and said, "Ah shit yeah! Clear the path! Sereia is coming!"

CHAPTER 12

The staircase had descended to the ground by the time Emblyn and I returned to the group. Petrafae gathered around the top, lining the sides where we would walk through. Lily gave me a soft smile and nodded, then turned without a word to ascend at the head of our group with Kerenza and Queen Deniza to either side of her. I decided it was probably a formality, that the order we walked up to greet the waiting Petrafae might matter. Yet another thing that would have been good to educate me on first, but I was quick enough to figure out that I should bring up the rear with Emblyn. Rachael and Maureen followed after the first three. Emblyn squeezed my hand and gave me a big smile. *This will be fun*, her smile seemed to try and assure. I grinned back, I knew she was excited about what experiences she might have here, and I wasn't about to ruin it for her. I would have fun, too, Emblyn seemed convinced of that. For her, I would make the most of it.

I tried not to swivel my head at the heights we were reaching while climbing the stairs. I had never been so high up, and we hadn't even nearly reached the top. My stomach dropped when my eyes wandered to the side, allowing me to see just how far down it was. I focused instead on the stairs themselves, the feel of the stone as I dragged my fingers lightly along the railing, the feel of Emblyn's warm hand clasped in mine.

Lily was just finishing her greetings, and must have been introducing me and Emblyn when we crested the last riser. My stomach once again clenched as all eyes swung to me. There was a moment where their gazes felt hard, discerning. Wind whipped through their bright, coppery hair as we stood at the crux of entering their domain. The soft, diffuse light from the mist-filled skies made their tawny skin seem to glow, as they stood stock-still assessing me. But their expressions soon lightened and they welcomed me with open arms, literally. There were no formal fists to their chests like Lily's mate, Rannoch, would do. Instead they took turns wrapping their bulky arms around me in exuberant hugs. Everyone in our party got the same treatment, a gesture which had Emblyn beaming from ear to ear.

As they led us further into the stronghold, I found my previous apprehension had melted away. My impressions were that they were overall kind, and tolerant. It was interesting how warm their greeting was after that initial moment of appraisal. When I thought about it, it almost seemed like that would be the approach that the Ignisfae would have, as a fire wielding and naturally warm race. Heat ran through their veins, their frequency—as Brokk had put it—meant that they were more akin to fire. And yet, their interactions with others usually felt more stoic. But, I had really only met a small few of them. Four at this point. Queen Deniza, Rannoch, Kerenza, and Emblyn. Though admittedly Emblyn's friendliness seemed over the top sometimes, she also seemed different, and offset from her kin in that manner. If I were to describe the Petrafae's appearance in one word, it would be stoic. Built like blocks with muscle mounded on top, the great stone wielders were not stand-offish at all, but very demonstrative instead. It seemed a curious contrast to the first impression of their stature.

Walls that had bordered both sides of us opened up to reveal a massive area, Lily motioned to it and told me it was the main courtyard. I stopped and stared at everything, as much as I wanted to carry on the illusion that it was not overwhelming to me, I finally could not fight that reality. It was absolutely stunning, with levels upon levels of carved stone, entrances into the inner keep on each ring up, and every opening bordered with elaborate carvings and detail. Some strange creature's likeness had been formed as support structures to several of the grander entrances, with wide open maws the width of their heads, and many legs lined down the sides of serpentine-like bodies. Countless clumps of plants grew down from recesses above each level, creating a cascade of greenery over the sculpted rocky surfaces and softening the otherwise imposing creatures' fearsome depictions.

A loud scraping sound behind us caused me to pivot on the spot. Dust plumed out from the hall we had just walked through, as the staircase settled in place. They had pulled the stone riser back up, and it swung neatly within the wall, enclosing the courtyard. I glanced up, noting four Petrafae on the top of the wall bordering the area. They must have been the sentinels that help move it when visitors arrive, and perhaps the ones that can move the whole city as well.

I turned back to the center of the courtyard, just in time to see my group disappearing into the main entrance. Rushing to catch up, I sprinted headlong into the darkened opening, straight into someone's solid form. I smacked into their back so hard my teeth rattled and I fell backward, dazed.

"Are you all right?" a disembodied male voice asked.

No, it wasn't disembodied, I just couldn't see properly yet. I blinked my eyes, trying to get my vision to clear. "Yes, I'm sorry, I couldn't see you."

A laugh, a rich chortle of a laugh echoed through the space. Then a broad palm appeared in front of me. "Here, let me help you up." He grasped my hand, though I wasn't sure I was ready to stand yet, however I didn't argue as he pulled me up. My eyes adjusted after a moment and I finally saw his face. Brilliant copper haired twisted in multiple braids, a few wisps of hair hung down, which framed stunning green eyes. His bronzed skin caught what little light there was, showing off a sculpted, bare chest. The taut muscles of his arm held firm as he steadied me, then my gaze fell past him. I saw Emblyn's too excited face looking back and forth from him, to me, and with a few obvious glances in between that dipped to his bulging biceps. She grinned and gave me an approving gesture along with an obnoxious eyebrow wiggle. I rolled my eyes and waved her off. She was much too giddy about males in general, but then I shook my head and laughed. *Of course* she would make her way back just in time to see this. He realized someone was behind him, then spun to see her.

"Greetings!" she said in that chipper voice that had me shaking my head again. "I just came back to see what was keeping my dear friend. Now I know she had good reason to be delayed."

I almost audibly groaned. *Nooooo*, I pleaded with her with my eyes. *Oh my gods, she's going to make this a thing.*

"Good reason?" he asked, swinging his head back to me. I quickly dropped the look I was giving Emblyn and put on a big, pretend smile that showed entirely too many teeth before his eyes had fully landed upon me.

Before I could respond, Emblyn reached over to thread her arm through mine. "Stopping to meet a handsome male such as yourself, of course," she said easily, like it wouldn't cause me any kind of discomfort.

He stared, his cheeks reddening as his mouth worked to form words.

"I bumped into him and fell down, Emblyn, he was nice enough to help me back to my feet."

"Ah, *well*, whatever the reason, I'm sure we'll see you later," she amended with a dripping, sweet tone. "We'll definitely make an effort to meet back up with you again. For now, Sereia and I must rejoin our group." Emblyn tugged me further into the hallway.

"Sereia, is it? Then later it is!" he said, his form backlit by the exterior light coming down the passage. I didn't respond as he shrunk in the distance.

"Are you serious?" I hissed at Emblyn. "Meet up with him later? What are you doing?"

She squinted her eyes at me and pursed her lips, making a kiss noise. "Here I was thinking I needed to help you find a male, and you found one even before me!"

"I hardly think that me tumbling blindly into him qualifies," I mumbled.

"We'll have to find out where the hangouts are," she mused, seemingly ignoring my comment as she walked me further into the building.

"What are those?"

"Hangouts? Lily told me that's where those that have

completed their growing cycles go, to "hang out." We don't really have a phrase so I always used it. There's got to be someplace where they go, to dance and party, some place where they can get away from the elders and have fun."

Before I could ask further questions, the area brightened and we caught up to Lily, Kerenza, Zia, Queen Deniza, Rachael, and Maureen. Beams of light filtered down from small vents high above the rotunda we were now in. Kerenza gave Emblyn an assessing glance, which Emblyn returned with an innocent smile, as if she hadn't been planning to escape their watchful eyes later. Fortunately Lily seemed engrossed in something a female Petrafae was saying to them. Movement from the hallway caught my attention, and I realized the male I had walked right into made his way to our group. He caught me looking at him and winked at me, before standing behind the female guide.

"Our stronghold has proven to be impenetrable, in more than five hundred cycles since it was first constructed it has remained unbreached," the tall, stately looking female said to Lily and the others. They were apparently listening to a history lesson on the construction of the city.

"What are the carvings on the walls? What manner of creatures are depicted there?" I asked. All eyes swung to me, but I ignored them. I turned my attention to the guide instead.

She angled her gaze toward me, gold face paint which I hadn't noticed at first glimmered in a shaft of light as she cocked her head. Delicate symmetrical designs below her eyes glinted like pure metal and shone brightly as she looked at me. "They are the revered denizens of the deep, the scolopendra. Mighty burrowing creatures that tunnel through the rock here in Northern Alternis. They guard our borders from below."

"From below?" I asked.

She nodded, her hands now subtly squeezed together from the previously relaxed way she had been clasping them at her abdomen. "Our great city is anchored into the ground, and though the entrances are along the upper courtyard, the city must have the underground protected as well, lest any ruthless foes decide to find an alternate route. Protecting our people from threats, providing food and clean water, there are many concerns for leaders to manage." She turned away from our group, lifting her arms toward a blank wall, palms upraised as she pushed an invisible force toward the stone. The male I ran into lifted his hands as well, assisting her with moving the stones.

A tremendous grating sound reverberated through the chamber, punctuating her words as the last slivers of light that remained from the outside were cut off. The great room had rotated the center column, which changed our orientation and blocked us off from the main exit. A set of stairs had been revealed at the same time, but different from the ones we had entered the city by. These ones seemed to twist up and away. The guide opened an arm toward the stairs, palm up with a serene expression in a seemingly benevolent gesture. Lily moved toward it without hesitation. I appeared to be the only one who paused, noting that our only way out was forward, and they controlled all entrances and exits. I sucked in a breath. Lily was smart, she wouldn't do something unless she believed it was safe. I had to remind myself again and again that we were here in part for *my* training. That Lily knew them and was my protector. And to remind myself of the warm greeting they had eventually given me.

Emblyn turned back and leaned over to me, whispering in my ear, "That is the Petrafae leader, Magistrate Zarneh. We should probably follow."

My eyes rounded, here I was throwing random questions at the head of the city while she was trying to take us on a tour. Emblyn walked forward, coaxing me onward. I nodded to myself as I brought up the rear with her, then started to ascend the tight spiral of stairs higher than I had ever imagined I could go.

CHAPTER 13

Emblyn flopped down on a huge bed, high up in a tower that she and I had been assigned to stay in. I had excused myself to wash up in the bathing chamber, it was my first time using an indoor bath. Equally strange was relieving myself indoors, where the waste went I had no idea, but it was a far cry from peeing in the woods. The whole experience of the washroom was unparalleled, I saw myself in the clearest, most crisp reflection I had ever seen. This was not like looking back at myself at the water's edge, this must have been the most accurate reflection possible. I could see fine details in my dark irises, which I previously thought were simply black. Not so, there were tiny flecks of bright silver in them. The sheen of my opal hair shifted with subtle colors of pink and turquoise, even though it was primarily white. Brushing back my wet hair, it dawned on me that I was starting to learn the limits of the time I could spend away from water. I had only officially bathed twice while on our trek here, and I was beginning to feel the dryness set in when we had arrived at our new room.

Adjusting the robe I had donned after bathing, I left the washroom, then walked over to the wall of the round main bedroom. I peered out the slit of a window, looking out onto the expanse of land. The Praegra Forest seemed to stretch on forever, so far that I couldn't tell if it ever ended, the ever-present mist enveloped it well before wherever the edge of the forest may have been. I didn't even know if I was looking toward Caer Lake, toward Lacausia, or toward some other direction that I was unfamiliar with. It all looked the same from this impossible height, in all directions from the various windows that opened out from the curved walls. The dark rotations were nearly upon us, with the light waning and turning from golden to a hazy lavender. We had left Caer Lake before the light rotations had truly begun, which would make sense that nothing would look familiar. We had traveled constantly for many rotations and were a long way from where we had started. If I had gone so far west, I wondered how far Brokk had made it in another direction.

"This bed is so comfortable! I could snuggle in for a nap if I wasn't so excited to go meet others." Emblyn stretched and kneaded her feet in the blankets.

"You mean males," I corrected, giving her a sly glance over my shoulder.

She sat up quickly, throwing the blankets off of her. "True! Then let's get to it!" Just as fast, she fell back into the bed again. "But just *feel* this first! I haven't had a real bed since I was in my quarters in TerraIgni!" She patted the area next to her, so I padded over to the empty side of the bed then laid down.

She was right, it was *luxurious.* My eyes closed involuntarily, why did we need to go out after all? We could just stay in comfort and not have to deal with anyone else. But, I knew Emblyn was anxious to meet other young Fae. I thought about the tenuous greeting I had received when we arrived, then worried the same thing would happen again. I opened my eyes and stared at the carved stone ceiling. "Emblyn, can I ask you something?"

I heard her turn toward me, but I didn't look at her. "Of course, anything!"

"Why were you not put off by me when we first met? Why was it that you could seemingly so easily look past what I am? Very few others seem to be able to." I moved my head to look at her finally.

She was still for a moment, then answered, "Because I know what it's like to have others assume they know who you are because of what you are. It is of course different for you than it is for me, but even so, I know the feeling."

"But you were captured and imprisoned by Umorfae when you were a youngling. Do you not hate all Umorfae because of that?"

"You didn't capture me, *you* were not responsible. The Fae are notorious for holding grudges, for *eons*. Yes, there were terrible things that happened. But we don't have to carry that generational trauma on top of our own life events. I think hate is too easy, and I know that Umorfae can be bad, but it's not fair to sum up the whole race that way, is it? It's a trap we too easily fall into."

I looked back to the ceiling for a moment, thinking about her words and weighing how truly wonderful she was. Her sentiments were almost exactly like what I had expressed to Brokk, so similar that I marveled at the serendipitous nature. How two females born under such different circumstances from completely different parts of the world, could have such similar views. I kicked my legs to flip myself upright, hopping out of bed in one motion. "Okay then, let's go."

"What? Really? I swear I thought you were going to try and

get out of it," Emblyn said as she sat up.

"And miss out on you charming some Petrafae? No way." I tightened the belt of my robe, smiled at her, then moved toward the door to leave.

"Not like that!" Emblyn exclaimed. "You can't wear a bathing robe out!"

"Oh. Then I'll put my dress back on."

She gagged, then chopped her hand in the air in an emphatic gesture. "*No.* Definitely not your dress. That thing is so dirty I'd wager only fire will do to get rid of the grime."

I folded my arms across my chest. "Well then *what* am I supposed to wear?"

She slid off the bed, then headed over to a boxed-off area that jutted out from the wall on the opposite side of the room. "Let's see if they have anything fun in here for us." Pushing, then pulling what looked to be a stone panel, Emblyn eventually worked open some sort of storage cavern. She put her fists on her hips and smiled triumphantly at folded fabrics held inside. "I thought it looked like a closet! I imagine it's much easier for a Petrafae to open that."

I walked over to join her, peering at the lengths of various cloth she had already begun rummaging through. Some fabrics seemed more utilitarian, simple weaves made from dry looking threads in bland colors. But there were a few pops of color that she was quick to weed out and heap in a pile.

"These are *definitely* TerraIgni textiles, I recognize the weave, but let's see if they're worthy TerraIgni fashions, shall we?"

I gave her a quizzical look. "What does that mean?"

Emblyn gave me a knowing smirk. "TerraIgni has *the best* clothing, by far. We wear a lot of linteums, of course, long pieces of fabric designed to wrap a particular way around the body. But on top of that, our constructed clothing is simply stunning. I know there has been trade with the Petrafae for a long time, so it would make sense they have received fabric from us. But let's see how these pieces measure up!" She squealed with excitement as she piled up the ones that she deemed to be of the better make, then carried the haul over to the bed.

After a lot of tying, twisting, testing, and audible contemplation on Emblyn's part, she decided I was nearly ready to be presented. She picked a dress out for herself and dressed quickly, then led me into the washroom. Keeping me turned away from the reflecting wall—which was apparently called a mirror—she applied color that had been left for us to my eyelids, cheeks, and lips. Emblyn told me all about "makeup" while she smiled at her work, explained how it is used to accentuate facial features, and how the colors are different in TerraIgni. Deeper, warmer colors like reds, bronzes, and browns. She mentioned how her maeder would dress her up and put makeup on her.

"I never had that," I mentioned. "I don't know if Syrenni used it in the past before leaving Lacausia, but they definitely don't now. At the most, Neila would brush my hair. I'd imagine my faeder's kind wear makeup, though."

She paused, looking me over for a moment. "Neila is not your maeder, correct?"

I nodded. "She was my maeder's sister. I never even met my maeder, she died before I hatched. And I don't even know who my faeder was. Lily knew my maeder, though. But if she knew who he was, she never told me."

Emblyn nodded. "I've heard a little about her. From the

stories, she sounds very brave."

I frowned. It wasn't easy to accept that I'd never know my maeder aside from stories, in spite of the fact that her effort had not only helped free the Syrenni from the Umorfae, but also helped prevent an evil Vale Born from taking over the realm. It's the familia ties that have to endure the loss, while the bravery of their loved one lives on in memory only. When experiences of life and key moments happen without them, their stoic death is little consolation.

Emblyn finished my makeup, then finally turned me around to face the mirror.

I blinked and went to rub my eyes, which then Emblyn promptly averted by batting my hands away.

"Don't rub, it'll ruin it," she advised.

"I can't believe that's me!" I sputtered. The color on my eyelids shimmered a soft pink, more saturated yet matching the color of my hair that shone depending on the way I angled my head. The teardrop-shaped pink swaths on my lids were punctuated by a thin, precise swish of black which swept across my upper lash line, then streaked slightly upward past the corner. There was a little color on my cheeks and lips, but what was really eye-catching was the dress.

It looked like bright liquid silver hugging the curves of my upper body, until it cascaded off of my hips and slowly transitioned to a crystalline blue. It reminded me of falling water, and of Brokk's eyes.

"I never knew I might look like this."

Emblyn smiled and took my hands, giving them a gentle squeeze. "*This* is who I saw when I met you, who you are on the inside. Now your appearance reflects that."

I tried not to let my doubt at her words show, not that I thought she didn't mean them, but that they were not true. How many times had I been dishonest? How many times had I misdirected Neila, lied by omission, or just outright lied? Too many to count.

She noticed the hitch in my breath, but I smiled and squeezed her hands back. I would *make* myself deserving of her admiration. Starting with this event. If dancing was what Emblyn wanted to do, godsdammit we were going to do it. "I think I'm officially ready, let's go do this hang up."

"*Hangout*," she corrected with a grin.

Leave it to Emblyn to somehow find a Petrafae who could tell us where a secret meetup was. She had intentionally skipped talking to two guards before finding a third whom she pegged as someone who would know. Sure enough, after he asked if she'd dance with him when he was off duty, he told her exactly where we needed to go. We'd descended what felt like thousands of spiral stairs down into the depth of the great stone city, when I heard the thud of a rhythmic beat. A glow from a rough tunnel seeped into the hallway we stood in, Emblyn looked at me with practically maniacal giddiness as she grabbed my hand to run toward the light together.

After several twists and turns, the hallway opened up to a great cavern with uneven walls, torches lining the sides provided barely enough light to see the writhing bodies. I stared at everyone, all moving with similar motions and dancing to the drums. Several

Petrafae stood on a raised platform on the far side of the cave, each lifting and dropping various sized stones, which they did either in unison or timed perfectly offset from each other. Females and males both sang, using their voices to complement the thudding stones. I had never seen or heard anything like it, hitting and dropping objects to make sounds. When a particular rapid succession of beats happened, the whole crowd sang the same phrase at the same time, adding their own sounds to the music. Emblyn tugged at my hand, trying to get me to budge from the spot I had become rooted to, I was too busy watching everything.

"Come on, let's *dance*!" she insisted.

I blinked, shaking off the trance the music had stunned me into. I laughed and then was the one to drag her out to the center. Countless Petrafae moved to the beat, now with Emblyn and me in the middle. Slightly awkward at first, it took a few times to find motions that felt natural to me. Emblyn spun frequently, causing her dress to fan out around her in a colorful, swirling circle. I found if I spun like that with both feet on the ground, my dorsal fin eventually got in the way, but a modified, fluid swish motion felt natural and flowed with the energetic rhythm. The beat ramped up again, reaching the crescendo I recognized as when the crowd would chant.

"Scolo! Scolo! Scolo! PENDRA!" Their voices dragged out the "A" at the end, which was punctuated by a deep bass thump.

The floor rumbled, shaking the torches on the walls and reverberating up my legs. The sensation came from directly below us, which sent cheers through the crowd. A thunderous, echoing boom shuddered through the entire space, followed by the sound of thousands of scraping clicks which felt like they came from the underside of the rock we stood upon.

Emblyn and I dropped to a crouch, my eyes wild with fear as we locked our gazes. She covered her head, which I copied, fearing the rocky ceiling was about to come down on us.

"What's happening?" she shouted, though I could only make out what her lips were forming, rather than actually hear her above the loud music. The beat abated, and the shuffling clicks faded from below the surface. I realized their music had called the guardian that the magistrate had spoken of, the scolopendra. Fortunately it seemed to be contained beneath the rocky cavern we were in, and did not have direct access to any of us.

A pair of muscled hands hoisted me up. "I am always lifting you off the ground, it seems!"

I gasped as I was placed upright again. "Oh! It's … you." I didn't know the name of the male I had run into—literally—earlier.

He flashed a brilliant, beautiful smile. How did his eyes look so bright in this dark cavern? They seemed to have a funny gleam to them. "Tyrus!" he said, then looked over my shoulder, waving to someone else.

I glanced to where he had gestured, but whoever it was he had motioned to had already begun dancing with a partner. I looked back, finding the male staring at me. It took me a moment to realize he may have been introducing himself. "Your name is Tyrus?"

"Yes," he answered, "I am here to dance." His speech was a little slow and slurred. "With you," he added.

"She'd love to!" Emblyn exclaimed, as she popped up from below.

"Faex!" I cursed, clutching my chest instinctively from being so thoroughly startled by Emblyn. She gave me a mischievous grin.

Tyrus laughed, then took my hand and tugged me into motion before I could respond. The room swirled around us, the beat quickened again, ramping up in a loudening crescendo. He pulled me into the thick of the throng, the bodies around us flowing to the rhythm. This time it was more familiar, more expected when the chant approached. By the time everyone called out in unison, I felt the rightness of it, the way it moved through the whole crowd. I joined in and belted out the chorus to summon the beast, it wasn't long before the thumping and the clicks of what must have been its massive legs returned. This time I was more prepared for it, and the joyous shouts of the Petrafae helped lessen the terror as well. I looked over and saw Emblyn had found a partner, and was busy delightedly kicking up her heels in a dance with him. The guard from earlier who had directed us to the cavern had made his way down to find Emblyn. I grinned as I saw the look of absolute joy on her face.

I danced with Tyrus for a long time, until beads of moisture collected along my temple. I became parched from all the activity, and the lack of moisture in the air. "Can I have some water?" I asked him, shouting over the music.

"Want some vocafortis, too? I was going to get myself more soon anyway."

I shook my head. I didn't know what that was exactly, but I remembered Brokk mentioning it as something that makes you feel off. Tyrus shrugged, then sauntered away to procure drinks. I watched him as he met up with a group of males by the beverage area, all cajoling with each other as they chugged clear liquid.

Emblyn spun in front of me, grabbing my hands. "Where did your friend go? Let's dance!"

"Off to get me some water and some vocafortis."

"Oh, I forgot to mention, be careful with that. It can really mess with you. I don't drink it, but if you want to try it I understand. It's powerful, it can really sneak up on you."

I waved her off. "I'm not having any, though he is, apparently." I nodded with my chin in the direction he had gone, still guzzling drinks with males. A female came over and looped an arm around his neck, trying to get him to go with her.

"Looks like he's popular with others," Emblyn mentioned. She looked back at me, with a worried expression creasing her brow.

I shrugged. "Sure, he seems likable." I decided I didn't care one way or another if he came back. "Where's the one you were with? You seemed to be having fun!"

She nodded emphatically. "Yes! He had to complete his guard duty, but he promised he'll be back."

"I thought he was coming here after his guard duty was over?"

"He took a break to come find me, wanted to make sure we found our way. Hopefully he'll be back soon."

"Now *that* is a thoughtful male." I made an effort not to roll my eyes at Tyrus, and smiled at her instead. "Might as well dance then!" I lifted my arms overhead and spun on one toe. When we had tried spinning before my fin always got in the way if I spun on both feet. I had a thought it might work better if I tried on only one foot.

"How did you do that!" Emblyn exclaimed. "I want to try, too." She proceeded to bend her knees, then lift herself off the ground, elevating up onto the ball of one foot like I had. She made it about a quarter of the way around, laughing as she came to an abrupt stop, though her dress twirled further in reaction. We traded competing spins, laughing when one was too wobbly, and cheering when either of us completed the occasional full turn.

A loud male laugh from directly behind us halted our spins. "You look so pretty dancing over here! You need some strong arms to assist you, though." I shrieked as Tyrus lifted me high, his hands pressed along my side waist, gripping me hard. Fortunately he only made it partway through one turn before he lost his balance, I managed to touch back down as he fell completely. The males watching him all burst into laughter. He stood up, dusting himself off and chuckling.

"What a charmer," Emblyn chided.

He attempted to give me that brilliant smile again, holding out his hands to start another round of dancing, but his eyes looked wholly glassy, like he maybe even couldn't see straight. "Let's take a break instead, I never did get that water," I said as I motioned over to the drinks, which his jaw dropped in realization that he had forgotten to get me anything. At least he was aware enough to recognize his error. I angled my head to Emblyn, trying to get her to join us, which she dismissed with a flick of her hand. She was clearly waiting for the guard to come back.

I shrugged, then walked with Tyrus to finally soothe my rapidly drying throat. The music died down to a gentle thrum. Whether it was a momentary pause or the normal end of the event, I wasn't sure, but my sensitive, pointed ears were glad for the rest. "Tell me about yourself, Tyrus. What do you do here in Adrilan? Do you serve a role or how do you spend your time?"

He swigged a cup of liquid, definitely not water, as I poured myself something from a carafe—which I sniffed first to be sure it wasn't vocafortis. Based on how he was handling it, I definitely didn't want to accidentally drink that. "I pick things up, then put them down," he answered.

I flashed a quizzical glance as I took a drought of water. "What does that mean?" I asked after I finished my gulp, since he didn't catch onto my confusion.

Tyrus flexed his arms. "I pick things up! I am able to lift some of the heaviest stone among the Petrafae. Magistrate Zarneh calls on me when the locks need to be moved."

"Oh! The locks! I heard about those. That was why you were in the passage, when I first ran into you? You were there to move them to allow the staircase down."

He nodded, not bothering with a verbal response.

"How does the combination work? I am interested to hear more."

He shrugged. "I do not really know, I just move them where they tell me to."

I was about to try and ask him more questions, thinking maybe a different subject would entice better conversation, when the beat ramped up again. He grabbed my hand and pulled me back to the dance floor, barely waiting for me to set my water down.

He looped his arms around my low back, the music was slower this time, more melodic. He smiled at me, that funny gleam in his eye even stronger than earlier. Nearby faces blurred as I took him in, time slowed for that moment as it struck me how handsome he was, how I was *supposed* to find him attractive. He was like a male specimen, with his bold, defined jaw, his muscular arms and chest, his striking coppery hair. And yet, I felt nothing, no desire to be close to him, no yearning to catch one more smile.

The song ended and I stepped back, bowing my thanks before

I moved away to find Emblyn. He stared after me confused for a moment, but it wasn't long before his group of friends were ribbing him and encouraging more drinks, quickly seeming to forget me altogether.

I looked all over for Emblyn, but she was nowhere to be found. I eventually decided to make my way back to our room.

By the time my aching feet had completed what felt like the thousandth step up the tight staircase, I was ready to flop down on our luxurious bed. But as I reached the door, I noticed someone else had let themselves in our room, and left the door ajar.

CHAPTER 14

"You didn't think it was important to tell me, Sereia? I'm responsible for you here! I'm your chaperone! And you just go tromping through the bowels of the city looking for a party? You somehow thought that would be okay?" Lily kept doing the same gesture over and over, her hands open yet angrily slicing through the air to make her point.

I debated how to explain myself, and I certainly didn't want Emblyn to take any blame for it, so I decided to leave her out of it. "I didn't realize I was a prisoner here," I said as I folded my arms. "I just went to explore the city a little, I didn't go looking for a party." A *partial* lie, but a lie nonetheless.

"Didn't go looking for a party, wearing that dress?" Lily gave me an incredulous look that told me she was smarter than the faex I was trying to sell her. She waved a hand, dismissing my next comment, which would have probably been another lie. She walked to the narrow window, looking out on the dark expanse with the heavy mist that shrouded the night rotations we were now well into. "We need to be careful here, Sereia. Something is happening, I can't tell what, but something feels different than the last time I visited. I understand being young, wanting to experience something, finally having an opportunity to see something of the world. I get it. But be mindful, things are not always what they seem. That is true for this entire world, frankly. That's good cautionary advice *anywhere*. Believe me when I say I learned the hard way. Learn from my mistakes."

"Then tell me more!" I shouted. "You brought me here and I slowly started realizing that there are so many things you simply glossed over, barely teaching me anything. How am I supposed to learn from your mistakes if you aren't teaching me in full?"

Lily's expression changed, her whole demeanor changed. Her eyes narrowed and her mouth curved up a tick, like she seemed to delight in something almost wicked. She crossed her arms and leaned back. "Challenge accepted. Get some rest, we start in one quarter rotation."

Emblyn had arrived shortly after Lily left, and somehow magically she didn't pass her on the stairs. Her new love interest, the guard named Trachen, had walked her up, and judging by her swollen lips he had given her quite the parting kiss.

"But what else did she say? Is she still mad?" Emblyn asked, now pacing the room.

"That was it," I said and shrugged. "I never told her anything about where you were—because I honestly didn't know—and I never said that you were even involved in the idea of going to find the party. I think she was only mad about me, because I'm the one who she is supposed to watch over. She didn't even ask about you."

"Well," Emblyn let out a breath, "never mind that we are *both* of age and should be able to go to a party unsupervised, but whatever. I guess I see her point about needing to be careful. Sereia, I'm so sorry, I didn't mean for us to get separated, by the time I tried to find you I think you were already gone. Trachen had taken me to *the most* incredible biblio. And said he'd take us both back there to explore!"

"That's where books are kept, right?"

She nodded. "You said you wanted to learn more, to maybe read about some of the mysteries of the world, perhaps you'd even find out more about Lacausia and the Umorfae."

I paused, looking her over as I thought about it. Then I laughed. "Lily just finished scolding me for scuttling around without her knowing, and we're going to do it again?"

She chuckled a little. "Okay, fair point. But you could ask her, then it's not doing it secretly."

"That's true." I went to the storage area on the wall looking for something comfortable to wear to bed. After finding some soft wrap pants and a matching loose fitting top, I tugged off my dress then donned the cozy clothes. "I have to train with Lily in a quarter rotation, something tells me she's not going to go easy on me, so I need to get some sleep."

Emblyn patted my side of the bed. "Come on then, get some rest. We'll find a way to do both what she wants, and what we want. Clear the path, right?"

I grinned at her and climbed into bed. "Right!" I snuggled in next to her, and she caressed my hair as I drifted off.

"Faster!" Lily demanded.

Sweat beaded on my brow and ran down my back from the countless laps I had run around the expansive training hall, hauling weights with me no less. The sore muscles from so much dancing didn't help, either, but I didn't dare complain about that to Lily as she was still a little irritated with me that I had gone out. I gritted my teeth, pushing myself harder to reach the speed she insisted upon.

"I'd say you're warmed up now," she called out to me. "I know you're anxious to start training with your abilities, but we're going to learn something else first." She motioned me over to where she stood in the center of the large ring. I welcome the light breeze that flowed in from the open arches at the top of the domed ceiling, which let in the misty night air. Braziers lit the perimeter of the room, casting an orange glow on the reddish stone. It was the same stone of the cavern we had danced in, though this rock had been carefully chiseled, erected in large blocks to form the geometric space.

We were in an uppermost area of what was apparently the south tower, the room I shared with Emblyn was in the much narrower north tower. I hadn't gotten to explore any further, other than the path from our room, to the dining hall for mane fare, then to the south tower to train. Lily seemed intent on minimizing my interaction with any Petrafae we passed, not stopping to talk with any of them and made a point to seat us at a small, hidden table in the hall when we ate. I had hoped it was because she wanted to use the time to talk to me, to tell me more information about whatever she planned to teach me, but that wasn't the case. She was fairly unresponsive when I would try to ask anything, she preferred instead to eat her meal of sliced fruit and baked rolls in silence, periodically sipping on capuli until it was time to head to the training ring.

I rolled my shoulders, trying to release the tightness that had crept in from mulling over all the things Lily failed to say to me. All the possible things she could have started teaching me more about. It was definitely *not* the way I hoped we would start out.

"Over here?" I asked flatly, as I arrived near to where she stood.

She nodded once. "Pick up the weapon."

"You mean the stick?"

"*Staff*," she corrected. "And, yes. I'm going to teach you how Kerenza taught me, using our ability in conjunction with physical maneuvers. Spending elemental magic is tiring, and you can exhaust yourself if you only rely on that. You need to learn to fight as well."

"I do know a little fighting," I said.

"A *little*," she agreed, "but not enough to really count in a battle."

I looked at her carefully. She had never mentioned I might need to know how to fight in a battle, and it surprised me that she thought it was necessary. But then again, she had a knack for leaving out critical information, even when I had already called her out on it.

I picked up one of the dry wood poles that lay on the ground at the center of the ring. Not a drop of water was left in the shaft.

It felt brittle inside, like I could sense its contents. I could certainly sense its lack of water. The dryness of it gave it a rigidity that felt distasteful to me, something about it made my skin crawl. Lily picked up the other one, then spun it with her hands, demonstrating switching between her rotating grips to keep it spinning.

"Copy me," she said. "Start to get familiar with its weight, its balance." She guided me through several exercises which built upon the first, adding more movement, periodically switching the direction the staff was going and sometimes including forward thrusts or parries. I certainly wasn't natural at it, but I started to get more comfortable and able to shift through the movements with her, which also helped to get past the icky feeling of the staff in general. When she was satisfied, she instructed me to put down the staff, then motioned to someone on the outskirts of the ring. Two well-built Petrafae came forward, lifting their hands in the air to hoist a stone trough between them. The basin hovered slightly off the ground, and though I couldn't see any water sloshing out of it, I could feel it as they approached.

They settled it in between us on the floor, then stepped back to the alcove they had been stationed in. The water rolled in soft waves after being set down, taking a few moments to calm completely. I felt the movement lessen as it slowed, watched it come to rest. I didn't even need to watch it to feel the movement of it, I could close my eyes and see it as if my eyes were staring right at it. I looked back up to Lily, who studied me carefully.

"I've never taught someone how to wield water before," she spoke after a moment. "I'm going to show you how I learned, but there might be some trial and error to find the best way to show you. I know you've had some instances of things happening without you trying, so the innate tendency will be there I'm sure, but it will be about learning control. It won't be easy, though."

I nodded, feigning ignorance about controlling water. I didn't want to let on about what I had already learned, and how.

Lily held her hand open over the water, palm up, then curled her fingers toward herself. The water bulged up until a sphere released from the surface, floating up to her. "Hold your hands open and ready. It's hard to pull up a sphere but much easier to maintain one. I'm going to pass this off to you. Take your hands below mine and *feel* the volume, test its weight and the tension on the surface." She used her chin to motion to my hands, directing me to bring them under hers.

I did as she wanted, preparing my stance like I was going to take over the control of the fist-sized sphere and try to keep it aloft. I nodded to her, which she then slowly pulled her hands away. The ball wobbled, then lost cohesion and slipped through my fingers, splashing on the ground. I made a show of looking apologetic, which she waved off.

"No worries, I expected this to take a few tries. That's why the sphere is small." Lily had formed another ball already, and wasted no time passing it to me again. It fell, or rather, I *let* it fall. She pinched her lips, but said nothing as she pulled up more liquid. I decided to hold onto it this time, two failures seemed like enough. Her face lit up with excitement as I held the ball of water steady, and a pit in my stomach grew. I faked a smile at her, even though I was dismayed with myself for misleading her. But, this way was better, she shouldn't know about Brokk and the time I had spent with him. Hopefully it would only be a few more purposefully thwarted attempts with my skill before I could abandon the ruse.

Lily held her hand over the water again, but waited before commanding it. "I want you to try pulling up some water yourself this time."

I nodded, wondering how far to take it. Should I just get it over with and pull some up? She demonstrated the subtle, claw-like motion she used to get a portion to funnel off of the surface, she let it pull up until a small amount had separated from the main body, then let it back down. I readied my stance, then copied her. In truth, my stance would have been different, my hand motion as well. I had already long since figured out what way was most responsive for me, what worked best with my physiology. My webbed fingers caused differences, but I needed to look like I was doing it *her* way. Nonetheless, a runnel came off the surface and came to my call.

Her jaw dropped. "You are learning fast!"

I tried not to look concerned that she might think I was learning *too* fast, and gave her a large, toothy grin. I decided against any sort of patronizing remark about having the best teacher, because I did actually want to make an effort not to outright lie to her. I let the water splash back down, and didn't bother to try and do so carefully. I figured that would indicate weak control over the volume I had pulled up. I spotted Emblyn waiting in the wings, trying to get a view of what we were doing. She made eye contact with me, then motioned to the exit, making an opening and closing sign with her hands that looked like a book. It took me a beat to realize she *was* making a book sign, and that it meant she wanted to hurry off to the biblio.

"I'm getting tired," I blurted. "Perhaps we can resume later?"

"Yes, of course!" Lily answered. "You should definitely be

mindful of using too much energy. You'll have to learn your limits on how much you can use at a time. We'll need to have a discussion about burnout."

I nodded, Emblyn once again catching my eye and jerking her chin toward the hallway. "I wanted to go with Emblyn to the biblio. I know I'm not supposed to wander the city, but she has a guard that is willing to escort us." Hoping my progress warranted a little relaxation of the leash, I decided to just ask Lily if I could go, rather than go and get another scolding again. Lily opened her mouth, her expression told me she was about to say no. "I promise to go only to the biblio," I added quickly. "I'd love to see the books you've told me about. I've never seen a whole collection! Only the ones you've brought from TerraIgni to teach me to read with." I closed my hands together at my chest, wringing them. Maybe I should have gone, then asked for forgiveness later. But, another unsanctioned outing could mean further restrictions, maybe even going so far as keeping me sequestered in my room, aside from when I go to train. Definitely *not* the trip Emblyn and I had envisioned.

She sighed. "All right, Sereia, you can go to the biblio."

"Whenever I want?" I asked, lifting my clasped hands higher to my heart.

"Don't push it," she warned. She laughed finally and pointed with her chin toward the archway that led out of the training arena. "Okay, you monster, get out of here. Have fun in the biblio, but be safe, be aware."

I chose not to pause at her wording, and instead nodded as I ran off to head down the hall with Emblyn.

"I take it you decided to ask her?" Emblyn asked.

"Yep, let's hurry before she changes her mind!"

Emblyn giggled, and grabbed my hand to hurry faster. "Trachen is waiting for us in the next hall."

CHAPTER 15

It was no surprise, but I had never imagined so many books. What was a surprise was the levels upon levels of them, descending down into the dark recesses of what felt like a depthless structure. The volumes were all stacked sideways on risers, and the flooring sloped down, down, down, spiraling lower into a cavern that appeared to be unlit.

"What's down there?" I asked, peering over the edge. The glow from the closest levels illuminated the empty core of the biblio, highlighting the edges of the otherwise smooth stone. But further down I couldn't see anything. I couldn't sense anything either, nothing with any moisture in it resided below.

"More books, older volumes are lower in the Pit," Trachen answered.

"I'm going to go with him to a secluded section," Emblyn said, her cheeks reddening. "Is there something particular you want to find? He can tell you where to find what you seek."

"Histories mostly," I answered. "Maybe information about the world, the mist, the history of it?"

"So natural history," Trachen responded, though his gaze was fully focused on Emblyn. "Four levels down, south side," he looked away finally, to point where it was. "I can show you, if you like."

"No need," I answered. I knew they were anxious to abscond to some dark corner, and I could make my own way just fine. I walked down the ramp, counting levels once I had passed below the one we had entered on. It didn't take long to lose myself in the wonder of it all. So many books, so many pages, all carefully written. So much time invested to make such tomes of thought and knowledge. I perused several rows, making my ways toward the section Trachen had pointed out. I eventually reached it and found that it didn't house the history books I was looking for, it had histories of war. I stopped to peer at some of the titles. Some were on the subject of the most recent war, titles like "The Attempted Umorfae Expansion" and "Water and Greed", I knew a bit about the noteworthy Magna Mori War between all Fae that had happened over five hundred cycles prior, the war in which the Umorfae tried to take over and rule the realm. But another title caught my eye, "Vitus Augustus's Peloponesian War." I had never heard Lily mention that one, and only knew of Vitus Augustus as being a Vale Born who had ruled many many cycles prior, and that his death had spurred the Magna Mori War, which Lily said meant Great Death. A part of me did want to read about it, to get a better understanding of what my Umorfae kin had done. I pulled it off of the shelf, opening to a random page. It had information about the Umorfae chain of command, about their titles and hierarchies in the military. Praetors, generalises, and spies, and how each one was used. There seemed to be the highest number of praetors, highly trained fighters skilled in battle, generalises were the tacticians good at strategy, and spies were sent out to explore and dig up information to return to the rulers. Many times spies were selected from within the royal family, if they were not particularly good at strategy but needed to be of use. Making them a spy usually meant they were spared from direct hand-to-hand combat that the praetors would handle. After a few pages of too much military information, I closed the book and slid it back into its spot, leaving the heavy reading for later.

A thump, followed by Emblyn's telltale laughter pulled my attention from the distressing subject. I smiled to myself, hopefully they didn't get caught. I moved farther down into the depths away from them, toward what was apparently called The Pit. A level further and I started seeing books that seemed like what I was looking for, encyclopedias with flora and fauna, so many texts on rock formations—which shouldn't be surprising given the interest the Petrafae would likely have in different rock types. The different rocks might actually require different levels of skill or force. I thumbed through one of the books that seemed manageable size, looking at the various sketches and diagrams. The drawings reminded me of Brokk, how he was always putting down what he saw on paper as a visual study, cataloging the known world. I sighed as I put the book back on the shelf, in a way the whole place reminded me of Brokk, of the thirst for knowledge that he had and because of the biblio in Lacausia he had mentioned. I wondered if this one was larger than the one there. Dragging my fingers along the countless spines, I couldn't help but think about him. Couldn't stop myself from wondering what he may be doing right then, if he was safe, if he ever found a place where he could settle and study things at his leisure. I pictured him drawing by a peaceful creek where he could siphon off some water to drink, with plentiful fish in it to catch. With no one nearby to judge him for being an

Umorfae. I hoped he had found that paradise.

I frowned, I was enjoying myself here, sometimes, but truth be told I wanted to be by that stream with him. It may have only been made up in my head, a pretty little image I imagined, but it sounded like a dream I wanted to be a part of. To be near water, with him, and not have the expectations of others pressing against us. Neila expected me to rise up and lead the Syrenni, the Syrenni expected me to simply disappear, Lily expected to teach me and watch me level up to some powerful force. I sighed, brushing aside the thought. I had to remind myself how Brokk and I parted, it was not some rosy-hued promise we had made to find each other. He had made a clear delineation: I was going one way, he was going another. I had grown fond of him in part because he was the first whom I had met where I could really be myself around. I shook my head, that hadn't meant much of anything beyond that. There was no declaration of feelings, no physical interaction. Nothing. That time was over, and I was now, supposedly, heading onward and upward to find my path in the earthen city of Adrilan. I needed to stop letting thoughts and memories of Brokk cloud my eyes, I'd be no better off than the Tamed Syrenni if I continued to pine away for him and not see what was right in front of me.

Like Tyrus. Quite literally now standing right in front of me. *Oh my gods, Tyrus, what is he doing here?* "Hello, Tyrus, how are you? I'm surprised to see you here." Frankly, the only reason I could see him coming to the biblio was if the magistrate needed to have some heavy stone moved. I imagined he never thought long enough to actually even open a book.

"Emblyn had told me where I could find you, I came looking for you."

"Oh, that's nice." I turned, pulling a book from the shelf. I had to do something with my hands, otherwise I might have ended up shaking my fist and muttering a curse at my dear friend who lovingly, continuously, meddled in my life.

"I wanted to ask if you would go to the turba with me."

"The what?"

"The turba. Where we danced and called the scolopendra. I wanted to ask you if you would come again."

"Oh, I see. I don't think I can come, I'm a bit restricted with where I'm allowed to go in the city now." Saying it out loud sounded so pathetic, to be unable to go out, like a youngling being disciplined by their elders and not allowed to go out and play. Pathetic or not, I was actually glad for the excuse, I didn't want to go party with him. Being forgotten while he went to drink didn't especially sound appealing.

"That is disappointing. I would have liked to dance with you again. And ... spend time with you after."

A gleam in his eye and quirk to his lips told me he didn't intend on *talking* after the dance. I humored him with a small laugh. "I'm sure you can find someone else to spend time with in my absence." I opened the book I had pretended to look at, flipping to the first page and ran my pointer finger across a line of text, which I failed to read.

"Yes, that is probably true," he said matter-of-factly. "I was with more than one after the last turba. And also a male. But they were not you. They were not *different*."

I dropped my jaw and snapped my gaze to him, and stared. *Did he really just say that?* To so casually drop that he had been with not one but at least *two* females *and* a male right after trying to court me …

It was the emphasis on "different" that snagged in an unsettling way. "Different," I repeated, wanting him to elaborate.

His smile showed his perfect teeth and softly pointed canines. All too handsome for someone who had just set off my alarms. "Your hair, your eyes. So beautiful, that is what I meant. No one has that look."

"And what else? What else about me do you like?"

"What else is there?" he asked, looking bewildered.

It was hard to believe it was possible, but my jaw hung open ever further than before. To him, apparently, being different was a token, a thing to possess and enjoy for a bit, to take what he wanted from it but to keep his enjoyment of me at surface level. Perhaps it was all he was capable of, anything further than that was outside of his thought process. I closed my mouth and shook my head, clearing away the momentary aghast reaction. In truth he had done me a favor, a fairly inept and unintentional favor. He had shown me who he was, that he really was only there to have fun for a bit, that I meant little more than a different experience for him. I was a curiosity, and he wanted a sample.

His unwitting admission made it so much easier for me to snap the book closed and turn my full attention—and my fury—to him. The sound of the heavy tome clapping shut echoed in the cavernous stone biblio. I sensed the water in his body, tempting me to yank it or push it, though pushing felt more appealing. Repelling him away seemed like a better plan. Instead I repelled the thought of doing anything with my force against him, and put my effort into my response instead. "As I said before, I am unable to go to the turba, and even *more* unable to "spend time" with you, perhaps more than that, I am also unwilling. I have studying to do now." I didn't bother with a pleasant parting, a formal goodbye, nothing. I turned back to the books then moved along the shelf toward other stacks of bound paper.

He waited for a few moments, I could feel him watching me, probably trying to figure out what had just happened. His footsteps echoed at last after I had rounded the bend and descended toward the next row. I decided to move a few more rows down, closer to the bottom and further from wherever Tyrus had just gone. I leaned out over the railing, listening to hear if his steps continued upward. I heard another thump, followed by Emblyn's giggling, so I turned my head up to look in the direction she was. It looked to be about eight levels up, when I felt a light breeze from below. The stale wind seemed to churn up from the depths, as I craned my neck I saw that I had neared the bottom. It appeared that the lowest level terminated into rough stone, but there must have been some sort of connecting passage down further or off to the sides for there to be any ventilation. I had clearly reached the oldest section of the biblio, not much lay beyond. I was about to consider stopping to go find Emblyn, when I glanced back at the shelves. My heart thudded as I noticed a book with a familiar looking sketch paper, with familiar looking drawings, sticking out from between the pages of an ancient book.

CHAPTER 16

The thick leather that wrapped around the cover was cracked in some areas, the corners worn down and overall was extremely dried out. The parchment inside looked beyond frail. It seemed to be hundreds of cycles old. Maybe more. But the excessive age wasn't why I hadn't yet picked up the book. Out of the top of the pages a square of paper had been stuck, a different, newer type of paper than what the book was composed of, and also a slightly different color. The visible sketches on the small leaf appeared cut off, continuing on the remaining slip hidden within the pages. A marked page would probably not be that big of a deal, but the paper was *exactly* what Brokk used to do his drawings on. The charcoal lines looked exactly like his style. Of course I hadn't compared it to what I remembered, as I still had not dared to pick up the book to look at the loose paper completely.

It was ridiculous. It couldn't be his, that would make no sense. Aside from the fact that we had gone different directions what felt like a lifetime ago, how would he even get into Adrilan, into this fortress of a city that was completely impenetrable with the Petrafae controlling all sides above ground, and the scolopendra burrowing from below? Impossible.

I sucked in a breath, reminding myself of the irrationality of even the thought, then pulled the book off the shelf to see what the title was. Whatever had been on the spine had long since worn off. The dust was disturbed from being recently read, some fingerprints were left where there must have previously been an ancient coating from disuse. Setting the book on the edge of the shelf, I opened it to the first page, reading the title, which caused the breath I had pulled in to immediately whoosh out of me. "The Taming of the Syrenni and Connexion to the Mist."

The lettering was of the old style Faelan, making it very hard for me to read, and some of the ways words were formed was very old, too. I didn't know much about alphabet and vernacular history, but I would have guessed the book could date back at least eight hundred cycles. To when Vitus Augustus had died, but the Great War had not yet happened. My eyes drifted further down to a date, 2535 D.V. I thought back to Lily's teachings. That meant it was written *during* Vitus Augustus's rule, when he was still alive. I didn't know when he had officially enacted the Taming of the Syrenni, but it must have been around that time. Whatever was in this book was likely highly dangerous information, and dangerous for the author to risk writing down.

I looked again at the paper, resting just before the quarter point of the page count. I almost didn't want to look at it. I rubbed my fingers together, staving off the grating feeling of something so dry and aged, everything about the book creaked and cracked. I split the book to the marked page, the small piece had a detailed drawing of a flower on it. Definitely familiar in its style of thick-and-thin lines, but in truth I couldn't tell for sure that it was his. There were no markings other than that, just a beautiful flower. I pulled it out, reading the page that it had been holding. An initial glance at the first few sentences told me enough, it actually was a historical recounting of what had happened when the Syrenni were Tamed, and what we had lost. I hauled the book completely off the shelf, then walked up a few levels up to where I had seen a place to sit and read. I wrinkled my nose at the amount of dust in the area, it seemed no one ever visited so far down into the biblio. Perhaps that was for the best, having a secluded corner where I could nestle in uninterrupted for awhile. A faded, deep purple velvet cushion sat atop a small settee, with an angled stone pedestal across from it. I propped the book up on the small ledge which jutted out from the surface, then flipped it back open to the page that had the paper inserted. Settling in at last, I started poring over the long and disturbing history of my maeder's people.

I lost myself in those pages for nearly a quarter of a rotation. I would have kept reading, if I hadn't heard Emblyn looking for me. I shut the book, then mentally noted the page I had ended on before taking it back down to put the heavy tome in its proper place on the shelf. I made sure to keep the bookmark where it had been, just in case. Who knew who was reading it, I didn't want to alert someone that I was studying it as well. Maybe it had been recently read because of my arrival? I didn't know if any Syrenni had ever visited Adrilan, it would make sense that if I was the first—even if I was only half—it would mean interest in finding out more about my race. As I thought about it, I decided it was probably highly unlikely there had been another Syrenni to come here. Before we moved to Caer Lake, we had been stuck in Lacausia Palace unable to leave. I *must* have been the first.

I dropped all thoughts of the what-ifs of the Syrenni when I found Emblyn and Trachen. "Find anyone interesting?" Emblyn asked suggestively. I stared at her puffy lips, clearly having been thoroughly kissed for who knew how long.

I narrowed my eyes at her. "Don't you mean find *anything* interesting ... as in books?"

She chuckled. "Okay, okay, I may have let it slip to Tyrus where you'd be."

"Well congratulations, he found me."

"You seem upset, I think he really likes you, you know. Why not just have some fun with him?"

"He doesn't really like *me*," I retorted. "He's only interested in one thing."

She nodded, lifted her shoulders and hands, as if to say "Yeah, and?"

I laughed finally. "Well I do actually have something interesting to tell you, but we should wait," I looked around to see if we were alone.

Life seemed to breathe back into Trachen, who had been only partially listening and functioning at minimal capacity since they had found me. Whatever he and Emblyn had done had clearly caused him to power down for a time. "I can walk you back to your room," he suggested.

Emblyn reached over to thread her hand through my arm, then stood taller and lifted her chin. "Yes, escort us back to our quarters, Guard Trachen!" She flicked her hand forward with her free hand.

Trachen and I gave each other a look and huffed a laugh. He looked back at her with a gleam in his eye that told me everything: her antics were only furthering his feelings toward her.

The whole way back up to the room I had debated telling Emblyn about the paper bookmark. Finally I decided that since even I wasn't convinced it was Brokk *and* it was so far-fetched, I left that particular part of the story out. Once we were alone in our room I did tell her in detail some of what I found in the book, and that someone else had been reading the same section recently.

"But I don't understand what that might mean," she mentioned as she stared at the ceiling. "The ancient Syrenni could connect to the mist before Vitus Augustus took away their power? But, he *created* the mist, right?"

"Yes, and it must have been that he realized after he shielded Alternis, the Syrenni could be a threat to that. He wanted to keep it intact."

"I still don't understand the purpose, why did he even want the mist so badly?"

I shrugged. "He must have been hiding Alternis from something."

"But even that doesn't make sense, our world exists apart from the human world with or without the mist, as far as I know."

I tapped my chin. "Maybe it was something other than the human world he was hiding us from." I started pacing the room. "Or who knows? Maybe he was just crazy!"

"I suppose that's possible, Lily has told me about the Vale Born that went insane with the power of five Vale Born inside her. Vale Born can absorb each other when one dies, and multiply their power. That Vale Born had tried to kill Lily for her power, was apparently already crazy and then would have had the power of six Vale Born if she had succeeded. I think Vitus Augustus had more Vale Born trapped within him than that. I don't even think they knew how many he killed, but it was a lot. By that reasoning he must have been completely insane."

"Maybe I should talk to Lily about what she knows, since it was a Vale Born that blocked the Syrenni's power. Maybe she might know more about that or about the mist,"

Emblyn watched me walk back and forth. "I am wondering," she said slowly, "why you are so hung up on the mist. It's been there your whole life, why are you so intent on learning about it now? It's been there for a millennia, our world has adapted to it, it's just the way it is now."

I stopped and looked at her. "Because I can feel it, I sense it. Sometimes I feel a pull to it, like it tugs at me for my attention."

"Well that *is* interesting." She hopped off the bed. "Okay, new plan, learn more about the mist, and figure out how to make Tyrus as interesting to you as this weather phenomena you're so obsessed with."

I rolled my eyes. "Oh come *on.* He's just ... he has about as many thoughts going through his head as those rocks he lifts."

Emblyn burst out laughing. "Okay, fair point. *But,* maybe

he needs a second chance. I know Brokk had the intellect that stimulated you, maybe Tyrus has the body?"

I cringed. "Oh my gods you, did not just say that."

She laughed again. "I actually am kind of serious. You do think he's attractive."

"I do."

"I'm just saying, keep an open mind. If you're … uh, *physically occupied*, it's not about the conversation."

"Fine, whatever. I will *consider* it. Now let's go to the banquet hall for nocte fare. I'm officially starving."

With plates loaded as we made our way to an open table in the dining hall, I spotted Lily sitting by herself. I glanced around, then noted the rest of our group had just arrived and was getting food..

"Emblyn, would you mind if I sat with Lily?"

She nodded, her expression seemed to note that I spied an opportunity to ask Lily some questions, some of them hard ones. "I will sit on the other end of the table. I'll get the others to sit with me as they come over."

I blew out a breath and thanked her with my eyes. The Fae so seldom used a verbal thank you, though sometimes I was tempted to do it. I walked over, then set my tray down across from Lily. I didn't ask permission as I slid onto the bench seat.

She gave me a wordless greeting with a nod of her head.

I started to eat, sensing that she wanted again to sit in silence, but I was having none of that. "Thank you for training me today, Lily. And, thank you for letting me go to the biblio."

She looked stunned for a moment. "I'm so used to no one ever saying thank you, it comes as a shock to hear you say it. Though, I appreciate it. It's a human custom that feels awkward to not do."

I nodded. "Speaking of … your heritage, I guess, I wanted to know if you'd tell me some things about being Vale Born."

She blinked. "Another surprise."

"What I mean is, I'm trying to learn about the mist, and since it was originally created by a Vale Born, I thought you might have more insight."

"That is curious, why the sudden interest in the mist?"

I took a bite of food, noticing how she had responded to me with a question. I decided against telling her about my connection to it, how I could sense it. "I guess before the Syrenni were Tamed by Vitus Augustus, they had some sort of link to it, and that was why he Tamed them. I'm studying it in the biblio, but it's written in old Faelan, so it's slow going. Since you're Vale Born, I thought you might know something."

She shook her head. "I wish I did. If I had to guess, I'd say he was more like the Vale Born that tried to kill me and less like me. He was power-hungry, ruthless, and most likely a madman. How he did it, and why, I don't know if that will ever become clear."

I sagged. Another dead end there, but at least she was talking to me. I then realized I had an opportunity to ask another long-burning question. "Then what about my heritage?"

"Your Syrenni heritage?"

I shook my head, and her gaze hardened, her jaw tightened.

"What do you want to know about your Umorfae half?"

I measured my words carefully before speaking. "I want to know about your history with them."

This stiffness in her jaw grew to an outright clench. Her brow furrowed, and she waited a long, uncomfortable moment before she spoke at last. "To get that knowledge, you'll have to earn it. Training, more training. I'll see you after mane fare in the hall where we met earlier. Come prepared to work."

With that, she stood, then left the table without a word to anyone else. I sat, bewildered for a time until Emblyn got my attention and encouraged me to slide down and join the rest of the group. As I finished my meal, I started to become angry. That Lily was now lording this information over me, and would only dole it out when she felt I had worked hard enough crept under my skin in an irritating way. I flexed my hand, then made a fist. *Fine, she wants me to train harder? She'll get more than she expects.*

CHAPTER 17

My muscles burned as I ran triple the laps I had run during my first training session. I wasn't sure why it was necessary to push my body to exhaustion *before* using my water skill, but I didn't argue. I didn't want to give Lily any reason she could wriggle out of telling me about the apparently bloody history she had been a part of. I hadn't let on that I knew anything, but if need be I could make up something so that I didn't have to mention my time with Brokk. I used my still pent-up angry energy from the banquet hall to fuel my legs. I'd anger-run myself until she said stop if I had to.

She called to me, then motioned to follow her. We passed the water trough ready for skill training, and instead walked to a wall on the opposite side. It had pockets a little larger than my hands scooped out in an alternating pattern partway up to the ceiling.

"Climb this wall, then grab that bar to shimmy across to the ramp, then come back down and do it again." She pointed to a narrow rod strung across the top of the right side of the wall which had no pockets.

I gaped at the wall, the pattern on it was for *climbing*. I had never really climbed anything. Syrenni like their fins in the water or their feet on the ground. The only heights they'd tolerate are that of the Great Falls near Lacausia Palace. "Lily, I've never climbed! I don't know how to do it."

"Hand over hand, one hand goes in the pocket, you lift up, get the next hand in the next pocket. Your feet do the same at the same time, repeat and alternate. This is not a difficult climb, sometimes climbing rock is like solving a puzzle, having to think a path out in order to complete it. This is as easy as it can be. It will build your arm muscles and help ease your fear of heights."

"Not likely," I snapped, as I readied to climb it. I closed my eyes and took a breath, *don't be a faexhead, remember you have to do this so she'll tell you what you want to know.* Without deliberating further, I blinked my eyes open and started up the wall. I focused on one hand after the other, rising higher and higher. I made an effort not to look down at the floor, which I could sense getting farther away. Reaching the top after what might have been nearly a hundred repetitions, I closed my hand around the bar that connected the pocketed wall to a narrow circular ramp, which wound around a corner column of the training hall. Leaning out to put myself in position to grab the bar with my other hand, I'd have to let go of the wall not only with the hand that I still had firmly in the last pocket, but also my feet. I'd have to fully commit and allow my legs to dangle in order to get across. I muttered a curse at Lily for this task, if building my arm muscles was the goal, I could have easily done something far more comfortable and safe. Neila would have an absolute fit if she saw this ridiculous maneuver. I let that curse push my determination to make it happen.

With one exhale, I let go of the last sense of stability I had, and now had both hands on the bar. I tried to lift my legs to anchor against the wall, which was now smooth in front of me, I had moved away from the pockets. I suppressed a whimper as my legs couldn't find purchase, then relegated myself to sliding my hands along the bar, moving dekkate by painful dekkate to get across. My dorsal fin hung limply, utterly useless so high in the air. At long last, I reached the end of the bar, then swung my legs over to reach the ramp. After another hard push, I managed to get myself upright so that I could descend the ramp. My heart thundered in my chest as I flattened my back to the wall and scooted down sideways, desperate to get as far away from the edge of the drop off as I could.

My nerves were shot as I reached the bottom, making an effort to calm myself as I walked over to Lily. "There," I said, my voice shaking, "done."

"Wonderful," she smiled. "Do it again."

"What! You have to be fucking kidding me!" I had finally lost it, absolutely lost it. There was no fucking way—

"Do it *again*," she demanded.

"That's just—no! Why are you being so hard on me?"

"Because, you wanted to go out into this world, yes? You want to break free. This world is *dangerous*. There is no part of it that is made with your safety in mind. This is the kind of shit you encounter in the world. I cannot send you out there unprepared. So. You. Will. Do. It. *Again*."

I wanted to scream. Or cry. Or maybe put up my fists and fight. Instead I curled my lips then let out a primal noise, making sure she heard all of my feelings as I started again.

Then again. And again. After my fifth round, she held up her hand. "Take a break. Magna work, Sereia."

My eyes rounded. I had been so mad at her, so frustrated and ready to lash out, yet one word of praise from her had floored me. I had never noticed how much I hung onto those words when she said them, memories flashed in of her teaching me to read, and write, how difficult it had been. I had been so small, progressively getting bigger, and every time, at the end she would tell me "magna work." So much time spent learning with her, looking up to her, hanging on her every word.

"Will you tell me now?" I whispered. In a way, I almost didn't want to know. To hear the reality of what my idol was, to have that stripped away. But, I needed to know. I could not move forward in ignorance.

Lily sighed heavily. "There's no taking this back, Sereia, Once you know … there are dark truths in our world. I've protected you for a long time, my filia. It's not easy for me to just pull back the curtain and let you see it all."

Clear the path. "I need to know though, Lily. It's the half of my heritage that I know nothing about. You've always been my teacher. How will I learn this if you don't teach me? Or more than that, what if someone else teaches me?" I gulped at the outright lie, because someone else had taught me. Had told me how she killed Umorfae.

She nodded. "You're right. I didn't know enough when I started out in this world, and it has cost me with wounds I can never fully heal from." She sat down on the ledge of the water trough, and I joined her. She told me how she arrived through the Vale, how she met Opius first and he tricked her. How she had spent time in Lacausia Palace not knowing she was being served by Syrenni slaves. That my maeder was the one to take care of her. My blood went cold at that truth, I had never known that.

She went on to detail how she got away from the Umorfae, about the great battles she fought in where many Umorfae were killed. Some by her hand, some by her order. Later she decided to free the Syrenni, and she went back to Lacausia to demand their release. The Petrafae—who had been their ally at the mountain battle against the Vale Born that tried to kill her—came to her aid. They started tearing down the castle from the outside until her demands for the Syrenni's release were met. Once again, many Umorfae died. After that the Syrenni were released, and she began the process of relocating them to where they are now at Caer Lake.

She held up her hands. "No more for now. This is a history that is very hard for me to relive. More training, then more stories."

I frowned. I still didn't know some critical details. At least I knew the truth about some of the Umorfae deaths she had been a part of, and knew that Brokk's feelings on the matter were warranted. Painfully lacking was information about my faeder, who he was and what the nature of his death was. I opened my mouth to object, to argue that I had done as she asked with the difficult wall climb.

She shook her head before I even got a word out. "Later, Sereia. Part of this is for your protection, aside from it being hard for me. I have just told you how I killed many of your people. The Syrenni are your people, but so are the Umorfae. And I think you need time to process what I've told you, before we continue." She stood, then walked to the exit. "No water training today."

I let out a relieved breath, with the mixed emotions I had over what she had told me, I was glad not to have to pretend. I glanced to the hall and saw Emblyn waiting. "May I go to the biblio again?"

She nodded once, then motioned for me to join Emblyn.

CHAPTER 18

It had apparently already become the routine for Emblyn and me, we'd go down to the biblio, where Emblyn would hide out in some nook with Trachen doing who knew what, while I studied several levels down. I carefully flipped to the next page, reading further from the same book. The history was boring and dry, nearly as dry as the book itself. I rubbed my fingers together, desperate for some semblance of moisture. I turned another page and stifled a gasp at another loose leaf drawing. It was another foliage sketch, leaves this time, with a grouping of berries. After a moment I realized it wasn't berries, it was beans. Capuli beans when they're still fresh on the bush. The slip of paper marked a page showing daily life, Syrenni living by the river drawn in a cross hatch style. The page was fairly unremarkable and looked just like our life around Caer Lake. In a way that was both heartening and at the same time disappointing. Heartening that we had returned to our way of life, but disappointing that in the millennia since this depiction was portrayed, we had not advanced. Our enslavement had arrested that development and we had reset to the time just before the Taming.

I leaned back and stretched, I had been sitting for a little bit and my muscles were starting to lock up from the strenuous exercise. I wished I had some water. Smacking my lips, I thirsted for something to stave off the dehydration.

"Sereia?"

I almost fell out of my seat. "Faex, Tyrus! You scared me!" I settled myself in my seat again. "Did Emblyn tell you where to find me again?"

"No, I did not know where you would be, I came here because you had been here before."

"Good guess," I said as I went back to reading.

"I thought about what you said. Or I should say what you asked."

I read a sentence that I didn't absorb, as what he said struck me. I looked away from the book and up to him. "You … thought?"

"A nearly impossible feat, I know."

I blinked and shook my head. "Wait, what was that? A joke? You thought, and *then* cracked a joke?"

He nodded and laughed nervously. "I can tell one once in awhile."

"Lily will be so pleased, she always told me the Fae lacked humor, for the most part."

"Only the ones not deserving of a second chance."

Second chance …. I am absolutely going to throttle Emblyn. "Is that so?" I said suspiciously.

"Well, I was not a good partner at the turba, I had already had a lot of vocafortis before I found you, and then I only got worse from there."

"Is that supposed to be an apology?"

"Not yet," his voice steadied, and the look in his eye made me pause.

Something about his response told me he was taking this seriously, as serious as he could, I imagined. "Go on."

"I was forgetful and careless. The next rotation when I found you here, you asked me why I was interested in you. I made a mistake there, too. That is what I thought a lot about, which is what I did instead of going to the turba I had invited you to. I sat and thought. What *do* I like about you? I like that you are smart, and inquisitive. You asked Magistrate Zarneh interesting questions when you first came, most do not even observe what you had noticed with the carvings on the walls. You are observant. I am both drawn to it and shy from it, because I feel you observe everything about me, too. You seem to notice everything."

He waited a beat for a response, but I was too taken aback to say anything yet. Of course Emblyn could have prepared him, told him what to say, that was my initial thought after all, but now I wasn't so sure.

"I *am* sorry," he continued. "I am sorry your first turba experience was diminished because of me. I am sorry I did not know how to respond to you when you asked me what I liked about you."

I appraised him for a moment, he did seem genuine. I gave him a small smile and nod of my head, not much of an opening, but a tentative acceptance of his apology. It was appreciated, but I was still unsure if I'd consider anything further. I rolled my lips, debating what to say.

"I have someplace I would like to take you!" he said quickly, his hand reaching out a little toward me. "That is, if you were willing. It is somewhere I think you will like, once we are there, that is."

I clicked my tongue. "Unfortunately I'm not really allowed, I don't think, but—"

"It will not take long! I can have you back to the biblio in less than an eighth rotation." He held out his broad palm, his eyes shining with hope that I would reciprocate the distance and take his hand.

I looked down at my clothes, dressed in taupe wrap pants and a matching, close-cropped top for training, I was not in what Emblyn would consider suitable outing attire. I laughed a little, I really didn't care what I wore, and I actually felt far more comfortable in what I was wearing now versus the gorgeous dress from the turba. If someone spotted us now, I was in clothes I could move in, evade in. Blend in with. Besides, I had at least a quarter rotation allotted to me in the biblio. I reached forward, then took his hand.

"All right, Tyrus. I will go with you."

His smile lit up his mind-numbingly handsome face. "Magna! It will only take us a little while to climb up."

"Climb?!"

I regretted everything, literally everything, while Tyrus laughed and hoisted us up a sheer rock wall. *Of course* it was rock, and of course it was a wall. Everything in this damn place was stone and everything was made with sheer drops. One wrong move and you'd fall to your death. Only, not with my present company, apparently. Tyrus boasted being the strongest stone wielder, being able to lift the heaviest rocks meant he could also use them to balance our ascent. I grabbed hold of him tighter, now convinced he had taken this ridiculous path simply so I would be tempted to reach my arms around him. What he probably didn't count on was me losing any semblance of sanity and practically choking him to make sure I was holding on tight enough. I clenched in so tight, my face so buried that I didn't even see how he was managing our climb.

"Almost there," he assured, though it had better be soon or I was likely to cut off his air supply all together before we arrived wherever we were going.

Second chance, my ass. Emblyn better not have told him what to say to convince me to go with him on this sadistic journey.

"We are here," he said close to me. A shiver ran down my spine at his proximity, at his warm breath against the shell of my ear. In spite of his assurance, I didn't dare let go until I felt the ground beneath my feet. "Open your eyes, look around."

I actually hadn't even realized how hard I was squeezing them shut. I blinked them open, and audibly gasped. I let go and spun around to see more, as he looped his arm around my waist and held me from behind to keep me steady. "What is this place?"

"The Spire," he answered, again dangerously close to my ear.

We were high up at the peak of the city, everything around us seemed translucent, with varying colors and striations running through it. Light from the nearby torches bounced inside of the surfaces, giving off an ethereal glow with mesmerizing color shifts. "What is it made of?"

"Crystal," he answered. "Our previous castle had been made almost entirely this way, but we learned from our mistakes. It is not safe to craft an entire fortress out of it, but we could add it in some areas and still retain control over the lower portions. Magistrate Zarneh is the best at forming crystals and gems, she has a trove of them in a secluded tower. Hers are unrivaled in sparkle and beauty. She uses gem gifts as a sign of her trust and to seal partnerships."

I had to admit I was surprised. This was the most eloquent he had been with me, the most sharp. Perhaps I had misjudged him. It wasn't that he said anything truly witty or thought provoking, but he didn't sound as vacant as he had before. Maybe the crystals surrounding us had brought clarity to his mind. Mine certainly felt enlivened as I took in the pristine view. "I've never seen anything like it," I said, staring in awe around me. We stood on a narrow platform, also made of crystal, and were sheltered by an angled, roof-like structure, held up by four shimmering, glossy pillars which reflected the flickering torch flame. I could cross and subsequently fall off the open air area in less than a pace. The walls of the city descended below us, graduating outward until reaching the great disc of the main plaza. From the highest peak of this great vertical city, the mist surrounded us, calling to me, connecting to me. In spite of how high up we were, I wished we had visited the overlook during the light rotations so I could actually see the view. But, there was something magical about being surrounded by the dancing flames of the torches, the darkened mist hanging in the distance. "I've never seen anything so *beautiful*."

"I used to say the same, before I met you."

My eyes widened. He could very well be that smooth, just naturally adept at saying something to a female that would evoke an instant physical reaction in her. I already knew he had been with multiple females after the turba. Aside from his devastating good looks, he was probably good at making a female feel special to get what he wanted. I could dissect his compliment, could distrust it. But maybe just letting go, and being with him while I was here would give me something I secretly wanted. It didn't have to be love, to Emblyn's point it didn't have to be great conversation. It could be something else. It wasn't wrong to enjoy myself if I wanted to. After Prant and the realization that I had practically forced his hand, it was welcome to have the unencouraged attention. I had given Tyrus very little and he still kept trying.

I turned to face him, and angled my chin up, looking in his sparkling coppery eyes. His chest swelled, and a triumphant smile crept across his face that told me he sensed his victory. His chase had worked. I didn't care if that was the truth, if I was only a conquest to him. I would take from him just as he would take from me. I made my invitation clear to him with a nod as I looked at his full, sensuous mouth. Tyrus leaned down and parted his lips, and then it all happened so fast. His mouth was upon mine, tasting me, consuming me. His arms flexed around me, drawing me in closer by my hips. It was not gentle, and was not tentative. His kiss was insistent, demanding. I had been unprepared for it, my previous experience was so subdued by comparison. It had been quiet, and soft with Prant, a gentle meeting of bodies, hidden on the far side of the shore of Caer Lake. This was several notches higher in fervor, and the spot between my legs warmed in response.

Our shared breath now quickened to something I hadn't experienced before, and Tyrus hadn't even laid me down yet. I could only imagine the frenzy that we would reach. But, here we were, up on the tallest peak of the city, with barely a place to sit down—let alone lie upon. That would not be happening here.

The kiss lessened, his hand swept lower over my backside in a smooth tug toward himself. The motion made me want to hike my knee around him, to push our bodies closer together. But I staved off the instinct, forcing myself to simmer. I pulled away, my lips tender from the friction. "I think it's time we got back to the biblio." My heart raced, and I tried to not sound breathless, but there was little chance of masking my heightened state.

He smirked, his eyes drifting lower to my heaving chest. I felt like my words were quickly ignored, like he was going to avoid taking me back right away, or suggest something else instead of returning me to the rows of books. He definitely seemed to have something *else* on his mind.

"You promised," I reminded him.

"I did," he agreed, then took my hand. We turned toward the side to descend, and my gaze took in the enormity of the drop below us.

"Oh, fuck." I had somehow conveniently avoided thinking about how we'd have to make the return trip from this impossible height. I looked over my shoulder to the mist and smiled. I hated heights, it felt unnatural, but being near the mist was a calming presence, like being near an old friend. It was a reminder of my goal, even if I enjoyed a side quest for a little while. *Soon, I'll know more,* I silently promised the mist.

CHAPTER 19

"And then what happened?" Emblyn demanded. "I want to hear every detail!" She sat on the bed as I looked out one of the high windows in our room. The darkness had only deepened, we still had not reached the zenith of the dark rotations.

"You are utterly obsessed," I laughed. I recounted the outing, leaving nothing out, and she fell back on the bed and sighed. "I knew it, I *knew* you'd find someone here."

I didn't want to tell her that it was likely only for the short while that we'd be here, and that I had no intention of making it anything more than that. "Okay so, deal time. I'm officially doing *whatever* with Tyrus, I guess. That takes away from my research time."

"Deal!" she exclaimed.

"You don't even know what I was going to say."

"Oh yes I do. You want help with your research, you want me and maybe even Trachen to find books that you can read to learn more. If we help find the *right* books, it will give you more time with Tyrus."

"Okay, sometimes it's a little creepy how spot on you can be."

She sat up again and smirked. "It's not like it's really some great mystery as to what you want to find down there."

"But what *is* a mystery is the mist, my Syrenni heritage, what Vitus Augustus actually did to take control over us. How did it all happen? Also, this may be my only real chance to learn like this. I don't even know when I'm expected to go back to Caer Lake, but when I do, this opportunity disappears." My face fell, the idea of going back was appalling. There was nothing for me there, aside from Neila. I looked back out of the window, though there was only the black, formless expanse to try and focus my gaze on. I stared blankly as I decided once and for all, I would not be going back. Brokk was right, the more you learn, the more you realize there is to learn. And I couldn't relegate myself to moving backward. The Syrenni's growth had been stunted by their imprisonment, but they did nothing now to move forward. I couldn't go back there, my soul would wither.

"I understand, Sereia. You want to know about what you came from. I said I'll help, and I will."

I had gotten lost in thought with the eventuality of returning to Caer Lake. I turned to Emblyn, who sat on the bed pensively watching me. I nodded my thanks. I didn't know what my future might hold, but the firm decision within myself to not return to the lake gave me a sense of relief. It would of course mean other problems: how would I tell Lily, what will happen to Neila, where would I even go? It would most likely mean more lies, but as usual, there would be some pressing need to hide my true intentions. At least Emblyn could be one person I didn't have to lie to.

"I'm going to get some rest. If I'm going to train with Lily, study in the biblio, *and* sneak around with Tyrus, I need some sleep!" I crawled into bed next to her then shut my eyes.

"Sereia," Emblyn whispered.

"Yeah?"

"How big was he?"

"Oh my gods. Go to sleep."

Lily didn't meet me in the dining hall for mane fare, she sent word by way of Kerenza that she wasn't feeling well. She had arranged for someone else to train me, and afterward I would be allowed to go to the biblio again. I wondered if it was because she didn't want me to ask further questions about the Umorfae, or if it really was that she felt ill. I shook it off. Just because I was a habitual liar didn't mean she was. I finished my meal as the others continued their conversation around me, then headed down to the training hall unguided. Strangely, I was actually getting used to being inside buildings, using staircases and feeling almost at home encased within walls. Learning my way had helped, feeling like I could get myself out of these places alleviated the initial tension I had when I first arrived.

I walked into the training hall, adjusting my top to try and cover more of my abdomen. It was the same style as before, a soft, sleeveless top that stretched over my upper body, however this one was not only a deeper purple but also somehow smaller. It left more of my waist exposed than I would have preferred. I entered the training hall, then stopped dead in my tracks.

"Tyrus, I'm not sure if I should be surprised or not." I debated whether I was glad or not, as well.

He grinned, all too proud of himself. "Princess Lily asked Magistrate Zarneh for someone to train you, my name was suggested."

I laughed and shook my head as I walked over to him. Dumb fucking luck. But, at least I knew him a little, and maybe that would make things a bit easier.

His gaze tracked mine, then swept lower to my lips, then to my visible midsection. His eyebrow arched in interest, and I recognized the expression right away. The same one Brokk would make when he saw me. Tyrus lifted his eyes back to mine, then leaned forward to whisper in my ear. "I am going to make you sweat, in more ways than one." A lock of his hair slipped forward, half of it was tied up in a knot, the rest of the copper waves were left down and unruly, gleaming in the torchlight.

My toes curled. I didn't know exactly what he meant, but I was sure the way I reacted was the intended effect. He smiled, showing all those perfect teeth, those pointed canines. *So, not easier at all, I guess.* No, this was probably going to be so, so much worse, because he'd be taunting me with this tension while he ordered me around.

He stepped back and procured a staff from behind his back, he must have been holding it out of sight the whole time. "Pick up the staff," he used his staff to point to another one against the wall, "we will be learning more advanced techniques. Fighting only, no use of skill. Lily said she needs to train you more for that first."

Oh right, that. I didn't know if the amount of control I had so far would be enough to go head to head with a Petrafae, using two skills against each other, but I didn't argue as he didn't need to know that I had any development there.

It wasn't long before I was sweating, as he promised. And every time I cursed or complained, he made me run five laps. If I protested in the slightest, he added on more to the tally. He taught evasion, which I started to enjoy, once I got past my irritation with him at being an absolute taskmaster. I found it fun to find creative ways of leaping out of range of his weapon, sometimes using the base of the staff to launch myself in a different direction. I cackled at a particularly good jump I had done, leaping over his wide swing and giving him a taunting grin.

He spun backward, his weapon tucked behind his elbows, but as he completed the turn, Tyrus whipped a fancy flourish and the staff was suddenly extended and finished the spin with him at full force. It whacked across my chest, stunning me and sending me toppling over.

I laid on the ground, gasping and trying to suck in air.

He rushed to me, placing a hand on my aching chest. "Are you all right?"

I couldn't answer him, not yet.

He looked me over carefully, then made circular motions with his hands in the air while breathing slowly, demonstrating to me to calm my breaths. "Slower," he said, "slower. Getting the wind knocked from you can cause panic. If you slow your breath, you will recover sooner."

After a few tries, I managed to get a breath down, though my lungs ached.

"That is not a fun lesson, I have learned it myself," he said. Tyrus gave me his hand, then helped me up to sitting.

"What lesson?" I forced out after a moment.

"That congratulating yourself can lead to your demise. You

always have to think ahead when fighting, see the next move. If you spend any time being pleased with yourself over besting a maneuver, you can put yourself at risk."

"I see." I couldn't manage more words than that, my ribs were beginning to feel tender. This injury was probably going to be with me for a few rotations. He helped me up to my feet, and didn't let go of my hand as he held me steady, and held my gaze steady to his as well.

"That is enough. I will take you to the biblio, we can check your injury there." He flicked his eyes to guards at the hallways, indicating we were being watched here. I frowned, this would undoubtedly get around that I had taken a rough hit during training.

The walk through the central building was painful, I tried not to wince as we made our way to the lower levels. A few Petrafae noticed us and stared at me, of course, but I kept walking with my head held high. I did not want to hunch over in the slightest and give curious minds something to chatter about.

Finally, we reached the biblio, and I exhaled a sigh of relief. Usually no one else was here, so I could probably let down my guard a little. I started to take a step toward the lowest levels, when he pulled my hand toward the wall bordering the edge.

"In here."

"Where?" I asked. There was only a block wall edging the perimeter.

He held up his hand and pulled back his elbow, slightly straining against the weight of the wall. A section of it swung open, revealing a room with a table with a stack of parchment on it, and a plush long seating area with pillows of rust orange and cobalt blue.

He walked in, holding my hand firm as he guided us in.

He pushed the door shut behind us, which I cringed at. Like the closet in my room I shared with Emblyn, this door was designed for a Petrafae to open, not me.

He noticed my concerned look. "Do not worry, we can leave anytime. I wanted some place private to check your wound."

I nodded, looking around the dimly lit space. A few small lamps cast patterned shadows on the walls. I didn't know how he'd be able to see anything clearly enough to make sure the injury wasn't bad. To that point, this was a room off the biblio, people read in here, right? How did they see the words?

Tyrus smiled at me as he pushed out a single stone from the side of the door, making an inset in the wall. "It lets others know it is occupied."

I hadn't really thought about it, but I guess making sure the door wouldn't suddenly open while he looked at my bare chest would be a good thing. I shuddered, thinking ahead to that moment. To say I wasn't used to a male undressing me was an understatement.

He walked to the table, then turned a small wheel on the side of the lamp, which lifted the wick up higher, brightening the room. I rolled my eyes at myself, having thought the room too dark for reading. Of course there was a way to make it brighter, though I wrinkled my nose at it, I would have preferred not being even more on display once my clothing was off.

"Just for a moment, we can turn it back down after," he said, noticing my expression.

I remembered again how I had felt he was thoughtless, and shamed myself for the assumption. He was actually quite attentive, it was as if the Tyrus I met at the turba and the one I was with now were two completely different people.

His fingers slipped under the bottom edge of my top, tugging gently to lift it higher. I stiffened for a moment, then lifted my arms to allow him to pull it off of me. As I did, I realized it did *really* hurt, and probably would have been hard for me to wriggle the garment off myself. He slid it off, the cool fabric sliding past my fingertips. I sucked in a breath, which I then winced at having inhaled too deeply.

I followed his gaze down, and saw the blue diagonal welt across the center.

"Blue," he whispered.

"What?" I didn't know what he expected to see.

"I thought it would be red. But, I guess maybe this is your … heritage."

Oh, right. Umorfae had blue blood, and if I had been hit hard enough to break tissue below the skin, that's what we would see. I remembered the first time I was injured as a youngling and bled, it frightened the Syrenni. Even my blood looked different from theirs. I looked up to his eyes, momentarily worried I would see the same fear there, the same that I had seen in the Syrenni's eyes before I understood how I wasn't like them.

"I knew you would be different," he said, his eyes softening. "I like it."

I blinked back tears that pricked my eyes. As much as I would tell myself that I didn't care, that someone could hate me for what I was, that I would be okay … it was entirely different when someone actually accepted me. Maybe it was a small thing, but when you've spent your life as the outcast, as the offspring of the enemy, the few who dared to open their arms earned a certain level of appreciation.

"It does not look too bad, the injury, that is. I think you are okay." Tyrus turned the light back down as promised, then stepped closer. His gaze pierced mine, as he lifted his hand to caress my bare shoulder. His fingertips trailed down my back, exploring the ridge of my dorsal fin, then back up again. He brought his other hand up to my collarbone, running the pads of his fingers along the peak of it, then moved both hands to cup my breasts. I inhaled sharply at the sensation, the breath making my ribs hurt.

He paused, his eyes searching mine.

I nodded to him to continue. "Don't stop," I whispered. A command, a demand, a plea. I wanted to feel everything he had to give.

His mouth crashed upon mine, the request was all he needed to hear to unleash his desires. The kiss heated my blood, quickened my breath, and warmed my whole body. My hands went to his backside, grabbing at him and pulling him harder into my hips. This time I didn't stave off the desire to hook a leg around him, I wrapped it tightly as I pulled him in close. Tyrus released his lips from mine only long enough to whip off his shirt. His hand went to my waistband, tugging with surety. It took him no time to loosen my pants, dropping them to expose the rest of my body. They slipped off of my feet and onto the floor, at the same moment he had undone his. His length sprang free, nudging against me. His arms wrapped around me, hoisting me up onto the table behind us.

I gasped as he buried himself in me. My body stretched to fit him, both pleasure and pain at the same time. My head emptied and all thoughts narrowed to where we were joined, the way he plunged in and out of me. The way he moved in a rhythmic cadence, lifting me up, pulling me down. His arms worked and his muscles flexed. I clenched my eyes from the intense sensation, then opened them to see him watching me. My eyes drifted past his to Tyrus's ear, to that ridged edge along it. I don't know what came over me, but I was suddenly tempted to lick it. I ran my tongue up the side, and in one motion, he grunted, thrusting forward hard. His whole body went taut, stiffening in me, around me as a surge spilled from him.

Panting against my neck, he sagged, letting the table hold me up. Feeling came back to the rest of my body, to my aching ribs, to a knot between my eyebrows. I had forgotten about everything else when we had started.

He pulled himself free, and suddenly I felt very conscious of how sticky I felt. Perspiring while at the same time feeling an incredible dryness in my mouth and along my fin. The scales that surrounded it felt tight and flaky, a sign that I needed water. This was not like my joining with Prant at all. This was hurried, and heated, and *drying*. Somehow I hadn't thought about that possibility, that me being part Syrenni might mean he might not fit with what I was. He made himself fit. Yet still, it felt *good*.

But I needed water right away. "Tyrus? I need some water. Really soon."

He looked at me, his eyes wide. "Oh! Yes, I will get you some. Here," he said as he pulled out a small folded towel from the pocket of his pants. "You can use this if you need. I will be right back with water!" He hiked his pants on, then threw on his shirt. I wiped myself down with the cloth, then dressed as he lifted his hand to open the door. I winced at my injury as I pulled the top over my head. He was gone by the time I finished settling it in place.

I made my way out of the room, then headed down the levels to where I had been studying previously. Hopefully he returned soon with water, it had better not be like the turba where he got distracted by everyone and everything. I might turn as dry as some of the parchment in the biblio if I didn't get fresh moisture soon. I tried to ignore the pressing need as I grabbed the book I had been reading, then headed to my usual spot to study.

The weight of the tome made my arm muscles complain, reminding me that I had exerted a lot of effort during training. And then exerted even *more* energy in that hidden room with Tyrus. I set the book down on the table, shaking my head as I thought about the encounter. Things with him seemed to be powerful, but only for a very short time. Our kiss at the peak of the city happened so fast, was intense, and then was just as quickly over. What we had done just now, how long was that? I supposed I could look at it as him being efficient. I definitely had some questions for Emblyn though, some of what transpired I wasn't entirely sure about. I held up my hands, reminding myself to stop muttering about the experience and focus on studying.

I flipped the book open to where I had left off, and found another slip of paper, this time with something written on it. My jaw dropped at the lettering, at the words written there, then spun to see who else might be near the books with me.

158

CHAPTER 20

There was no one else in the biblio with me, not a sound from any direction, save for a subtle wind from the depths below. I looked back at the paper grasped in my fingers, then held it close to read it again. It only had two words on it, "I'm sorry." My hands shook as I wondered if it could be him.

The type of paper, the drawing style, the charcoal used, the way the words were written. Other Fae would write "I am," not "I'm", the only others who might write this way were myself, Lily, Emblyn, and Brokk. I supposed Lily's maeder and aunt were possibilities, too, they were here with us and they both spoke this way. I could easily assume they wrote this way as well. However I quickly eliminated them from being the potential note givers here. I had barely seen them outside of the dining hall. Emblyn had certainly been in the biblio with me, but she had no reason to write an apology. Lily *might* have a reason to write one, she had admitted to me that she had killed many Umorfae. Or she could be apologizing for canceling training and sending a replacement. Unlikely, but I supposed it was possible. But who would have a better reason than Brokk to write an apology? Still, the sheer unlikelihood of it, when I looked at the facts of what would have to have happened for that note to be from Brokk, it all but eliminated him again. Lily had been the one to teach me to read and write, and she did sometimes have some unorthodox ways of giving me lessons. I had already realized that the papers indicated that someone else was reading the histories at the same time as me, it could have been Lily. After all, the paper was simply new by comparison to what was in the book, it could possibly be made the same whether it was paper from Lacausia or from TerraIgni, I had no way of knowing.

But the drawings. I had never known Lily to sketch, to put down images as she saw them. That was such a Brokk thing to do. I set the paper down and began reading. I didn't have unlimited time and I had things to learn, mysteries to solve. Maybe the marker was there for a specific reason, maybe it was to make me pay attention to those particular pages. I focused on reading for a time, until Tyrus reappeared.

"Your water is here!" he proclaimed proudly, like he deserved an award for procuring something I physically required.

I nodded my thanks and wasted no time as I downed the glass. It frankly wasn't enough.

"What are you reading?" he asked with a sour look on his face. As if me reading an actual book was abhorrent. I almost choked from my laugh.

"A book, with words," I answered.

He looked around blankly, already bored with the situation. I ignored his inference at the books holding no interest to him, just as he ignored my sarcastic—and *funny*, if anyone asked me—reply. So much for him understanding humor. Maybe that was only when he had a goal he had set his sights on, like a predator using all abilities to hunt with. He had wanted something, got it, and now maybe the chase wasn't as fun. Why try anymore?

"You don't have to stay," I mentioned, "I know this isn't your thing. I can find you again later."

"I have another idea."

I raised my eyebrows as he walked off, seemingly heading up the levels. I started reading again, catching up to where I was before. I was reading a passage about how the Syrenni first encountered Vitus Augustus, when he was angling to crown himself ruler. The realm had been called T'al Belgranrael, before he changed it to Alternis. He claimed it honored his roots to a place called Brundisium, though it was noted that he said that neither the land nor the inhabitants resembled it. I assumed that meant it was the place he was from in the human world, before crossing the threshold into the realm. In a way, Tyrus was a little right, it was kind of boring. What did it help me to learn about the place Vitus was from? What was interesting however was that at first he was allied with the Syrenni, along with a female whom he spent the majority of his time with. So he had befriended them before he betrayed them. But beyond that, I didn't know how that might be useful information. There was probably going to be a lot of that, sifting through knowledge and histories to find what mattered. Maybe another conversation with Lily would help give some clarity, but, if she was ill, I was probably on my own for awhile. I sighed and rubbed my temples, fighting off a headache. Maybe I overexerted myself. Or maybe I was overthinking these historical texts, or these bookmarks for that matter.

Tyrus came back holding a heavy-looking stone box. Heavy to me, that is, he of course lifted it with ease. "I thought of something to pass the time while you studied!" He was entirely too happy with himself as he set the box on the table with a loud thump. Pulling the lid off, he revealed sets of squared rock blocks, all lined up with markings on them. He pulled some out, arranging them in a formation. "Caudex! I can play while you read, if that is what you *must* do, or you can have more fun and play this with me."

I eyed the set up, then looked up at him. "I'll keep reading for now." If I was going to ever get to the actual usable portions of information, I had to keep going. I didn't know at what point—if at all—I'd have a breakthrough.

He shrugged, then started arranging the blocks, building them higher. When he managed to get markings to match up, they would click into place. Click, click, click. I kept reading.

Tap, tap, click. He built higher, becoming more animated as his block structure rose from the table. The base started encroaching my space, forcing me to scoot to the corner to keep reading. The structure was becoming unstable, which he had to start using his skill to balance from multiple sides. "One more stone!" he said, as excited as a youngling playing with a toy.

I rolled my eyes, but laughed a little. At least he was having fun. Tyrus lifted the last stone with his hand raised, forcing the stone up with those invisible threads of power. The blocks were about the size of my fist, so they couldn't take too much effort, especially for him. It raised up to the topmost portion, then he attempted to get it to click into place. It turned halfway around, barely balancing, then made a tap sound rather than a click. He must have misheard, thinking that it had settled properly into place. It fell, striking the layer below it and causing a chain reaction.

The whole thing tumbled toward me. I shrieked, grabbing the aged book to prevent it from getting damaged. Fortunately, Tyrus reacted quickly enough and thrust his hands forward, arresting the falling motion of all the stones. He stood, cringing, and scrawling his fingers to try and keep the connection to all of the small blocks suspended in the air..

"Need help?" I asked. He merely nodded. I laughed, starting to pluck them one by one from the air, snapping his connection to them and then set them back in the box. Once there were only a few left, he was able to manage those just fine.

"I think this means we need to play a round together," he said with his eyebrows dancing.

I sighed. "Oh all right. Can't have my book getting pummeled by these now, can I?" I moved the book out of the way. We started to play, and though he explained the rules, I already understood the logic. It was pretty simple, match up the symbols and they stay together. "I'm surprised that the small stones seem hard for you to control. The last one, just before it fell, needed to be turned a little more."

He nodded. "I am not good with things that require precision. Something big and heavy, that is my talent. Small? Not my skill set. The game does help me practice, though."

"And the city locks are like that? Big pieces only?"

"For the outer wall locks, yes. And the main structure inner locks. But things that Magistrate Zarneh locks away, whether documents or even if someone were to be imprisoned for tribunal, those locks are delicate and complicated. I could never open those."

"So never get imprisoned for tribunal, check," I said with a smirk.

"No," he affirmed seriously, "never. Tribunal is just a formality for a death sentence. It is one and the same."

I had been joking, but he clearly was having none of that. I shuddered, thinking of being trapped within stone before they decided to execute me. Good thing I was on their good side, and had come here as a part of Lily's diplomatic envoy. I wondered who had been caught within their borders before and faced the punishment Tyrus alluded to.

CHAPTER 21

I gulped glass after glass of water at nocte fare with Emblyn. I ended up finishing the one round of caudex with Tyrus, before I became ravenously hungry and just as thirsty as when we had gotten ourselves entirely worked up in the little room. Emblyn came to find me as we finished the game, and I decided it was time to go to the dining hall if I wanted to still be able to walk for much longer. Tyrus was called away by the magistrate, and Trachen had to return to guard duty.

"You aren't drinking another glass to avoid telling me more, are you?" Emblyn asked.

"No, why?" I gulped more.

"Because! All I got was essentially "We did it" and nothing else!"

"Oh, right. That's true." I nodded in agreement. That was all I had said to her.

She stared. "That was subtext for "Give me more information before I die, please." In case you didn't know."

I laughed. "Okay, fine. But hey, question actually. Is there like… an ear thing? I had this weird temptation to lick his ear, which I did."

She covered her mouth. "Oh my gods. I bet he came right away."

I winced, she was way, *way* more comfortable talking about this stuff than I was. "Uh, yeah, I guess he did."

She laughed so loudly that faces turned toward us, watching for a moment before going back to their food.

Fuck. Hopefully they didn't also hear what we were talking about.

"So, yeah, the ear thing," she said, motioning at me with a piece of dried meat. "Touch a Fae's ears if you want an instant reaction. Whether you want to get something started, or to finish it. Either way, it's almost as sensitive as, well, you know." She took a bite of the jerky, chewing and smiling at the same time. She swallowed. "Which, by the way, might include you as well. You have Fae ears, not Syrenni."

I wrinkled my nose at her, shaking my shoulders to shimmy off the off-putting insight. "Ew, too much information for nocte fare."

She giggled, fortunately not nearly as loud as before. "So, any new information from your studies? I'm sorry I wasn't there. Trachen wanted to take me somewhere special."

"That's okay, after, you know, we were in *the room,* I managed to get some reading done. I don't know how much usable knowledge I found, but I did make progress." I decided once again to leave the bookmark papers out of the conversation.

It wasn't long before Emblyn swung the conversation back to what had happened between Tyrus and me, so I finally, begrudgingly, gave her some details.

"So, wait, he just had that towel ready to go? Like, he already knew this is what you'd be doing?"

I shrugged. "Maybe he always has it?"

"I don't know, Sereia. Now I feel worried, like I shouldn't have told you to go for Tyrus. It now sounds to me like he does this a lot."

"He does."

"What! Wait, how do you know?"

"Well I think he does," I mused. "He made some comment about being with multiple females, and even a male, after the turba that I danced with him at."

She choked, clearly grossed out by the level of action he must get. "Oh no, he's going to hurt you."

I waved a hand, dismissing her worried comment. "I don't care about him, I don't need some promise from him. It's fine. It's … just whatever. He was looking for an experience, and I guess so was I."

"I'm not so sure," she said warily, slumping back in her chair. "If Trachen admitted to being with other females around the same time as me I'd be mad. Real mad. I'd lose it."

I widened my eyes comically. "Oh no, you have *feelings* for him!"

She bolted upright, staring at me at the realization. "Oh faex, I do." It was as if she hadn't thought about that possibility until this very moment.

The rest of our wayward group appeared at the entrance to the hall. I motioned with my chin to Emblyn. "Look alive, your maeder just arrived."

She immediately changed her expression to that of a charismatic, carefree female who was enjoying her meal. I laughed and shook my head. She was a master. "Greetings, Maeder," Emblyn said in her lilting tone once they reached our table.

"Greetings, my filia!" Kerenza returned.

I bobbed my head in a hello to them all, content to let them fill in the table on the other side and have their own conversation. But then I remembered the bookmark papers, and that technically speaking they were written in a way Rachael and Maureen might write. I leaned closer to them. "Have you seen the biblio here? There are so many books!" I made an effort to seem like a wide-eyed female who had never seen such things, even though I was a duplicitous one who wanted to know if they'd been there or not so I could eliminate them from the list.

Rachael shook her head, but Maureen nodded and spoke, "Well I haven't *been* there yet. I did request a stack of books be delivered to our room. I am still perusing them, deciding if I need to go to the source to find something spicier."

"Spicier?" I asked. "Like, spice for food?"

Maureen chuckled. "Spice for the mind! I did find a particularly good one. It was a courtier's journal of all of her conquests." She fanned herself, while Rachael rolled her eyes. "I am almost done with it. I could send it your way after, it has some … intriguing entries!" She waggled her eyebrows, and Rachael rolled her eyes again.

"You are the *worst*, Maur. Maybe she doesn't want to read that smut! Not everyone wants to read romance novels like you do."

I considered it. "Who knows, might be educational."

Maureen burst out laughing. "Oh, you'll learn something, that's for sure!"

I mean, a little reading for reference with it might give me some ideas. I weighed the thought in a mental committee for a moment. By the look on Emblyn's face, she might be interested in the book, too. At the very least, I now knew it wasn't either of them that had been putting the paper bookmarks in the pages.

It was no surprise when Tyrus was waiting for me in the training hall again. More drills, more godsdamned sexual tension. He taunted me the whole time, even went so far as to flick my ear when we were twisted around each other in a sparring match, proving to me what Emblyn had guessed about my ears being sensitive like the Fae. The zing went straight through me, making me slick between my legs. He cocked an eyebrow and slung his weapon over his shoulder as he walked away, annoyingly proud of himself for sending me into a frenzy.

I hollered and sailed through the air at him, which caught him completely off guard. He startled, then dropped his staff and held up his arms to block me. I cackled as I launched myself away.

"Oh you will *pay* for that one!" His words were threatening, but he had a huge grin on his face.

"Of that I have no doubt. Now pick up your weapon."

"Giving me orders now? I like it."

I laughed. I was so charged up that I was ready to demolish him, in one way or another. We faced off, trading jabs and blocks. Several times I was tempted to use my skill to push him, to redirect his body or his swing against his will. I could feel it there, telling me when it would work perfectly. Every time I could see the opening for it, and every time I had to side step my sense, ignore it. Undoubtedly word would get back to Lily. I probably could spin some faex-filled story about how I simply felt when to use it, but I didn't feel like having to do all that extra work to cover my tracks. It might open the way for a whole lot of questions I wasn't ready for.

We finished up training, then headed to the biblio. Emblyn's worry and caution echoed in my mind, but I swept the thought away. If he was using me, I was also using him. It was fine if neither of us really cared. I was enjoying his company—and the looks of him—and that was enough for me for now. He pulled open the wall to the small room, and this time we spent the entire time we were locked in there on the narrow couch. It was not enough space, but it was made of stone so it was stable enough. I was thankful for the plush pad on it, no doubt the stone would have been grinding into my back without it.

Breathless, and sweaty for the second time that rotation, we exited the room, then descended the levels to my favorite row of books. I wondered if I might be better served to try a different book. I had thought I'd find more helpful information in the thick, old text. But so far I hadn't seen anything that really answered current questions. I pulled it off the shelf anyway, noticing a new bookmark had been placed.

Tyrus took the book from me. I dropped my jaw, thinking he was trying to keep me from reading it. "Any more you would like carried up to the table?"

It took me a moment to realize he was being thoughtful. I wasn't used to anyone being accommodating. I shook my head, then motioned to head up to the study area. I was still a little stunned by the sweet gesture. His expression changed once I cracked the book open however, and he fidgeted while I tried to read. He moved over to behind me, playing with my hair and rubbing my shoulders. It was both distractingly welcome and annoying, that he couldn't leave me in peace to read. But, the massage to my neck eased the tension that had been building up for what seemed like my entire life.

I flipped the page and a new bookmark appeared. There were no words on it this time, only a drawing. It was upside down, so I turned it, and stifled a gasp. It was me. A few lines for my hair, my small nose, the pointed shape of my eyes framed by arched eyebrows. I was looking over my shoulder with what might have been a sultry expression. I blinked. I looked beautiful. Did I really look like that?

"Is something wrong? You are suddenly more tense!"

I tucked the paper in closer, keeping it from Tyrus's view. "No, I'm fine. I just need some water. And food, please. Can you bring some? Both food and water."

He lifted his hands from my shoulders, moved my hair aside then kissed my neck. "Whatever you need."

He disappeared out of the study area, I waited for his footsteps to fade before I took the paper out again. I could ask Lily if it was her, but there was no point, I knew now, it was Brokk. Somehow, he had made his way in here. But I would do one last test to be sure, I had to know if it was him.

I looked at the page he had marked, and the blood drained from my face. A drawing took up the entire page that had been marked, the old parchment had been hand sketched with careful crosshatched lines, depicting a Syrenni floating in the air, her arms outstretched. Incredibly thin lines connected her to the sky, which might have been the mist. And in her hand was the sigil, *my* sigil. The one that had been passed down through the generations, what looked to be the same one I had inherited from my maeder. I couldn't see that it was the same silvery metal because the image had no color, but a sketch on the facing page had a close up drawing of it. The carved lettering in old Faelan was the same.

Bravery of the heart is rare, the sigil shares the power when it is there.

I thought back to the last time I saw the sigil, left in my room at Caer Lake. Much of the lettering had worn down, it had been hundreds of cycles that we had possessed it. Neila had told me once that the Azal Familia had hidden the sigil for the entire time the Syrenni were imprisoned, that was for around a thousand cycles or so. It had been entrusted to our familia by Queen Sereia just before the Syrenni were imprisoned. I ran my fingertips over the detailed sketch of the palm-sized metal disc. Some of the letters that were on the real disc I hadn't been able to read before, I never knew all of what it said.

How did Brokk know to mark this page? Was it a mere chance? I had never told him I had the sigil. Perhaps it wasn't the sigil, but the image of the Syrenni suspended, apparently controlling the mist. Showing proof that the Syrenni *did* do something with it. And I had felt a similar connection, it felt like threads to me, like a giant net over the whole world, with thousands of taut lines funneling down to me. But how was she floating? We couldn't lift ourselves or fly, in water we were very fast, but even if we swam as fast as we could go we would only make it a little way out of the water with a leap. This picture showed her hovering.

I flipped a few pages back when I saw Tyrus approaching. "You're back!" I said, eyeing the plate of food and the decanter of water as he set it down. "Magna, Tyrus, I need water so badly." I made an effort to fawn over the delivery. He puffed up his chest with pride. I picked up the water, then made a show of taking a big swig of it, but didn't drink much. "I need to make some progress and focus, can I meet you later?"

He looked a little stunned that I had basically asked him to leave, but he bowed without complaint, then he left. I couldn't really deal with listening to another game of caudex, or join in on one for that matter. I breathed a sigh once I knew he was gone again. I also needed him away so I could try and prove my theory.

I grabbed the tray, then carried it down to the lowest levels, to where the last torch cast its light. I edged toward the darkness, setting the tray down just out of sight. I looked out to the unlit rough tunnels. They *must* have been tunnels and not simply the dead end of the base of the biblio. I backed away from the provisions, balling my fists to prevent me from wringing them.

It had to be Brokk, it just had to be. But then, I thought of the sigil. Brokk didn't know I had it, but Lily did. Lily knew Neila had brought it with her from Lacausia when Lily had guided the Syrenni during their exodus. Lily was, in fact, the only other one who knew about it. My face fell, all this time I had been hoping it was Brokk in the biblio. I had wanted it to be him, so I kept going back to the possibility. That he was the one apologizing, and that maybe I would get a chance to apologize to him. That maybe I would get to see him and tell him things I should have said before.

I turned my back on the dark depths, then returned to the study area to put away the book. If it was Lily leaving bookmarks,

I was going to find out for sure. No more of this 'being ill' excuse, I wanted answers.

CHAPTER 22

Emblyn had come back to our room late and was still sleeping, so I tried not to disturb her as I dressed, then headed straight to the dining hall. I had already decided that if I didn't find Lily there, I'd eat and then seek her out. Yet, there she was, quietly sipping a steaming beverage as I approached. I put on a pleasant face as I walked over, reminding myself to have patience before I demanded information.

"Bonum mane," I said as I sat down. "Enjoying some capuli?" I glanced at her plate, she hadn't put much on there, and seemed to have only pushed around the few potatoes.

She shook her head. "Just tea."

"You never drink tea! I thought you only like capuli."

She gave me a slight smile. "It helps me feel better. So, how has training been going?"

I looked down at my arms, muscles already visible from all of the work I had been doing. "Good, I think. Learning some new moves." I smirked at the truth of that statement, new moves both in the training ring and in the secluded study room.

"And how has your time in the biblio been?"

My eyes twitched at her change in tone. Something was there, something underneath the question. "How has *your* time in the biblio been? Is that where you've been, going in when I'm not there?"

Lily huffed a single laugh. "Answering my question with a question? You've learned much from me, I see."

"And you didn't answer my question," I shot back.

"And you didn't answer mine." She paused, then sighed, rubbing her head. "Don't forget that we are visitors here, and that I am responsible for you. So it is completely fair for me to ask about these things. The same is not true of you, however, you do not need to know about my schedule or my comings and goings."

So that's how it was going to be. Fine. I crossed my arms and leaned back. "The biblio has been magna. I've read some books. A particularly interesting book about Syrenni heritage." I did little to hold back the venom in my tone. So quickly the conversation had turned sour, a bitter, silent undertone to any words spoken.

She nodded, keeping her expression flat and unreadable. Then I wondered, did she ask about the biblio because of the books, or because of my time with Tyrus? I fidgeted, realizing she may have found out about what I was doing with him. She had asked the magistrate for someone to train me, and somehow the male that I had bumped into, who had then met up with me at the turba, and *then* secretly took me up to the peak of the city, is the one to train me? Suddenly I felt foolish, it probably wasn't a coincidence. I had to remind myself that Lily was a lot smarter than that, and very perceptive. I probably wasn't nearly as clever as I thought I had been. Now it all felt like a terrible mistake, and because I had been sneaking around with Tyrus I might not be able to figure out exactly what Lily might be alluding to. And if I asked ... well I wasn't going to. Because that would shine a big light on things I don't want her knowing everything about.

"Finish up your food, it's time to go train," she said.

I squared off with her in the training hall, the slow current of irritation that had been building up in my blood turned to a raging storm. I gripped the staff, my fingers tight around the center. Her eyes flicked to it, noticing my white knuckles. We danced around each other, trading hits and blocks. The sparring started to level up in intensity, I began to go harder, striking with more fury each time. I could see her straining, and I could feel something different, something off in her blood. It sang to me, tempting me to use it. The call was powerful, intoxicating. I wanted to feel her movement stop at my command, to be the one that had that control.

Lily spun, then whipped out toward me. Her staff whacked my hand. I yelped, then my anger really flared. I gritted my teeth and attacked again. She blocked every hit, though her steps were more careful, slowly backing up to absorb my attack, rather than meeting me head to head.

We traded more hits and blocks, endlessly circling, swiping, and I started to lose my patience. I wanted to know what she knew, and I was tired of her antics, of her controlling the flow of information. She had done that my entire *life*. She had never been truthful about her involvement with the Umorfae, never told me what she knew about my maeder's death. She only doled out droplets of truth from the veritable river of knowledge she possessed.

I swung down, which she blocked from above. I pushed my staff harder into hers, forcing her down, down, down.

"What is it you want to ask, Sereia?" she asked through clenched teeth, trying to hold out against my force.

Was it a trick? A way to distract me and get me to back off so she could do something like swipe my legs from under me? I wasn't falling for it. I pushed harder, her knee bent and she started to crumple to the ground. I had grown stronger, and I was winning.

"Ask me your questions!" Lily shouted at me.

"Are you the one reading the book? Leaving the bookmarks for me to find?" I pushed my weapon further, not waiting for a response. "Did you manipulate the situation so that Tyrus would be with me?" I pushed the shaft against hers again, and she buckled, falling to the ground. I stood over her, whipping my staff around so that it was now at her throat. "Did you kill my faeder?" I asked quietly.

Her eyes were round, staring up at me. She was quiet, but then I saw it. The anger behind her gaze. She went to leap up, but I used my free hand and thrust it between us. I closed my fingers in the air, wrapping my power around her blood, finally giving in to the call, that beckoning song that I couldn't ignore any longer. All her movement stopped and her eyes flew wide with fear as I stopped her blood flow.

"No," her voice quaked.

I narrowed my eyes, gripping harder against her as she fought to free herself from my invisible hold.

She struggled to get up, I could feel her heart begging for movement, her body desperate to allow the blood to flow again.

"Sereia! What are you doing?"

Kerenza came running in from the hall, arms upraised and ready to fight. I blinked, releasing Lily's blood as my power ebbed. Lily gasped for air, then sobbed as she tried to get up.

Kerenza reached her, helping her off the ground. "Are you insane?" Kerenza seethed. "She is pregnant!"

I backed up a step, then dropped my staff. That's why she had felt off to me, why she seemed different. Lily finally looked at me, then pulled herself up the rest of the way to standing. She took heavy breaths as she evaluated me standing there, her expression now that of someone who saw me for what I was, the slow realization that I had known how to use my power for much longer than she knew. "Looks like you've been keeping a lot of secrets, Sereia."

I opened my mouth to speak, but instead turned around and fled.

CHAPTER 23

I would have run away from the city, but I couldn't. I was stuck here. Trapped, until they opened the stairs for me. Maybe I could find Tyrus and convince him to help me escape. I couldn't be here any longer, not with what I had done. I had almost hurt Lily, almost hurt her unborn child. I had lost control over myself and nearly did something that I couldn't take back.

I didn't know where Tyrus would be, so instead I ran to my room. Ran however many thousands of steps to get there, I ran up the whole way. My legs were screaming to rest by the time I reached the top of the stairs, but I didn't care. I deserved to feel pain, discomfort, however I received it. Whether I did it to myself or if someone else inflicted it. I threw myself down on the bed as I couldn't hold back the tears. They were hot and salty on my face, my eyes burned from them. I cried until I had none left, until I was drying and flaking, needing water immediately. I didn't get up to get myself some. Who cared if I let myself completely wither on this bed? I'd do it. Just wait it out. I'd let myself dry to a husk as punishment.

Emblyn came into the room and stood in the doorway. "Everyone is waiting for you. I'm supposed to bring you with me," she said quietly. She walked in, then saw my disheveled state. "Are you all right? You look terrible!"

"Good."

"You need water, look at you!"

She rushed into the washroom, then brought a filled cup out to me. Pulling me by the shoulder, she forced me to sit up and drink. I didn't want to, but damn my body and its natural reactions, I drank it all. She went back and refilled it, then made me drink a second one. She wetted a towel and patted my face with it, cleaning off the salty tears and returning more moisture to my skin. I flopped back, breathing as the liquid did its magic. My skin felt less tight, and my lips felt less crusty. Usually I could go rotations without water, but crying everything out of me had left me spent and dehydrated.

"Is Lily okay?" I asked finally. I was terrified to think I might have caused permanent harm to either her or the baby.

"She's fine. She was shaken up, and I'd say mad, I guess. But I don't want to speak for her. They're waiting for you in a private meeting room, somewhere we can talk. She doesn't want anyone knowing about … certain things."

"You mean about what I did?" I asked quietly.

"More than that, unfortunately. Things are not looking good. You'll have to come with me to talk to Lily yourself."

The rest of our group had gathered in an enclosed room at the center of the city. The room was well away from any exterior walls, and a massive table with a map inlaid into it took up the majority of the space. Emblyn, Kerenza, and Zia all pushed the door closed with their shoulders, grunting until it was in place, a task that would have been much easier if we had a Petrafae with us. I stood, my arms straight down at my sides while Lily cast her eyes on me from where she was seated. I merely looked at her, Rachael, and Maureen, while the everyone else finished shutting the door. Lily motioned to an open chair across from her, indicating she wanted me to take it. The others finished with the door, then seated themselves, Emblyn taking up the seat next to Kerenza on the other side of the table. I felt very conscious of the fact that they were lined up on one side, leaving me to sit alone on the other.

"The situation has changed," Lily spoke up, the tone in her voice stern and resolute. My heart sank, as if it was possible to sink lower from where it already was. What she didn't say was that it was my actions that had made the situation change. "Aside from … recent events, which the Petrafae know nothing of," Lily said as her eyes flashed to me, "we have intel that may change us being able to stay here longer."

I looked at Emblyn, trying to figure out what was going on, what Lily was talking about. At first I was sure it had to do with what I had done. Emblyn looked right back at me, but shrugged her shoulders. *She doesn't know, either.*

"I found out there may be someone dangerous after you, Sereia," Lily continued. "Word has gotten out that you are here, and it may bring a confrontation to the Petrafae's doorstep, which we don't want. Or it could be something like an attempt on your life. I really don't know for sure. We need to leave soon."

My heart beat faster. And time slowed. And every fucking alarm in me flared to life. "Who?" It was all I could say, my heart skyrocketing from the pit of my stomach all the way up to the top of my throat caused me to nearly choke on it. I started to panic, thinking that somehow they had found out about Brokk and assumed he was here to kill me.

"Someone I should have told you about a long time ago. Empress Celestine, the leader of the Umorfae. She has bad blood with Queen Deniza and me. A very old feud from when the Syrenni were freed. You were kept a secret from the empress, Neila managed to get out of there without them finding out about you. However, somehow she has learned of your existence. I don't know how, but the fact is as long as you are here, it puts the Petrafae in a bad position."

I gulped, my mouth going dry all over again.

"But, wouldn't she be safer here, within the walls of Adrilan?" Embyln asked. "Out in the forest she could be easily caught! Also, sorry for saying this, but it sounds more like this is your problem to deal with, being that the feud is between you two and Empress Celestine." Emblyn motioned to Lily and Queen Deniza. Embyln gave Queen Deniza an apologetic look, but gods love her for saying what she thought in spite of the obvious issue of it being someone so important to her.

Lily stood. "The reality is, we cannot stay here, and though I am usually not one to back down from a fight, we are not prepared to face her. I do not have any knowledge of where she is right now, or how many warriors she has under her command, but with my current state, I'm at about half of what I usually am strength-wise. Queen Deniza, Kerenza, and Zia are formidable fighters, Emblyn is as well. Sereia has definitely *grown* in her ability. And my mom and Aunt Maureen … well—"

"—We're great for entertainment," Maureen chimed in.

Rachael elbowed her sister, who only grinned in return.

Lily sat back down, her hand cradling her lower abdomen. "The point is, we've got to leave soon and quietly, returning to Caer Lake as quickly as possible. From there we'll decide what to do."

My head swam from the news, and conflicting emotions pummeled me in waves. She hadn't made any mention of Brokk, or of what I had done. I should have been ashamed—and part of me was—but overall I was relieved. How was I relieved that some psychopath empress was after me? Was I glad I was not the villain here? Probably, but in fact, I was not exactly on the "good" list. Just the "less bad than the empress" list. But, Brokk … if he was here, I needed to find him, or send a message to him, and let him know what was happening. I needed to find some way to scrape a little time to steal away to the biblio.

"Lastly," Lily continued, "I'd like to answer your questions, Sereia."

I raised my eyebrows, unsure what she meant. "I don't even know what to ask."

"I was referring to what you had asked when we were training. Regarding a book you have been reading, and something about a bookmark. The answer is no, I was not reading down in the biblio and leaving bookmarks for you to find, I wasn't sure what you were talking about."

I nodded, realizing that this was further proof of who it might be.

"The second question: did I set up the situation so that the handsome Petrafae you had run into when we had first arrived was the one to spend time with you? Yes, though I heard afterward that he had in fact found you in between that time."

My mouth twitched, I was momentarily annoyed, then just as quickly dismissed the interference. I had much bigger problems to deal with right now, Tyrus might as well already be with someone else.

"Finally, the third question: Did I kill your faeder? I honestly don't know, it was certainly possible. I did admit to you that there have been a lot of Umorfae deaths at my hands. Your maeder never even let on that she had carried on a relationship, or that she was with child. I only knew your faeder wasn't Opius. Just before he … killed her," Lily gulped, then looked away from me, "he taunted your maeder, saying how she betrayed her love and because of her he was dead. He never said who, but I knew then that it was probably Opius who had killed him. I think it was Opius who killed your faeder, but I don't know for sure."

I clenched a fist, not knowing if I was mad, or sad, or frustrated all over again that once again I had no exact answer to this question.

Queen Deniza reached across the table, cupping her hand over my fist. "I think I know. I was in the prison when your maeder was brought in. I could never see her, but we were close by each other and we would talk. I encouraged her when I could, we were there together for many rotations. She was strong, right up until they took her away. There was something that she knew which Opius tried to break her for, to get the information, but she never gave in. He killed her love, your faeder, not right there but Opius brought back his bloodied, chopped hair as proof. He said his name was

Locrien. Even knowing he had died, she still did not give up."

Lily's jaw dropped. "I never knew that! I did know him!" She turned to me. "He was one of Opius's guards, I didn't get to know him well, but I remember thinking he was kind-hearted."

I put my hand to my mouth, processing everything for a moment. "So Umorfae *can* be good."

Lily started to respond, when a loud bell clanged. It seemed to echo from everywhere.

"What is that?" Emblyn yelled, covering her ears.

Lily's face went white. "The summoning bell. Something has happened."

188

CHAPTER 24

After pulling the door open, we all exited, then headed toward the droning sound. Voices echoed throughout, the entire city was being called to the open air courtyard where our group had first been welcomed to the city. Petrafae gathered all around, crowding on the terraces and overlooks, trying to get a view of what was happening.

Magistrate Zarneh appeared on a narrow platform that jutted out high above the masses. Everyone jostled for a position, though the center was kept clear except for some surly looking guards, who stood stock-still, waiting for their leader's announcement. Lily put a hand on my shoulder, I wasn't sure if she was trying to calm me or calm herself. Everyone in our group looked pensive, worried while we waited. My mind started to tumble through the possibilities, but I kept landing on the fact that Empress Celestine knew I was here, and my presence hadn't exactly been wanted since I had first arrived. It probably wouldn't take much of a decision for them to ouster me. I looked back up to the magistrate, then saw Tyrus standing behind her, his eyes locked to me. His face was as solid as a stone, not a flicker of emotion, but I could read the concern in his eyes even from a distance. Something was happening that had him very worried. His eyes flicked to the side, which I caught as him trying to get me to follow his line of sight. I glanced to where he looked, at another Petrafae who stood near him, to the other side of the magistrate. Tall and slender, with his hands upraised and tapping his dexterous-looking fingers below his chin. I looked back to Tyrus, who gave me a single shake of his head. I wasn't sure what it meant, but it felt ominous, like a warning.

The magistrate raised her hands, and the crowd quieted at last. "We have the honor of living in the greatest city in Alternis. We Petrafae have built Adrilan with care and ingenuity, with mindfulness toward the future and with the highest security." Her commanding voice echoed across the square, all faces looked to her with admiration and reverence as she spoke. A cheer went through the crowd, praising their leader for her bold belief in their stronghold.

I couldn't help but notice Lily stiffen, and Queen Deniza bristled at the mention of how she considered their city to be "the best." Kerenza and Zia whispered something to each other, no doubt talking about the declaration when clearly there were visitors from TerraIgni in attendance. *Pretty rude of the magistrate, honestly.* But still I waited, I was certain we weren't all gathered for her to throw barbs at other dignitaries. This had to be something bigger.

"And though we can claim to have such great defenses, there has been a breach in our security. An unwelcome visitor is among us."

A murmur swept through, and I suddenly felt thousands of eyes land on me. My hair, my skin, every part of me felt like it was in stark contrast to every visual marker that made them Petrafae. My white-opal hair. My pale, almost greenish skin. My large, dark eyes. No part of me matched their bronzed, coppery looks. I could be picked out of a crowd of thousands in an instant.

A sound rippled through from across the square, followed by shouting and booing as the crowd parted. A pair of guards hauled out someone shackled at the wrists. My heart stopped as I saw his head hung low, his opal hair messy with blue blood crusting one side of it. I didn't need to see his face to know who it was.

They came to a stop near the center, facing the magistrate and a mere thirty paces from me. He lifted his head finally, bright blue blood dribbling from the corner of his mouth. His azure crystal eyes darted around, then finally found mine. My heart, my spirit, my *everything* cracked as Brokk and I stared at each other.

All sound dulled: the crowd, the magistrate, my companions. They had obviously injured him when they captured him, but his eyes were as clear and sharp as ever. My heart came back to life, beating with fervor as we looked unblinking at each other from across the courtyard. I wanted to run to him, to tell him everything—the good, the bad, the shameful. I wanted to lash out and hurt whoever had assaulted him. I shifted my gaze to the guards that held him, marking their features. Whatever they had done to him had woken something up within me, something that wanted violence.

"This *Umorfae* has invaded our great city!" The magistrate's words filtered back into my consciousness. The crowd chanted and threw things. "But, we will serve justice. It is what is right. He will face a tribunal!"

The word "tribunal" echoed in my head, stirring up the memory of what Tyrus had said to me. I looked up to him again, and found his gaze still locked to me. He shook his head once, the way his mouth twitched down, his whole expression told me everything. That if Brokk were to face a tribunal, they would kill him. Tyrus's warning glance about the other slender Petrafae now made sense, he was probably the one who would control the prison locks. Once Brokk was in, there was no getting him out.

The chanting turned to a hum in my head as my power raged. I felt everyone and everything as the frenzy escalated. Their blood became a song of screams, all of them telling me exactly where they were, how I could push them, how they could fall. I felt the mist, high above and yet connected *everywhere*, millions of points all funneling down to me.

I clenched my fists, ready to pummel anyone in my way. Blood, I *wanted* their blood. I wanted to dance in that symphony and be its master, to free their blood and make it flow to my will. A hand on my shoulder snapped me out of my tunnel vision and redirected my attention.

"Don't do whatever you're about to do," Lily said quietly, looking around as she pretended not to speak.

"They will *kill him*," I hissed.

"There must be some way you can intervene," Emblyn said to Lily.

"There is nothing I can do," Lily said. "This is beyond anything I might be able to influence."

I curled my lip in disgust and looked back to Brokk. I couldn't let this happen.

"Don't do it, Sereia," Lily ordered. "Don't throw away everything for a monster. You are smart, powerful, and beautiful. And you have a chance at something good."

My blood twanged, and my magic thrummed as I felt

everything my power told me to do, everything I *could* do. I didn't look at her, I kept my gaze steady on Brokk as it all became clear. The truth of me, of what I was capable of, of what I wanted to do. Blood, blood, blood, I could almost feel it. "Maybe he is the beautiful one, and I'm the monster." I tightened my fists, then crouched slightly, readying myself. I looked over at Emblyn. "Clear the path, right Emblyn?"

She nodded, her expression sad, but understanding. "Clear the path, Sereia. Go be everything that you are."

I didn't wait. I burst forward, thrusting my arms out and lashing my power around anyone and everyone in my way. I yanked and threw whoever was between me and Brokk. Bodies tumbled, voices shrieked, but I didn't slow down as I charged toward him. Weapons flew at me as I reached the first row of guards. I pushed their blood, causing their swings to miss and nearly hit their own warriors. I dodged and evaded, just like Tyrus had taught me. I clashed with very few, using their own weapons to fight nearby guards off. I didn't let them slow me down as I charged through them, pushing them out of the way with my power. If they were bigger than me, it merely meant they had more blood for me to control.

I reached the guards who held Brokk, both of them ready to fight me. I *thirsted* to rip their blood from them, to slice a wound and then funnel their blood away from their bodies. To feel the liquid thread around my fingers as I pulled it free from their veins. I wanted it so badly I seethed for it.

But I didn't. And I only tempered my lust for blood because of Tyrus and Trachen, because these were their brethren. Instead, I shoved the guards aside with all of my might, then grabbed Brokk and ran with him for the edge of the city. I had no direct plan, no idea if we would live, but I wouldn't let him die in a stone prison. Something clattered on the tile as we ran, then one zipped by my face, nearly missing me. They were shooting fucking *arrows* at us. Those bastards.

"Sereia! What are—"

"—We're going to live. Hopefully."

"Hopefully?"

I didn't answer him as we reached the edge. I leapt up to the wide stone railing and hauled him with me. I didn't think or deliberate further as I jumped, and pulled Brokk with me over the towering side of the massive city of Adrilan.

CHAPTER 25

The wind howled in my ears as we fell so much faster than I was prepared for. My fear of heights blared to life again, all the caution that was absent before I jumped us to our demise now caused my panic to rise. But there was no going back, we were plummeting to our death. I tumbled with Brokk, managing to get underneath him, then shoved my arms through the gaps along his waist made by his hands bound in front of him. If we were going to die, it would be while I was holding him.

Instead of wrapping my arms around him, I reached up past him, toward the sky. With him over me, I clenched my eyes and tried to connect to the mist. To those million of points that had beckoned, promising their tether.

Brokk yelled my name, shouting about the rapidly approaching ground. In mere moments we would be dashed to bits.

There was nothing much to see above, the sky was still dark, only just barely beginning to brighten for the light rotations. A glow of torchlight cast from the terrace of the city, but it only got farther away. I stretched and splayed my fingers outward, trying to find purchase with that formless expanse in the night sky that I had so often sensed. I felt the connections form, one after another, so fast that it became a blur. I felt those millions of threads holding fast, like a web pulling down to me. I snatched my fists shut and pulled with all my might, yanking those threads. My eyes drifted shut. I felt weightless, my hair floated around me now, rather than whipping straight up past me. A stillness washed over me, though I knew we were still falling. But there was a buoyancy to the fall, like the threads held us aloft and slowed our descent.

"What's happening?" Brokk asked, his voice somehow sounding far away even though he was right on top of me. I slipped out of time, out of the space we were in. I could see everywhere, below the mist, above it. Somehow there were tiny, bright flecks suspended in the sky everywhere, all set against a backdrop of velvety blackness. I wanted to reach out and touch them even though they were much too far away, but my fingers were rigid, held in place by my tether to the mist.

I felt Brokk jostle above me, trying to flip me over. "The ground, Sereia!" My connection to the threads vanished at the same moment the world went black.

I blinked my eyes open, then bolted upright. "Brokk!"

A hand to my shoulder calmed my racing heart only a little, I needed to see him, to know he was okay. "I'm here, we made it. You did it, Sereia. You saved us."

A single, stifled cry heaved out of me. I turned, throwing my arms around him, burying my face into his neck. I could *smell* him, feel his solid presence. We were sitting on the ground, with me nestled in his legs as he held me. We were somewhere away from the city. I couldn't see the wall we had fallen next to.

I cringed, my head throbbed with pain. I let go of him, putting a hand to the back of my skull.

"You hit pretty hard," he said. "I tried to turn us to take some of the impact, but you were impossible to move. It was like you were locked in place."

"I was," I said, turning and leaning back to look at him. I could barely make out his features in the darkened night.

"The mist, just like in the book, you connected to it. You used it to slow us down," he said the words with awe and admiration.

I nodded. "I thought it would work, I've felt the possibility but never tried it."

He smirked, then tucked a lock of hair behind my ear. I shuddered at the touch. "Ballsy time to try it, when we'd literally die if it didn't work."

"Well, I guess I figured we were about to get arrowed the fuck up, we would've died if we didn't jump, so I just went for it."

He ran a knuckle along my jawline. "You were brave. But you should have let them take me. They wouldn't have done anything to you."

"I couldn't let them kill you. I saw what they did to you, your injuries, and I lost it. I wanted to kill them for it. Are you okay?" I lifted a hand to his head, barely touching where I had seen the blood. I looked at his wrists. There were sores from where the ropes were, but he had gotten them off.

He reached up, taking my hand, slipping his fingers around my palm, caressing my skin. "I'm okay, I promise."

Brokk's touch was both warm and cool, and utterly intoxicating. His fingers trailed down my arm. "We should get moving, if you can." His voice shook me out of my momentary stupor, I wanted him to continue touching me, to hold me, to tell me he wasn't going anywhere.

The sound of grating stone sounded from a distance.

"I think they're opening the city to look for us," he said, his eyes sharpening as he looked to see where the noise had come from. "I got us away from the direct area, but we aren't very far. We should move before they come looking when they don't find our bodies."

Right, bodies. They would likely have expected to find us dead at the base, and given that it was still night, they couldn't have been able to see where we would have landed if they looked over from above. They may not be in a rush to come looking, expecting simply a recovery operation. We might have a small window before they sounded an alarm and started a search party for the escapees. I almost laughed, I got out of their prison-city after all, even if I almost had to die doing it.

"I think that weird contraption is over here somewhere," Brokk said, pulling himself up to standing. "I'm not exactly sure where we are, but I think it's not far." He helped me up, steadying me to be sure I had my balance.

"Contraption?" I asked. I was definitely woozy and may not have heard him correctly.

"Some strange metal creature, it has a bunch of supplies in it."

"Oh fuck, I forgot about that. That's Lily's metal arthropod." Somehow I had not even thought about the fact that we just left it on a hill near the city when we had gone inside.

"Well thank the gods for it, I managed to use some of what I found inside of it to survive below Adrilan for a time. There was still a lot left inside that I didn't use, I had closed the hatch, so it should all still be there."

"Speaking of that," I said, starting to walk with him along a narrow path, "how did you—"

"—Later. I will tell you all, but later. We have to start moving. We don't want to be caught by them." He wrapped his hand around mine, and pulled me behind him as he picked a direction.

"Right, of course."

Fortunately the arthropod wasn't far at all. We scavenged everything we could: food, cooking implements, clothing, bedding, water. Then we took off into the night. A short while later a long, droning sound echoed through the forest from the city. They must have realized we survived, and had issued the alert to begin the hunt.

I curled my lip in their direction. If it was a fight they wanted, they'd get one. But first they'd have to catch us.

CHAPTER 26

We hiked until I was stumbling, heading what seemed to be east from Adrilan, toward the ever-so-slightly brightening spot on the horizon. The sky had only just started to lighten, indicating we were heading toward the light rotations. That would make our crossing much easier, but would also make us easier to track. We hadn't heard anything in a long time, no far off noises of a pursuit, no closer sounds like snapping twigs or movement of brush. I also couldn't sense any bodies nearby. Only the trunks of trees, and Brokk's comforting form were all that I could feel. We seemed to be completely on our own in the vastness of the Praegra Forest.

"Brokk, I'm tired." I tried to avoid saying the words for as long as I could but I had reached the point of exhaustion. My legs couldn't carry me further.

He had already packed all the gear onto his back, taking what little I carried so that he hauled the bulk of what we had grabbed from the arthropod. I should have felt guilty at taking the group's supplies, but I didn't. I knew the magistrate or someone in Adrilan could easily furnish Lily with the items she needed to make the return trip to TerraIgni. I also should have felt bad at leaving her, at not listening. But had I listened, Brokk would be shut away in a prison cell with a complicated lock that Tyrus couldn't break for me. Assuming he would, that is. And then they would kill him. So I couldn't feel guilt over saving Brokk, for protecting him. He was the better of us. If I had to be the villain, I would. I'd do it again to keep Brokk safe.

Brokk stopped, turning carefully to avoid jostling the supplies and faced me. "We can't stop yet, but I can carry you."

"Brokk, that's crazy, you're already weighed down."

He stepped closer, his free arm encircled my waist, his chin just above my eyes. I looked up, pausing at his closeness, at the look in his brilliant blue eyes which I had missed so much. "It'll be okay," he said quietly. "Just so you can take a rest. I'll start looking for a place that is hidden for us to sleep. We're practically out in the open right here. A little further. We need to go a little further."

I nodded, my gaze dancing between his eyes, dipping to his mouth, then back to his eyes.

"Good," he said and smiled. Then with one fluid motion, the arm that had been around my waist hoisted me over his shoulder, and he started walking again.

I closed my eyes, trying to use the time to recover so that I could walk on my own again. He was right, we couldn't stop yet. It had been perhaps a half rotation that we had trudged through the forest—the first part of which was practically at a run—so we had made it a good distance from the city. But we needed to press on. I hadn't yet asked where we were going, what our plan was. I figured, first thing's first: survive and get away, then decide what to do next.

I had him set me down after I had recovered a bit. It wasn't enough, but I could at least walk for awhile. I could only make out Brokk's outline in the inky darkness, and could see barely enough to recognize the gentle slopes in our path.

The region transformed into steeper hills, making them more tiring to climb, but the descent would give my burning thighs a rest. Brokk moved toward an outcropping of tree trunks on the far side of a hill, it seemed to be fairly dense from a distance.

Brokk untied the supplies from his shoulders, then dropped the pack at the edge of the copse. He stretched, then held up his hand to me to wait. He disappeared into the thicket, I heard rustling but felt no other life around him, save for the foliage. He returned a moment later. "There's a shallow cave behind these trees, not much, but it is protected and offers a little shelter."

I nodded. "I couldn't see you at all in there. I think it's good." I only hoped we were far enough away from the city that if there was a search party, we would at least have a reprieve to rest before they picked up our trail. We silently began moving our things into the hidden area. The low-lying foliage took extra work to get through with the supplies, but I knew the leaves they offered would hide us from any passersby. I pulled the bundle that was our bedding into the hollowed out cave area. Calling it a cave was generous, it was really more of a recess into the hill with an overhang, but the leaves that had dropped over time made the ground very soft. It would make a nice underlayment for the bedding, and further muffle any sounds from walking on it. It wasn't the crackly, dry sort of foliage I was used to from the area surrounding Caer Lake. This offered a sort of springiness to the ground, which was definitely appreciated by my aching limbs. I knelt down and started unrolling the bound up blankets, putting the rope aside to use for something else if needed.

Brokk opened the pack with food. "It's not safe for a fire,

unfortunately," he said with a frown. "Only the dried fruits, nuts, and dried meats for now. Hopefully soon we can enjoy one."

"Maybe we can even find some capuli eventually," I said, smiling. The thought of drinking capuli with him by the fire brought back good memories.

He grinned. "I'm thrilled to say I swiped the capuli that was stored in the metal creature, we shouldn't have to look for any for some time!"

I laughed quietly and shook my head. "Of course you managed to find some." I finished laying out the bed, realizing how small it was. Only a little wider than what one person would need to sleep on. The blanket could be laid down to make a second bed perhaps, but it wouldn't be much and then both wouldn't have a covering.

"I can sleep on the ground," he said, "I don't mind."

"You most certainly will not! You, who would go so far as to make yourself an elevated bed because "the ground was too uncomfortable." No, we'll share it." I smirked knowingly, remembering how he had accidentally disclosed that he was actually pretty sensitive to what he slept on back when he built his camp near Caer Lake.

"Well the ground there was a lot harder," he noted. But a faint smile crept over his expression that I had caught him at his own game, then he looked at me with that one eyebrow arched. It always did funny things to me when he made that face.

"I know you're trying to be considerate, but share the bed with me. You need to get some good rest." I sat down on the blankets, then folded my legs under me. I patted the spot next to me to encourage him to sit down.

"Oh all right," he relented. He sat, then offered me some food. We ate in silence, listening to the wilderness around us. Far off there was the sound of some twittering creature, something small and docile. I breathed a sigh. Animals like that were good to have around, if they ever went utterly quiet you knew something was approaching.

We finished eating, and I was tempted to ask him questions. There was so much I wanted to know. Why he had decided to follow me, how he got in, how they caught him. But, we were tired, and staying quiet would probably be wise, so I decided to leave the questions for later.

I sat up on my knees and reached across Brokk to a bag on the other side of him, then pulled a set of clothing out which I had found in the arthropod. I was glad to have something comfortable to wear and relatively clean. Thinking back on how long I had been wearing my current clothes, I cringed. I was still wearing the same clothes from when I trained with Lily. That felt like a lifetime ago, before I had nearly lost a hold of my power and almost irreparably injured her. Peeling off the layers sounded like exactly what my spirit needed, casting aside everything that had happened so that I could sleep, at least for a little while.

Brokk dipped his chin in a nod as he saw the clothing, though his eyes traveled momentarily down my body. I stood to dress, which he then did as well, turning around to give me privacy while I changed. We had only found a pair of sleep pants for him, and they would probably run a little small. I had just finished pulling the soft top on when I turned and saw him take his shirt off after he had finished tying the sleep pants low on his hips. The sky was barely light enough so that I could make out the muscles of his back, the chiseled lines showing how strong and cut he was. My mouth dropped open as my eyes traced the curves of his shoulders, the way his sides narrowed down to a strong low back. I shifted my glance away as he turned around, and I kneeled back down on the bed, readying the blankets.

I peeled back the covers and slid in, then held it open for him to join me. I kept my eyes averted as he settled in next to me. It took me a moment to work up the courage to twist around toward him, then lay my cheek on his bare chest. His arm circled around me, holding me close.

It took effort to keep my breathing steady, but his proximity, his scent, the feel of his chest under my hand, all combined together leaving me wanting more. It was overwhelming and alluring. *He* was alluring. I closed my eyes, fighting off the cascade of whatever was going through me, but there he was, in my imagination when I shut my eyes. That arch to his eyebrow, the way his perfect lips quirked ever so slightly when he looked at mine. I wanted to run the pad of my thumb over those lips. My hand reached up in my vision, and I did exactly that. His lips parted, and the edge of his tongue swept forward, still barely visible. I ached to kiss him, to feel those lips against mine. To part my mouth and let him sweep his tongue into me.

"Oh!" I said suddenly and sucked in a breath, opening my eyes.

"Are you all right?" he asked, concern edging his voice, though I thought I sensed he was perhaps smiling when he asked.

"Yes, yes of course. I'm sorry." I settled onto his chest again. *Good gods, calm the fuck down.* I had to get past this … whatever this was, if I was ever going to get any sleep.

"Sereia?"

"Yeah?"

"… I'm so glad you're okay, after everything. I was so worried about you."

"I was worried about you, too," I said truthfully.

"You were?"

I nodded. I knew he couldn't see me, but I figured he could feel the movement. "I thought about you a lot, even before I figured it was you leaving me bookmarks."

He sighed, then squeezed me tighter. "We'll be okay. We just need to get further away from *everything*. And everyone."

I rocked my head in agreement, as sleep was finally starting to claim me. I jerked and twitched a few times, and each time he held me closer, his thumb sweeping mindless, gentle passes against the back of my hand.

CHAPTER 27

I startled awake, but Brokk was right there to comfort me.

"Shhh, you were having a bad dream, that's all," he whispered to me, holding me closer.

The dark images haunted me still, stone walls sliding closed with no way to escape. The only window of an otherwise empty room briefly showing the mist beyond, being shut permanently, cut off from the outside world, with no ability to connect to the mist. No water. Nothing.

I shuddered, shaking away the last of the ominous nightmare. I had known when I was entering the city of Adrilar that it meant letting go of nearly everything that I've now learned brings me comfort. But the sense of terror when I truly realized how they could make that permanent, to lock me or Brokk away and control every aspect of our lives, it shook me to the core. There would be no path forward if they caught us.

I pulled myself away from him, then sat up from our makeshift bed. "We have to get going."

I looked back at him, and my heart stopped. He had propped himself up on one arm, the pose practically inviting me to climb on top of him, his opal-white hair cascading down the side. The dried blood was still there, but had been cleaned up a little. His uncovered chest was nearly luminous in the low light. I gulped, then looked up to his eyes, those piercing blue eyes. A subtle twitch to his eyebrow had me about to change my mind about leaving. But the risk was too great. I may have accepted how selfish I was, to always lie to get what I wanted. But I wasn't selfish enough to let him be harmed by the Petrafae.

I stood, then grabbed some clothes from the bag. I turned and didn't wait for him to move before I took off my top, dressing with my back to him, whether he was watching or not. I swished my fresh shirt over my bare upper body, then pulled on new pants. I worked the fluttery tail of my dorsal fin free, letting it hang under the top and over my pants. I looked over my shoulder at him as I tied the waistband, and could almost make out his expression clearly. His gaze dipped low, and the look on his face was nearly savage. He looked how I felt before we fell asleep, fighting against a powerful urge. His eyes met mine, and I stopped all movement.

Brokk's expression shifted, then he pulled himself up and started to get ready. Maybe I had seen what I wanted to see, maybe I wanted him to feel what I had been feeling. He picked up his clothes, then silently started dressing while I rolled up the bedding. I made an effort not to look at him, though I desperately wanted to peek. We finished gathering everything, ate a quick bite, then headed back out into the forest.

It was as quiet as when we had snuck in for a rest. The only other beings were the small animals rooting around or chirping in the distance. We started off toward the east once again, heading toward the lightening sky.

We traveled in silence for quite some time, when I finally broached the questions burning a hole in me. "Brokk, how did you get into the city?"

He looked over his shoulder at me. "It wasn't easy, but I found a way in through a cavern below. There was this huge creature. It was *terrifying*, but something called it away and I managed to get past the point that it definitely could have caught me. After that, the caverns ended below in what turned out to be the biblio. I didn't go beyond that."

"That was the scolopendra, I think. Massive, and with thousands of legs?"

"That's the one. There was some rhythmic thumping, then it went toward the sound. I used the window to sneak by."

I laughed. "The turba. Those stultuses. They were having a party called a turba and they made this music that calls the scolopendra. Funny that their party to celebrate the creature ended up risking their border from below."

He smirked and shook his head. "Well I used their mistake to my advantage, but had it caught me ..." He shuddered. "I've never seen anything so fearsome before."

"I'm glad you made it through. When I first found the bookmarks, I thought it was you, but it took me some time to be sure. I kept telling myself it wasn't possible. Why did you follow me?"

He turned to me. "Why do you think?"

I opened my mouth, unsure what to say. "Because you were worried?"

He faced ahead again. "Of course. I was worried. And to tell you …"

"Tell me what?"

He paused, and the wait to hear what he was going to tell me was unbearable. "… That I was sorry," he finally said. "I was sorry how we parted. That wasn't what I wanted to have happen at all."

I blew out a breath. It took me a moment to process, but then I was confused. Was I disappointed? Relieved? I was not sure if that's what I hoped he would say. He had eventually left an apology on a bookmark for me, so maybe I shouldn't have been surprised that he would say that as a reason that he took such a risk to get into Adrilan. But why go to such great lengths to apologize to me? I thought about everything that had happened again, about the sequence of events and how I finally found out that it was in fact him in the biblio. Suddenly a memory slapped me sideways. With everything that had happened, I had buried the revelation that Lily had told us all, just before we had been called to the city center and I found out about Brokk's capture. "Someone dangerous is after me!" I blurted.

He spun, grabbing my hand and looking around wildly. "Where?" he hissed. "I don't hear or see anyone else," he said after scanning the area.

"No, I mean, somewhere. I found out before we went to the assembly where the magistrate announced that they caught you. Lily told me that someone named Empress Celestine is after me. She's the leader of the Umorfae. Do you know about her?"

"Of course I do," he said, his face darkening in a scowl. "I'm an Umorfae, after all," he added quickly.

"Right," I said. "Of course, but, do you know where she might be? I guess she somehow learned of my existence."

"How? Last I heard she was still in Lacausia, I can't see her actually leaving the territory. She usually sends others out to do her bidding. I'd be more worried about hunters and bounties." Looking around again, he tugged my hand. "We should go."

Brokk stewed for our long trek through the forest, it might have been a half rotation or more. He seemed pensive ever since I had told him about the empress, but maybe that shouldn't be surprising. His mention of hunters made a lot of sense, of course she would have warriors in her employ that she could simply order to go out and track down whatever it was that she was after. Unfortunate for me, because I was only partially trained in weaponry. And with my greenish-white Syrenni skin, black Syrenni eyes, opal Umorfae hair and Fae ears, it was obvious who and what I was. The only thing helping me blend into my surroundings was my soft, gray-brown short top and pants. Fortunately Lily and Kerenza had packed some functional clothes from TerraIgni which I took, but I had left behind the beautiful, shimmering linteums that Emblyn loved to wear. My heart sank a little as I thought about her, hopefully she was doing okay, and hopefully I hadn't caused any issues for her and the rest of our group. But, I had acted alone when I had blasted all those Petrafae out of the way, then jumped with Brokk to freedom. Also, I had specifically *not* killed anyone, even though I wanted to at the time. I muttered a prayer to Goddess Tahia that Lily and the others would be safe from the magistrate's wrath. So what if she was a Syrenni deity, she could spread a little love to those that had helped Syrenni in the past, even if they weren't Syrenni themselves.

Brokk slowed, looking around then started untying the supplies he carried. "I think we need a short rest."

I couldn't argue that, my feet ached from all the walking. Our pace had been fast, too. This hadn't been some leisurely stroll. Brokk took long, quick strides the whole time, pushing us to the brink of a run sometimes. I wouldn't complain though, we had to get as far away as we could.

He pulled the bedroll out and sat on it without unfurling it, using it like a log. Brokk made space for me, motioning with his chin for me to sit next to him. Opening the pack of food, he portioned some jerky out for each of us.

After I finished mine, I cleared my throat. "What was it like hiding in the biblio?"

"Lonely," he answered without missing a beat. "And also dreary. It was very dark down there. I have discovered I really don't like the dark. But, I liked learning things, and when I saw you come down there, it was all worth it. I had been figuring out how I would risk venturing out of there without being seen to try and find you."

"Why didn't you just come and tell me then, when you saw me?"

"Because *he* was there."

I gulped. "Oh. Right. His name is Tyrus."

"Impressive physically, and certainly handsome," he commented.

"True. But dumb as a bag of rocks."

Brokk laughed and smiled at me.

"Kind though, he was kind to me," I said. "At first a little … unaware, I guess. But overall, he was thoughtful." I paused, about to slap myself for so easily talking about Tyrus to Brokk. What was I even thinking? I realized Brokk's comment may have been a test to see what I felt about Tyrus.

"And what else?" he asked.

My blood went cold. *And what else?* I had asked that same question to Tyrus when he had told me I was beautiful. He had told me he liked my looks when we were in the biblio, *after* the turba. After Brokk had made his way through the caverns. "And what else do you like about me?" I had asked Tyrus, and Tyrus had stumbled over the answer. Brokk must have seen the whole interaction. Brokk likely knew about a lot more than I wanted him to know regarding me and Tyrus.

"What else is there?" I asked Brokk in return, and he gave me a knowing smirk. That had been Tyrus's response, too.

"Was he good?" he asked quietly. "In that little room, was he good?"

I looked at Brokk unblinking, my eyes dancing between each of his. He had told me I was brave when I forced us to jump off of the lip of the city. I could be brave now and be truthful. For once in my godsdamned life I could be honest. Because I hadn't done anything wrong, Brokk and I had no promise to each other, even though my heart had been with him the whole time. Brokk had asked me, and I wasn't going to lie to him now. "He was good, I think. He wasn't my first, but my only other experience was with a Syrenni male. That was wholly different and I guess by comparison unimpressive. I would say it was shallow with Tyrus, he wanted very little from me, and I wanted little from him. I can't say it was meaningless, because that wouldn't be true, but it wasn't emotional. I think I felt no connection to him."

Brokk nodded, his eyes darkened as he looked away from me. A muscle feathered in his jaw.

"Are you mad?" I asked.

"It wouldn't be fair to be mad."

"That doesn't mean you aren't," I said. "Fair or not, emotions don't follow those rules."

He huffed. "Once again with the occasional overly-wise comment."

"I'm pretty fucking brilliant sometimes."

He laughed finally. "That you are." He looked at me again, and that sparkle in his eyes had returned.

I breathed a sigh of relief and put my hand over his, which rested on his knee. I was tempted to lean forward and kiss his cheek, to give him another physical sign that I cared. But given the conversation we just had, it felt off to do anything like that. I stood instead, then picked up the supplies I had been carrying. I didn't want to talk any more, it was too awkward. Distance, more distance was what I wanted. I wanted to get as far away from that place and those memories as I could. The whole experience of Adrilan was a lot of things, both good and bad, and now I wanted to leave it behind me.

We hiked in silence for another half rotation. My feet were dragging by the time he stopped. We found another spot to set up a quick camp, which wasn't nearly as secluded as the first one. We only had a few tree trunks for cover, but it would have to do. I drank some water, trying to quench my thirst. Swishing the water skin, I weighed what was left. I frowned, we would need water soon, and we hadn't crossed a source yet. I was also starting to dry out, I could feel it at the base of my fin. I didn't mention it as we ate. I changed my clothes into the sleep set, then made the bed, opening the covers to him expectantly.

He had changed into the sleep pants, but still had his shirt on. He stood there, waiting, perhaps deliberating.

"Come on in, Brokk. We should sleep."

"It's not a good idea."

I stared at him. Was he really going to do this after I had told him about Tyrus? I pushed down the upset feeling that started to well up within me. The feeling that now that he knew for sure, I was somehow tainted. Besmirched, because I had lain with a Petrafae. Or maybe he was just mad at me, and wanted to keep me at a distance now.

He held up his hand, looking like he was trying to decide what to say. "I think that I need to keep watch, I mean. We don't have enough cover in this area to hide us well. I will stay up and monitor, so that you can sleep."

My face fell, and my spirit guttered. It didn't feel like that was the reason he avoided climbing into bed with me. "You need sleep, too." I gave up quickly, not wanting to push the issue. "Wake me to switch off with me."

He nodded. "I will wake you if I get tired."

I rolled over with my back to him, and tried not to be upset so that I could rest.

CHAPTER 28

I slept fitfully, if at all. The feeling of tightness from my fin only grew worse, causing me to half-sleep with worry. I needed water, soon. I sat up finally, having dozed several times but never really falling asleep well.

I turned over to look at Brokk, who sat propped up against a tree trunk, pointed away from me and looking out in the direction we had come from. "What's wrong?" he asked over his shoulder.

"Nothing, just not sleeping well. Do you want to rest?"

"No, I'm fine. Let's just pack up and move on."

I silently rolled up the bed, changed my clothes, then heaved everything I had carried before onto my back. I cringed at the feeling, at the way my skin had no flex. No doubt the scales along my fin and probably at my hips were starting to flake.

Brokk eyed me as he adjusted his items, with that downward slant to his eyebrow when he suspected something was amiss. I gave him a half-grin that showed no teeth, then set off walking without engaging him further. Getting moving sounded preferable, it might mean we found water sooner.

He didn't talk to me at all, focusing instead on moving forward, making progress. The longer he went without speaking, the more upset I became. Plus my skin absolutely ached now, it was making me irritable. I knew it was causing my temper to flare, but I couldn't help it.

I stopped in my tracks. "Are you going to ignore me from here on out?" I tossed my things on the ground. I was sick of the silent treatment. I had been honest with him, and now I was paying for it ten fold. I hated to think it, but for a moment I said to myself that this was one reason I would lie. He wouldn't be acting this way if I had dumbed down what had happened between Tyrus and me. But, he knew what we had done in that room. Lying would have been worse. Logically I knew that, but my unbearably dry skin, and my withering insides made it difficult to think straight.

He swung around, glowering at me. "Not so understanding of my feelings now, it seems. Or do you just want me to pretend? Carry on like you didn't get involved with another male?"

"Well I'd hope you would talk to me about it. Rather than holding me at such a distance."

"You want me to get closer?" He stomped forward, coming to a stop right in front of me. "Is this better?"

His eyes, his tone, they were like blades. Sharp and ready to cut.

"We had parted under not the best terms," I said, "and further than that, you never said anything to me about ... *anything*. Nothing to make me think that my being with Tyrus would be a problem, or be something that I would have to explain to you. I actually don't owe you an explanation."

"No, I suppose you don't. Then why are you still talking about it? I am mad, okay? But I'm mad at *myself*. Because you're right, I never said anything to you about it when I could have."

I curled my lip, my annoyance had finally gotten the better of me. I went to elbow past him, when he grabbed me by my upper arms to keep me where I was. I winced in pain, my skin pinching because of lost moisture.

His expression changed completely. "What's wrong?"

"Nothing," I snapped. My head swam, and I felt woozy.

"Stop lying."

My heart sank. Godsdammit I just couldn't stop, could I? "I need water, right away. Like a lot of water. I need to be submerged."

"What? Why?"

"It's my Syrenni half. Syrenni have to be in water every rotation. We start to dry out, moving is hard and painful when that happens. The longer we go without water, the more unlikely it becomes that we can recover. I never really knew how long I could go, because of my Umorfae half. I can go about five rotations, depending on the circumstances, it seems."

Fear filled his eyes. "How long do we have?"

I cringed. "Maybe a rotation. Maybe less."

He didn't wait another breath. He picked up the things I dropped, and then swung me over his shoulder faster than I could blink, taking off running through the forest. The trees became a blur. I had never seen him move so fast. I knew the Fae were capable of unbelievable speed when needed, but this was unreal. I clenched my eyes shut, staving off the pain from being jostled so much. But if I had tried to move this quickly on my own ... I knew I couldn't. My legs wouldn't have cooperated, and I likely would have had to sit down soon after.

He charged with purpose for so long that I noticed the environment had lightened further, another click closer to the light rotations. I was becoming delirious from lack of water, I drank everything we had and it was nowhere near enough.

Then I sensed it, I felt the tug of a large body of water. Shortly after, I smelled it. That beautiful fresh smell of a softly moving river. I remembered this river, the one we had crossed when I traveled west with Lily. Everything was hazy as we approached, my eyes were not functioning well from dehydration. Brokk threw down our supplies on the bank, then dove in with me. I gasped as my body greedily sucked in fluid, replenishing what had started to crack and contract. He held me as we floated, keeping us aloft in a slowly churning eddie. I closed my eyes, resting my forehead against his as I recovered while we rotated around.

"You're okay. You're going to be okay." He said it over and over, like he was convincing himself with the mantra.

I opened my eyes, droplets dripping from my eyelashes as I looked at him.

"I'm okay," I said, not breaking eye contact with him. He had done it, he had raced us through the forest until we found water. He had not let up until I was safe.

His lower lip strained in a way I hadn't seen him do before, like he was fighting off something. "I followed you into the city because I can't live without you, because life is meaningless without you in it," he said as he lifted his hand and cupped my cheek, running the pad of his thumb along my jaw. "I couldn't bear to lose you, Sereia. I'm madly in love with you."

The air went out of me at his words. I searched his face, every beautiful line that I had studied so achingly. The swoop of his eyebrows, the slight curl of his eyelashes framing his unimaginable blue eyes, the curve of his enticing lips.

The pad of his thumb grazed my lip, just like I had done to him in my imagination. Something about the motion untethered me, breaking free the thirst that truly lurked within me. The need for water had taken over me physically, but nothing compared to this need. To the burning, desperate desire to claim him. This was a secret I could no longer keep to myself, could no longer keep myself from acknowledging. No more stolen glances, no more imagined scenarios. I wanted him and I wanted him to know it. "You're all I've ever wanted, Brokk," I confessed. "I need you so badly it hurts. I'm in love with you, too."

I became aware of our closeness, of my arms looped around his neck, of his arm drawing me in close at the hips. I leaned in even closer, opening my lips slightly to meet his. My eyes closed just as his mouth met mine. The fit, the taste, it was more than I had imagined. I opened my mouth wider, inviting him in deeper, our kiss not frantic, not hurried, it was *thorough*. His tongue grazed mine, and my heart fluttered for him, the spot between my legs warming, my breath quickened. My hands reached for more of him, moving from being around his neck to grasping at his back, his hips, drawing him in tighter.

It was a confession of the spirit, that I had loved him for so long, long before we had gone our separate ways. Love that didn't care whether he was Umorfae or I was a mestisius, whether I was good or bad or something in between. It was a power greater than anything we had control over and could wield. It was a power and potential beyond anything I had ever imagined. It wasn't until that moment that I knew how desperately I had desired him, I hadn't allowed myself to admit it completely before, because that raw need was tied up in whether or not he accepted me. And that want, that aching, previously unrequited want would have dashed me to nothing if he hadn't returned the feelings. I had grown so accustomed to lying I had even lied to myself.

My eyebrows drew together, as an emotional tidal wave rolled through me. I released the kiss, gasping and nearly weeping at what he had told me. I pressed my forehead against his again, and he stroked my back. Tears streamed down my face, finally I had enough moisture that I could let my emotions flow from me.

"Don't cry," he said, using his thumb to wipe the tears. "We just got you rehydrated."

I laughed, and cried a little more. But I could feel my beaming smile at him, it shined through in the gradually growing light.

He smiled back at me, placing his hand along my neck as he admired me. "I didn't know what I sought when I left my home, I didn't know it until I found you."

I breathed a sigh, trying to steady myself and my surging emotions. Home. I was home with him. But we had no place to live in peace, in safety. We had to continue our journey to find that, to cultivate it. To create a place where we could live and love away from the harsh, judging eyes of the rest of our world. I took his hand and squeezed it, then kissed his knuckles. I made a silent promise that we would find that home. That stream that I had pictured us next to when I would get lost in my imagination, when I let my thoughts run away with me way up in that tower bedroom in Adrilan. We would make that dream real.

I tugged his hand. "Let's ready our things."

He looked around. "But it's so beautiful here, and I do need a rest."

I wanted to facepalm myself, *of course* he'd be tired. He hadn't slept and then ran for who knew how long through the forest to get us to the river. I agreed easily. "Let's find a good spot then."

We decided to cross the river, ferrying our things to prevent the bedding and the food from getting wet. There had been a land bridge that Lily had used when we crossed, but that was out of the way further to the north from where we were currently. Brokk and I decided it was best to simply swim across the rapids. It would mask our trail and slow down any Petrafae that may still be chasing us. In reality, they may have already given up, we must have been a fair amount of the way through Praegra Forest. I thought back to that map I had seen on the table in the Adrilan war room, picturing where the first river crossed through the trees. There was more than one heading east from Adrilan. If that map—and my memory— was correct, then we had definitely crossed at least a quarter of the forest terrain. I hadn't realized when I looked at it that it was information that might be important later. Being observant and curious certainly had its merits.

We found a small hidden bay slightly to the south and just past the widest point of the river, even further from where the land bridge was. Tucked back out of view, it offered a beautiful canopy of leaves and a soft grass pathway that led up to an elevated flat area. After peeling off my wet clothes and getting my dry sleep clothes on, I flexed my hands as I felt the thin saplings that grew around the secluded spot, and the water their trunks held. I pushed then pulled them using that water inside, gently tangling them together to form more of a screen to hide our sleeping area better. I did the same with the branches overhead, pulling them down and twisting them around each other, creating a net which formed a natural ceiling, enclosing the small space even more. By the time

I was finished, you could only see the nook if you walked all the way around the wall of greenery and then along it for a few paces like a tunnel.

Brokk walked over and marveled at it, nodding his approval, then beckoned me out to show me something.

CHAPTER 29

Brokk had changed out of his wet clothes as well, but there was only a pair of woven pants for him to wear. I watched the muscles of his back and arms shift as he led the way. Around the bend further away from the river he had hung up our clothes—which he had washed—to dry on some low bushes. But it wasn't the drying clothes he wanted to show me. He had made a small ring of stones, and prepared fish wrapped in wide leaves to cook over a fire, and had set up the small pot we had taken to make capuli.

"I caught some fish, I thought we could hazard a small fire, if only for long enough to cook and make capuli." He sat down near the fire pit on a rock, and motioned for me to sit near him on an adjacent stone.

I settled in my seat and beamed, reaching forward to take his hand. "Magna!" It was a risk to have a fire, but we couldn't go on forever only eating the dried rations, the supply would run out much sooner if we did. "If only we had found some bisporus, too."

He wrinkled his nose, and I laughed. In a few moments, he had the fire lit with the flint we had taken, and the dry grass he had placed at the base of the sticks crackled to life. I watched it, mesmerized and anticipating the meal. I thought about the fire and the fish he prepared, then processed how quickly he had completed catching *and* preparing the food, and giving the wet clothes a scrub while I worked on the sleeping area. "How did you catch the fish so fast? I mean, I know you're a fast swimmer, but you're not Syrenni-fast."

He smirked. "True. It's not quite fair to the fish though. Once I spotted a good one I wielded my power, controlling the water around it. I lifted up a sphere out of the river, then just plucked the fish out of there. They don't have much chance once I've homed in on one I want to catch."

"Merciless," I joked.

"If I don't have a net, or rope to make a net, I do it that way. It's not always fast, though."

I watched the flame lick the stones that the fish lay wrapped on. "I'm looking forward to it, I had fish in Adrilan a few times, but not much."

He looked at me incredulously. "How did they even get fish? They have no hatchery nearby, I've never known Petrafae to eat it. Then again, it's not like I was ever invited in."

I shrugged. "I wondered the same. I hadn't seen any rivers close to the city. I even asked an attendant in the dining hall and he didn't know, he simply said they suddenly had some and also had bread, which they didn't often have. I let it go since I was hungry at the time and more focused on getting my plate to the table."

"Interesting," he said as he prepared the pot to brew the ground capuli beans, setting it near the fire to start the process. "The Umorfae eat fish for almost every meal. They have a surplus of fish grown in their hatcheries, it takes a lot to feed a whole population. Plus fields of grains to make the breads, lots of areas for crops in the outlying areas of Lacausia. Where do the Petrafae grow the food to feed all of them? I didn't see anything outside their city walls."

I pondered for a moment. "I didn't see anything either, but then again I didn't see the whole city. They must have had some way to manage their crops. There didn't seem to be a shortage of food."

He nodded, then smiled at me. "I missed this."

"I did, too," I said frankly. And as much as I loved talking with him about *anything*, I was glad for a subject change. "There's no one else I can talk to like I can with you. I learned that in Adrilan. I missed not hearing your thoughts, your opinions on things." The air hung heavy for a moment. I couldn't help but think of Tyrus, how I quite literally struggled to find anything to talk to him about, so instead it was purely physical.

"I was jealous," he admitted. "I reacted when we talked before about your time in Adrilan, because I was jealous. I wanted to be in there with you, too, in that little room."

I gulped and blinked my eyes, surprised that he had thought of Tyrus at the same time I did. I released a breath and nodded, I understood completely how hard it must have been to see what was unfolding. It was perhaps unfair that he had spied on me, that he watched me without my knowledge. But I wasn't going to harp on that, not if he was confessing and not blaming me for being with another in his presence unbeknownst to me. His words settled over me as I processed what he had just said. "Wait, you wanted to be in there, too? Like with him also?"

He shrugged. "If it meant I got to be with you. I'm not against it, but you're who I want."

My cheeks reddened, picturing what, exactly, that would even mean. However, since our admissions of feelings, Brokk was the only one I wanted to do anything like that with. I glanced from the fire back up to him, and gave him a look that I had only done in secret before, and perhaps one that he had imagined as well. A look like the one from his drawing of me, with that glance that conveyed so much more than words. A gaze of desire and invitation. His eyes connected with mine, and every part of me came alive with awareness. I flicked my eyes to his lips, and bit my lower lip. I wanted him and I wasn't ashamed to admit it, to show it. I leaned forward, hovering near him. He met me halfway, and his mouth found mine.

Right away the kiss was stronger, fiercer. Like it started in intensity from where we had left off. His hand reached under me from behind, and pulled me easily into his lap. I slipped right into place around him, my legs hanging to either side of his hips. It felt like I was made to fit right there. His palm glided along my back, his fingers grazing the fluted edge of my fin, sweeping toward my waist, then up my side further. Our mouths opened deeper, sharing breath and tasting each other, and his hand exploring more, reaching up my side waist. Brokk's thumbs swept over the peaks of my breasts, waking the tips of them in a sensation that had me releasing the kiss and gasping.

My mouth crashed back into his, an insatiable desire welling in me, needing him as close as he could get. The wound that had sat inside me—the one that had been cut when we parted and I left for Adrilan, the one I had ignored as I went about moving forward like I was supposed to—I felt it begin to close. I had needed him so badly, but I was forced to quiet that hurt. He had left, and I had left. But there the hurt had lain inside me, that dull pain that created the ache for him, it now finally quit its pulse. The throb that would spark a memory of him, anytime I did something of note, or read something I thought he would like. The reminder of his absence had made the wound a little deeper each time. And now, each kiss healed it that much more.

I lessened the kiss, leaning back to gaze at him. The corner of his mouth lifted up while his opposite eyebrow arched. The look had my blood heating, a rush went through me at having him so captivated.

The smell of smoke wafted over, for a moment it smelled so delicious. Then it smelled like something burning.

"Faex! The fish!" Brokk leapt up with me in his arms, a purely athletic move as he set me on my feet outside the rock ring, then swooped in to save the fish from certain ruin. I was already flushed from the kiss, but that move … it had me watching every nuance of his motions, the way his forearms flexed with corded muscles. He flicked the leaf packages away from the flame, then patted them with a quick smack to put out the crackling edge of fire along the leaf edges. The capuli was steaming and ready, and fortunately not burned, so he moved dirt over the fire pit with his foot, snuffing out the flames. He and I looked at each other, and then burst into peals of laughter. He held out his hand to me, which I took, then stepped back over the stones to stand with him.

"I got a little distracted," he said with a grin.

"Same here." I sat down, then wriggled my fingers at the food. "Can we eat now?"

He tested the pouches, making sure they weren't too hot, before unrolling them. I fanned the air, swishing away the last remnants of smoke. I looked up at the sky, at the trees to see if the signs of our little fire still hung in the air. Amazingly, barely a hint of it remained. Hopefully there hadn't been any watchful eyes that were keeping a lookout for our possible location while it burned. But, the Praegra Forest was vast, I certainly didn't know how far it extended, and it was dense. Someone hunting us would probably have to be fairly close to even spot the smoke. The smell though, that may have been able to reach further depending on winds.

"Do Petrafae have a good sense of smell?" I asked.

Brokk looked at me, nearly laughing in surprise. "I have no idea, what an interesting and sudden question."

"Well, the fire," I answered, motioning to the fire pit. "I don't see much smoke left, but the smell might linger or spread."

"Ah," he said as he handed me my opened leaf, "it's possible of course, but I think we had it lit for such a short time, we should be safe." He reached over to behind the stone nearest him, then pulled the two metal cups out we had swiped from the arthropod. I cringed, hopefully Lily would be understanding when she finds out how many provisions we took. I knew her mate had made those cups himself. Brokk poured us both capuli, and the core of my being melted at the sight. At the return to what was always our time, our moments to connect and laugh, to talk about the interesting things in the world or to tease each other. They were the times I had truly lamented and felt their loss. When having capuli in the dining hall in Adrilan, or anywhere else for that matter, it felt like a small portion of what capuli time was with him. None of them could measure up to how I felt when I was with Brokk.

He motioned to the fish, for us to eat while the capuli cooled. I took a bite, and it was worthy of closing my eyes to enjoy. Even the way he made food had something about it, a sense memory that rooted me back to when we first met. I was famished, and finished it quickly even though I wanted to enjoy it, but I was looking forward to that first sip of capuli hitting my tongue. We were supposed to rest soon, so it probably wasn't the smartest choice for a beverage, but I didn't care. I leaned closer to him, and we watched each other from over the rim while we drank.

After a few sips, my wants shifted *very* quickly. I had so desired to share capuli with him, it was a sweet, mild craving. And now a savage craving woke up in me. One that caused my eyes to drift down his body, lingering on his bare chest, then further down. The corner of my mouth kicked up as I looked at that little string tied low on his waist. Dragging my gaze up, our eyes reconnected as he watched me watching him. Brokk finished his capuli in one gulp, then set the cup aside without tearing his eyes from me. I finished mine as well, but I didn't bother with the pleasantry of gingerly putting my cup down. I tossed it, then closed the distance between us in a split moment. That was the Fae in me kicking in, perhaps fueled by the capuli stimulant, but the desire stirred up that potential to speed up my movements, to better my odds when I hunted something I wanted. I *wanted* Brokk.

His hand swooped in behind my head, clasping me at the nape of my neck. I thrust my arms forward, quickly gripping him from behind, and we were a frenzy of lips and tongue, sometimes teeth. He released my head and reached down, pulling me up to lift me off of the ground. I wrapped my legs around him, holding him tight at his shoulders. I became vaguely aware of him walking away from the campfire. The kisses never slowed as he moved us from the fire pit to the tiny, natural bedroom I had made. He stopped kissing me long enough to lay me down on the bedding, nestling himself atop me on the layers of soft padding. I was already panting feverishly, needing so much more of him, hyper-aware of how he fit right into my spread legs.

Instead he slowed our pace, reeling back the kisses slightly. He tugged at my shirt, pulling it up to expose my midriff. I sat up, pulling it off the rest of the way over my head. His eyes dipped, taking in my breasts, the pebbled peaks of them. Brokk lifted his hand to cup one completely, and the feel of his slightly calloused hand made them grow heavier with want. I closed my eyes, feeling him feel me. It was a wholly new sensation.

He ran his fingers along the top of my waistband, looping them under to glide across my lower abdomen. Brokk's gaze rose to meet mine again, and that subtle arch of his one brow sent a thrill through me. I finally knew what that look meant. It was a question, and a statement. All that time he had been indicating that he wanted me, and questioning if I wanted him, too. I nodded, silently telling him to pull down.

Brokk didn't look away from my eyes as he pulled the string, then slipped the pants down from my hips. Down further, sliding them softly along my legs, his hand caressing as it went. Lower still, until he swished them off of my feet. He brought his hand back up, grazing my calf, touching my thigh, sweeping toward the inner upper thigh. I gasped as his fingers swept in, to the apex of my legs, to that spot which ached for him to touch. He rubbed, casting his thumb gently back and forth with a few passes, before he finally lowered his gaze from my eyes, down my chest, to that spot which he was currently focused on. He shifted his body, moving closer to my hips. Angling my bent knees aside, he dropped his mouth to that spot where his thumb had been, and kissed me there. I closed my eyes, never having known this possibility. It was nearly more than I could handle, the feeling lighting me up from the inside out. He passed his tongue softly, so softly, across the bud at the center. I gripped the blankets to either side of us, hanging on for dear life as he escalated the motion. Something was happening, it was a quickening. A rapid crescendo that had hidden behind a veil before. Whatever this feeling was, it was also new. I felt like I was approaching a precipice and about to leap off.

"Wait!" I said. I needed to slow or I would fall off of that cliff, whatever it was that loomed before me.

He looked up and smiled at me. "Let it happen. I want to make you come."

I breathed hard as I watched him, I didn't know what it meant, but I didn't want to do whatever it was alone. "Not without you."

His eyebrow twitched in that way again, and the opposite side of his mouth curved up. He busied his hand with his pants, untying them to free himself of their restraint. In one motion he placed his hands on either side of me and lifted himself so that we were again face to face. His eyes searched mine and our breath synced.

"Touch me," he said. It was a quiet, gentle command.

I didn't know what he meant, I ran my hands down his arms. He shook his head, then flicked his eyes downward toward the length between his legs. I looked, and my eyes bulged at his rigid, proud shaft. Wrapping my hand around his considerable girth, my mouth went dry. His size, the feel of his length under my fingertips, it made me thirst for him in a way I never had before. I needed him to plunge himself into me. That raw desire for him to fill me was unexpected and insistent. This felt like a need as vital as breathing, as water. I looked back up at him, his eyes were closed and his eyebrows pinched. I could sense his pleasure as I stroked him. He groaned subtly, and the sound turned me molten hot. I wanted to be the reason he made so many more noises like that. He opened his eyes, the connection was electric as he pushed forward. I let go, and nothing had ever felt quite like it as he entered. His lips captured mine as he set an ardent rhythm, moving slowly and descending as far as he could go, before moving out again. My heart threatened to explode with the elation I felt at his closeness, *finally* as close as we could get. This was no mere physical act, this was an expression of the soul. Of our souls.

There was the precipice again, my breath, the sensation steadily ramping up, up, up. He gripped my bent knee, pulling me toward him. Something was happening that I was losing control over, the increasing sensation, the involuntary widening of my legs. A cascade hit me, waves coursed through me as release radiated out from my center. I may have shrieked, or gasped, or yelled. I wasn't sure. All I knew was that my consciousness had shot forward from myself when it happened, seeing something beyond the mist: brilliant flecks of light and the feeling of a breeze blowing across my skin, waking alive every nerve. I was both very aware of my own body and feeling out of it, suspended in the sky at the same time. I shuddered and held him, as he continued, his sounds ramping now, too. Hearing him, hearing the cue of what he might be feeling, what our joining was doing to him, it was enough to bring me back to that precipice to begin climbing again. I felt the possibility, though at the same time the sensitivity was too much, I was still riding the waves of the first release. His hand clutched my leg as he slammed hard, twice, and his other hand contracted into the blankets beneath him.

Brokk collapsed on top of me, breathing heavily as he then rolled to the side so that his weight was not pressing down on me. He ran a hand through my hair, admiring me, smiling.

I wanted to say something, but I didn't have words. I couldn't form them as I looked back at him, thinking about everything we had been through to get to this point. To be able to admit how we felt, and to be brave enough to put the truth of our feelings out there. My eyes drifted to his ears, and I realized we hadn't even touched each other there, that hadn't been a factor. I wondered what I had experienced, how I had felt that cresting surge, and how it had felt so, so good.

"What is it?" he asked, tucking a hair behind my ear which sent chills through me.

"Well, I felt something, and I wasn't sure what it was. It felt like it kept getting stronger, and stronger, and then it felt so good as I felt waves of something, pleasure I guess."

He stared at me. "You mean … wait, so, you've never …"

"What?"

"Had the physical release. You've done this, but never experienced what it could be."

"I guess not," I admitted. I honestly didn't know I was missing anything. But maybe this was why I wasn't really *that* interested in the physical act.

He smiled widely and kissed me. "This is so magna, that I could give you that. That you had your first one with me." He hugged me, his elation palpable.

I laughed a little, slightly embarrassed by the fact that I knew so little. That I didn't even know when it was good or not. Some of Emblyn's questions made so much more sense now. He noticed my momentary pause, and gave me a warm smile of encouragement. That he liked that I hadn't known and he had shown me. It wasn't a shortcoming in his eyes. I smiled in spite of my ignorance, at the feeling I had just experienced with Brokk. "So, *definitely* doing that again!" I said with a grin.

He chuckled, hugged and kissed me. "Damnatus, I love you, you're … everything. You are everything."

He pulled himself free then shifted onto his back, sighing as he curled his arm around me, drawing me close. It was exactly what I wanted, where I wanted to be. I nestled into his chest, then fell asleep to the sound of distant twittering animals.

CHAPTER 30

The second time was as magical as the first, if not more so. We awoke, then explored each others' bodies, and now were preparing the area to leave. He had joined me in the river after, washing off and basking in the majesty that was this great flow within the Praegra Forest. Were it not so close to Adrilan, I could have stayed here forever. I soaked up all I could, making sure to take full advantage of the river while we were here. After getting dressed and packing up the bedding, we walked out of the little nook I had made for us. I smiled at the private space, the place where we had officially joined, before I started to clear away signs that we had been there. I carefully undid the tangle of branches, releasing them to reach their full height. Pulling at the ground cover, I fixed the mussed ground, fortunately there was enough moisture in the fallen leaves to drag them into place. Satisfied that we had sufficiently covered our tracks, I went down to the waterside to find Brokk.

I found him washing our sleep clothes by the waterside. After wringing them out, he held up each item with one hand, pulling in a downward direction with the opposite fingers without touching the fabric, drawing the water down and out.

"They're still a little damp, but they should dry out while we walk," he said.

I looked at the fabric, then felt the water within them, my vision transforming to viewing the dampness as points suspended in the air. I realized that maybe I only had to move those points elsewhere in order to dry them completely. I fanned my fingers out, pushing the points up into the air, forcing them higher to disperse into the atmosphere. I blinked, my vision returning to normal.

"How did you …?" He stared with wonder at me.

I shrugged. "I hadn't thought about it before, I suddenly thought to try it."

He nodded. "This is what I was saying, a long time ago, with how you being a combination of Syrenni and Umorfae would shift your power, make it different."

"But the Syrenni have no power."

He leveled a serious look at me. "Are you so sure about that?"

I thought back to that sketched image in the huge, old book, the one of the Syrenni with the sigil. I decided against mentioning anything about the disk, about how I had stored it in my room back at Caer Lake. That fact mattered little now and as far as I knew, it was a long-dead power—if it ever had power at all. And I hadn't gotten to finish reading what was in the book, though I couldn't say I was disappointed that the trip ended early. I looked up at Brokk, thinking about what he said a bit more. "Maybe the Syrenni had power long time ago, but who knows now?" There was no evidence they could do anything, at least not with an elemental skill like the Fae had.

He looked deep in thought about the prospect, so I stepped down to the waterside then bent forward at the waist, flipping my hair down to soak it in the sweet-smelling river. I twisted it, wringing it lightly so that it was still mostly wet, before I tied it on top of my head. I glanced back at Brokk who watched with interest. "Just trying to stretch out the time we have before I need to submerge again." We had done all we could at this point to give ourselves a good buffer. All the waterskins were full, I had fully submerged and soaked until I didn't absorb anymore, and my damp hair would probably offer a little more time as well. There was no other reason to stay longer, other than every incredible moment that had happened here. I looked around, at the trees, the water, the mist in the sky, Brokk. I soaked it in like I could absorb that, too, holding onto the moments.

Brokk's smile shifted to a hard, discerning gaze as he looked toward the forest. "We should go."

My breath sped up as I heard it, too. Nothing. I heard *nothing*. No chirps or twitters of the peaceful creatures scratching around in the trees. They had quieted. My eyes rounded as I looked back at Brokk. He held his finger to his lips, shook his head once, then took my hand as we walked quickly away from the water's edge. At first we were careful, picking a path that made little to no noise, avoiding disturbing any brush or branches. The area opened up the further we went from the river, less water meant less undergrowth. By then, we were flat-out running. Brokk had restrained the metal items on his pack to keep them from clinking, making sure we didn't give away our position with unnecessary noise. We ran without stopping for at least a half rotation. I periodically fixed the path behind us, dragging the moss and leaves back into place to hide our tracks.

We finally stopped, my hair long-since dry and my mouth smacking for water. Fortunately my skin felt fine, and as long as we stopped regularly to drink water, it would hold off the drying a bit more. We said nothing for the entire trek, keeping our focus on the path ahead, still to the east and to the brightening sky. It was now light enough to easily see each other, which was both a blessing and a curse. That would mean whoever was tracking us would be able to see us easier as well. Our next stop would need to be much more secluded.

Brokk paused, looking around at the trees. He glanced back at me and motioned to the south, indicating we should switch directions. I thought back to that huge map on the war room table, I remembered briefly looking at the southeast corner. There had been a tangle of waterways and estuaries drawn out on that section of the table. No doubt plenty of places to find a spot we could call home—as long as we managed to lose whoever was tailing us.

I nodded. South it was. Hopefully the Petrafae didn't know much about Syrenni, because, if that map was accurate, to the north there were far less rivers and streams, it might be easy to guess that someone reliant on water would go south. But as we would need to be at another water source in about five rotations—six at the most—south was the smarter choice anyway.

We headed off at another fast clip, rushing through the forest with nearly silent footfalls. Brokk's opal hair streamed behind him, glimmering in the low light. I kept my attention on the terrain as much as possible, my training had built up a lot of strength, but I wasn't as sure-footed when loaded with supplies.

Brokk slowed, looking up at the tree tops around us. He looked at me, pointing two fingers at his eyes, then pointed up to the branches, telling me without words to look high. After a moment, I saw what he pointed out, but I didn't know why it was noteworthy. A fluffy animal with a long, swishy tail bounded along a high branch. I shrugged at Brokk. It was just a sweet little thing, probably only ate foliage.

He shook his head and motioned to look again. A thick, green cord with thorns on it looped down out of the leaves overhead and snatched the creature mid-bounce. It wrapped around it, squeezing it like a vice. I heard a weak squeaking sound as it tried to scream and struggle, but it was no use. Whatever is was had ahold of him and was only getting tighter. As its sounds died off, the rest of the forest quieted, too.

"What is it?" I whispered.

"Carnivorous prehensile vines. I know of an area in the southern Praegra Forest near Lacausia that has a large nest of them. Be careful, they'll snatch you right off the ground."

"The southern forest?" I frowned. *Scratch living in the south off the list.* Lily's words echoed in my mind, warning me of the dangers of the world. She wasn't kidding, there really were threats everywhere.

He proceeded onward, skirting the area where we had seen the animal become a meal for the vines. Once I knew they were there, I started to notice the signs of them, their gentle swaying in the canopy, the light rustle that they made when they retracted again. Unfortunately they moved so fast that there was no sound preceding their lethal strike, but when I cast my senses out, they *felt* different. "Brokk, I can tell where they are. I can feel them."

He paused, looking over his shoulder at me. The subtle quirk of his lips and slight nod of his head sent a thrill through me. His expressions conveyed so much with no words needed, it was a look of recognition and appreciation. That my skill, however strange and different, made a *difference.*

"All right, alert me when one is close by. I'll keep watching as well," he said. I smiled to myself, maybe now that I knew I could sense them, perhaps the south wasn't such a bad possibility for a future home. Maybe these vines could make a perfect perimeter to keep unwanted individuals out, while Brokk and I lived in peace and solitude in their midst. A "terrible" Umorfae and a two-faced Syrenni-Umorfae mestisius. Where better for a supposed villainous pair to live than in a den of plant-based serpents?

We continued on for a dreadfully pensive, long time. I constantly cast my senses out, seeking out the vines and navigating a path around them. After awhile, my feet were dragging, the uninterrupted search had drained me. "Brokk, I'm tired. I need to rest." I didn't want to say it, but using my skill for so long had depleted me. He didn't comment as he made a spot for me to sit, arranging the bedroll for my back as he fished out a bite to eat from the bag.

"I'm going to scout ahead, see if I can find a place for us to sleep."

I gulped down a sip of water as I eyed him. "Okay, but be careful about the vines, since I won't be there."

He flashed a cocky smile at me. "So worried about me, are you?"

I simply smiled and shook my head as he swung around to head off further into the forest. I mused at the unsettling feeling of having so much concern wrapped up in another being. I remembered how Emblyn realized she had feelings for Trachen, how they seemed to sneak up on her. I laughed and shook my head, how far I had fallen. All of those thoughts brought me back to Emblyn, to her bright smile, her raucous laughter, the light that she brought to every moment. I hoped she was okay, and hoped she was still with Trachen. If she wanted him, she deserved to be with him. I leaned back against the soft bedroll, letting my eyes take in the treetops, listening to the sounds of the forest.

246

CHAPTER 31

Brokk shook me awake, startling me back to the present. I didn't even realize I had drifted off. "I found a rocky area with some caves, it's perfect to sleep in, very secluded." He beckoned with a quick curl of his fingers, then looked around, checking the forest for any sign of a disturbance.

"Rocky?" I repeated. "Is it far? There don't seem to be any rocks nearby."

He nodded. "A bit, anyway. It's about an eighth rotation away, to the north slightly. It veers away from the dense forest."

I got up, arranging what I needed to carry as he picked up the main pack. He swung in for a quick kiss before we set off again.

It wasn't long before the path transformed. Large, angular rocks jutted out of the ground at haphazard angles. Their surfaces glittered with some rare mineral embedded within them. As pretty as they were, they were definitely a nuisance, they slowed us down as we had to navigate around them to stay with the path. It took extra effort not to catch anything on them when passing by, and to keep anything metallic from clattering against the stones.

The path gave way to tall, crumbly reddish passages. Brokk led me through a winding trail, bordered with walls that were more than double our height and made of sandy stone. He grabbed some dry bushes on the way, pulling their dead roots free of the loose ground, then holding them high to prevent their branches from dragging and leaving tracks. "Just a little further," he said with effort, trying to keep the twigs from snagging on the loose stones that seemed to defy falling out of the wall. One slight brush and they'd come sliding down the steep embankment. I knew without him telling me that any of those missteps could easily indicate that someone had walked through the area recently and give away our proximity.

He stopped in front of a narrow opening in the wall, then motioned with his chin for me to enter. It was only a little wider than his shoulders, and so low we'd have to stoop to enter.

"Is it safe?" I asked quietly, trying to look into the dark cavern.

"It is, it goes pretty far back. I already explored the whole thing, you can actually see in there as well, once you're inside."

"How?" It looked impossible to see anything, the sky still wasn't light, there was no way what little light emanated from the mist could reach so far back.

"Trust me," he said. His words hung there for a moment. I looked away from the cave and back to him, at the seriousness in his eyes.

I nodded. "All right, Brokk." I turned back to that unnerving, dark passage, then crouched to work my way in. As unsettling as it was to squeeze through the small opening, it at least didn't look like a possible entrance for Fae of our size. It could easily be overlooked by someone looking for a more reasonably-sized gap to find a place to sleep. Or more accurately, overlooked by someone looking for their quarry who would need a place to sleep.

He followed closely behind me, pulling the bush into the opening as he shuffled backward until it wedged at the narrowest point. Turning to look back, I could tell that the opening probably didn't look like much at all now, with the bush appearing to grow out from it and disguise it nearly completely. I dragged my hand along the wall for balance, sliding my feet forward slowly to gain safer footing. Blinking, I tried to get my eyes to adjust. I wanted to pull my hand away from the dusty, rocky surface, it felt terribly dry and brittle as I moved along dekkate by dekkate.

Squinting at the indistinct forms of the cave walls, I looked ahead to what appeared to be a bluish glow. Another step forward and the edge of the rocky wall was visible. I wrapped my hand around what seemed to be the end of the wall, and could feel moisture under my fingertips and something spongy on the unseen side. I would have jerked my hand back, were I not so glad to feel something other than that dreadfully dry stone. It wasn't a slick, gross feeling. It was more lush and verdant, like some life had found its way into that dank cavern. I could feel points of moisture suspended in the cave before I even made my way fully out of the narrow entrance tunnel. I pulled myself around the corner to peer at what lay beyond.

Plush, luminescent moss grew down the walls and across the ground, the occasional drip, drip, drip of water from a hidden source wound its way down large roots that forked into the rocky, mossy cavern.

"What is it?" I whispered, staring in awe at the subtle glow emanating throughout the surprisingly spacious cave. The entrance certainly belied what was hidden deep in the walls of the canyon.

"It's the sublayer, there are some plants that can channel the energy from it."

I couldn't tear my eyes from the view to look at him, thoughts swam through my head with questions. "I don't even know what that is."

"It's what flows through the core of the world, what the Maeder Tree is connected to, supposedly where we all spring from. I've heard its like pathways and streams of energy."

I walked forward, mesmerized by the light. Placing a hand to the center of the brightest glowing patch, I felt the surge of power through it, the pulse lit up around my fingers, making an imprint of where I had touched it. I closed my eyes, feeling the waves of gentle power thrum through it, coursing like a river of untold strength.

I blinked, bringing myself back to the present. "I've never seen such a beautiful sight or even heard of the sublayer, it's incredible." I turned around, reaching out to cup Brokk's cheek when I noticed how close he had moved in. But as I looked at him, something sparked a memory. "River of power … Goddess Tahia swims a river of power. "In the ancient way" it was always said."

"I don't follow."

"Goddess Tahia," I repeated, "she is revered by the Syrenni. A made-up goddess perhaps—or at least I had always thought that— she has the ability to swim a river of power and channel its energy."

"There are beings that can traverse the sublayer, called the Amibilis. Perhaps there were once more than just them?"

I smiled and shrugged. "Perhaps." One thing was for sure, I loved learning about the world and pondering possibilities with him. I looked down, he had pulled the pack with the bedroll in behind him. I motioned to the blankets. "Will we damage it if we sleep on it?"

His mouth curved up. "I guess it depends on how actively we sleep."

I scrunched my eyebrows at him, but then burst out laughing after his comment sunk in. We worked in unison making the bed, then ate a small bit of our stored food. After I had several large gulps of water, I decided it was time to undress. I stood, instead of reaching for my sleeping clothes, I pulled off my shirt, then tossed it onto the bag that held the extra clothing.

Brokk was seated on the bed, lounging back with his weight on one hand behind him. He lifted his eyes to me, letting them drag up my chest to my eyes. I undid my pants, then let them drop, puddling at my feet. I kicked them off with one toe, the fabric piling on top of my discarded shirt. He leaned forward, then undid his shirt. As he whipped it off, he sent it flying to land perfectly on top of my clothing without even looking. He folded his legs underneath himself and shifted his weight onto his knees, then pulled my bent knee to drape over his shoulder. I almost lost my balance at the unexpected motion, but reached up to steady myself on the cave ceiling, my fingers finding more of the soft moss.

His tongue dipped in, and I was so glad I had just found something to steady myself on because my eyes rolled back in my head. My awareness narrowed down to the in and out of my breath, the up and down of the tip of his tongue. One of his hands touched me gently from behind, caressing along my leg, while the other reached higher, casting his fingertips over my peaked breast. The sensation caused my breath to hitch, then speed up. I wanted to release my hands from the ceiling and dive my fingers into his hair, but I would have lost my balance as he continued passing strokes straight up my center.

I was reaching a fever-pitch, that imminent cascade that I had felt my first time with Brokk. Part of me wanted him to keep going, the other wanted him to slow, to not have it happen without him inside me. I pulled away, he gave me that knowing smile that said he could tell I was rapidly approaching that release. He leaned back, moving his legs from under him and flicking his eyes to his waiting, very exposed lap. I bit my lip looking at him in all his glory, his length twitched, beckoning me. Brokk gripped each of my hands, and guided me down on top of him, my legs to either side of his hips. I sucked in a sharp breath as he slid in, my weight settled on top of him and made him seat all the way in. That spot at my center dragged along him the whole way down, ratcheting me back up to nearly losing control over myself.

Brokk seemed to sense my impending pleasure, and he waited, kissing my neck, his hands trailing up my back, along my spine, down to the fluttering ends of my fin. I angled my chin down, then captured his lips with mine, sharing breath as I sat atop him, with him nestled deep inside me. His arms flexed, and he started moving us in a slow rhythm, pulling me up and then back down again. The sounds coming from him, they were enough to send me over that point that loomed so close. Waiting with him inside me had barely backed me away from the heat that had built up between us.

His hands swept low, his fingers reaching in and underneath me so near to where we were joined that it sent me straight to an unstoppable climax, but I wanted him to go with me. I didn't know why I wanted it to be at the same time, but I wanted him to feel what I felt as one. I remembered how sensitive Fae ears were, then swept my lips along the ridge of one, nipping the tip gently. He hardened further within me, causing me to stretch in the most merciless, decadent way around him. My nub that grazed the top of his shaft finally sent that explosive release crashing through me in waves, right as he thrusted hard into me and let out an unbridled sound of his own pleasure.

I gripped his shoulders, not ready to let go of him or completely stop movement just yet, pulsing once, twice, before slowing to a stop. I stayed in place, holding him while he held me, basking in our nakedness and carnal connection while our heartbeats calmed.

My knees started to ache, having been bent at a hard angle for too long. In truth I had forgotten about them, forgot about everything else on my body aside from where we were joined and how we moved. Anything besides that was extraneous, inconsequential. Anything else would have only gotten in the way. It was a hunt unlike any other, and during the height of that critical moment, all other senses had been blotted out. I moved off of him, then snuggled in with my arms wrapped around him. Brokk heaved a breath, still calming himself after the energetic coupling. His arms encircled me in return as he buried his face in my hair, breathing me in.

More of the cave was visible now that my eyes had fully adjusted. The blue light of the moss cast an ethereal glow on our surroundings. The space didn't go much further back, we had settled on the only level area. I eyed the entrance, I couldn't see anything of the outside world, the bush must have pretty well blocked any light that could have made its way in from the canyon. There was no doubt, however, that the leaves did little to hide any noise we had just made, so hopefully there were no keen ears nearby. I listened for a moment, straining to hear any disturbance or sign of another being. I smiled to myself at our luck of once again finding a safe place to rest—even if resting was not what we had done as soon as we settled our bed in place. I supposed it wasn't all luck, Brokk had gone ahead and made sure to find something suitable.

I began to drift off, when I felt a slow, steady beat from somewhere. It might have come through the walls, or from the ground, or from the moss itself.

CHAPTER 32

I should have been alarmed by the droning sound, but instead, it lulled me to sleep faster. It wasn't footfalls, that would have caused me to bolt upright in a panic. This was more of a melodic beat, one that soothed with its pulses. Brokk's slow, steady breathing told me he sensed no danger either, and had fallen asleep. I finally gave in to the rhythm, and allowed it to carry me away to a peaceful slumber.

The waves of energy lapping at my feet felt like water, but not. My fin flowed out with each surge, then floated back to hang down along my spine. It reminded me of sitting in the water at the shoreline of Caer Lake, letting the soft current drift in and out around me. The colors were brighter than what I had seen in the moss, and much more varied and vivid, with wisps of nebulae threaded throughout. When a pulse traveled, the brightness became almost unbearable, a quick flash and then it would subside. A sound crackled at the same time, the pulses affected all senses when they passed by. I faintly heard the calling of my name in my dreams, a female's voice that rode on the cresting electric waves. "Sereia, Sereia," she sang over and over. Was she looking for me? Or was she trying to wake me? The voice was muffled, like it filtered through multiple layers before reaching me, through the moss maybe. Was that the sublayer? I stirred, coming out of my slumber.

"Sereia." Brokk shook my shoulder as he whispered in my ear.

My eyelids sprang open, I heard something else at the same time that he said my name. It wasn't through the mysterious moss, but through the layers of the walls beside us instead. A thumping noise, and voices.

Footsteps.

I looked up at Brokk. He lifted a finger to his mouth and held me tighter. They had found us, through all of these jigs and jags we had taken our journey, and all of the care we had taken to mask our trail, they had *still* managed to track us. I rolled my lips inward and puffed a breath through them, slowly releasing my frustration—even though I really wanted to scream—because they were so close to finding us. *Fucking Petrafae.*

My irritation subsided as fear set in. What would they do if they caught us? Drag us back to Adrilan probably. But then more questions started flooding my thoughts. Why did they track us for so long? We were now a great distance from their city, why wouldn't they just retreat to their stronghold and leave us be? It made little sense to spend resources to haul us back there to face our punishment. I frowned, it was true that we were outlaws in their eyes, we had wronged them. But now we were gone and far from their borders, what gave them the right to hunt us so fiercely? Brokk had infiltrated their city, and I had then broken free someone they intended to execute, but neither of us had really hurt someone. I wrinkled my nose, correcting my thoughts. *He* hadn't hurt anyone, but I had. I had fought Petrafae guards to get him free.

Brokk squeezed my shoulder again. Looking in his eyes, I nodded once. He was saying without words for us to keep calm and be steady. I silently agreed. The sounds died off, they had passed us and continued on ahead. I closed my eyes again, focusing on keeping myself centered and quiet. Maybe we could use this to our advantage. They had inadvertently gone too far ahead, we could use that and switch directions from here. Maybe backtrack through the canyon and go a different way. At this point, we'd have to wait them out. There was no way we could sneak out and go an alternate route now. We would have to let them get far enough ahead before attempting that, then we could sneak out. I could have laughed, the other direction was south, at least, I was pretty sure it was. I never had to know my directions well when I lived at Caer Lake, but I did develop an innate sense for how certain directions felt. It somehow amused me to think that going south was our fate.

He tilted his head down, kissing me silently, gently. It was a prayer, and perhaps it was a diffuser to help calm my thoughts. I hadn't realized my fists had clenched and my whole body had gone rigid, it was only when his lips pressed against mine that I started to unfurl. The effect he had on me was impressive. Moments before I had been practically tumbling down a theoretical hole of next possible pathways, worrying and making mental plans for how to get us away from our hunters. But now, I found my eyes fluttering closed, brought back to the moment with him and away from my cascading thoughts. Maybe all we had was right now. We could wait, then leave, and then get caught. Then everything would change, our imagined future together would be just that, imaginary. I had to take in every moment I could with him, our future was tenuous and unpromised. But if that heart-stopping possibility of capture did happen, they could count on me fighting with everything I had in me to keep us free. The next time we go head to head, I wouldn't hold back and avoid killing, I'd tear their blood from their bodies to keep us from their rocky prison.

Brokk's arms slipped around me further, and he deepened the kiss. I had launched into yet another mental tangent, which he was now getting incredibly adept at circumventing. I focused on the closeness I felt with him, both the physical and emotional. If waiting was what we needed to do, I would enjoy every moment of it.

We crept out of our hiding spot, that glorious, mystical cave where I had been so near the core of the world, so near Brokk. It invigorated me in a way I didn't expect, prepared me for whatever may come. If I needed to fight, I would. If running would secure our safety, we would run. I would be like the water I was so connected to and take the path of least resistance.

Not a sound greeted us as we stood in the canyon, swiveling our heads to check for any sign of our hunters. Brokk used the broken branch of the bush we had plugged the cave entrance with to carve what looked like footprints in the canyon wall, making it appear that we had climbed up the wall and out of the area. He then pointed with his chin to the direction we had first entered the narrow walkway from, to the south. We started our trek, picking a careful path back toward the forest to the south, obscuring our footprints behind us to try and hide our tracks.

Once we were clear of the rocky area, we broke into a run,

dashing through the edge of the trees. Wind streamed through my hair, whipping from the swift motion. Fortunately we had thought ahead this time, wrapping our metal cups, the pot and anything else that might make noise inside of the bedroll. We ran until exhaustion set in, until my legs could carry me no further—at least not at that pace. Brokk threaded his fingers through mine, being careful of the delicate webbing between my digits. He kissed my knuckles and I smiled at him. We didn't have time to stop, but the small gesture sustained me, bolstered me for another push forward along our path.

I had already lost count of how many rotations it had been since we fled Adrilan. The evasion from our pursuers was becoming wearisome, sometimes I wondered if they would ever stop. Perhaps we really did have to find someplace in the southern forest surrounded by the dangerous vines. Maybe that would be the only way to have any peace. We kept a brisk pace walking side by side, not worrying about our trail for the moment. Sooner or later the Petrafae would figure out they were no longer following us, maybe their lost time would make them decide to turn back finally. It may have been a fool's hope to think that might happen, but I needed to cling to any semblance of hopeful thoughts. I had to admit to myself that I may not have had the fortitude to keep up such a long, arduous trek if I didn't believe in at least a slight chance of success.

My hopes were instantly dashed as a figure emerged from behind a tree in front of us.

CHAPTER 33

I clenched and unclenched one fist repeatedly, still holding Brokk's hand with the other. I stared at who had relentlessly pursued us and finally caught us, weighing my options. I had planned to run, or fight, now I wasn't sure which—if anything—I should do.

I decided to talk to the single Petrafae before us instead. "Tyrus," I said, by way of greeting, though the tone in my voice indicated I was anything but happy to see him. "Always showing up unexpectedly, I see." Brokk had stiffened beside me, no doubt recognizing Tyrus as well. Not only was he our pursuing Petrafae, he was the one Brokk had spied on me becoming entangled with.

Tyrus held up his hand, then opened his mouth to speak, but paused for a moment, clearly collecting his words before proceeding. I wouldn't think it would take long for him to collect his words, given that he didn't seem to have many at his disposal— based on how conversations had gone with him in the past. I was still deciding if I should fight him, or run with Brokk as fast as we could.

"We have been looking everywhere for you," Tyrus said finally.

"Obviously." I rolled my eyes, annoyed with his dim-witted ability to state what was already quite clear. Then my thoughts snagged on what he said, "we." Who else was with him? Trying to keep my body still and not make a show of swiveling myself around, I did my best to search the trees, to see who else was nearby.

I tightened my hand that still held Brokk's, squeezing it once to somehow send a silent signal to run. There were more Petrafae than just Tyrus, we needed to get out of here. My body tensed further, and I bent my legs slightly, preparing to bolt away from him. I readied to leap away toward the opening to our right.

But at that exact time, in the exact spot I eyed for us to escape through, the bushes rustled. And right after that, another Petrafae appeared through the foliage.

"Trachen," I said, dismayed. What a disappointment. I would have hoped he would honor what I was sure Emblyn would have asked of him, to *not* follow the magistrate's orders and hunt us down.

The other direction it was then. The underbrush was far denser to the left, and the route looked like it would be difficult to navigate. But, as long as we could possibly slip through their fingers now, an escape attempt *must* be made.

I tugged Brokk's hand ever so slightly, trying to indicate where I would suddenly run toward.

"We bring a message!" Tyrus said quickly. "A message from Lily."

I stiffened. "What do you mean?"

"We are here, in part, because of her," Trachen said.

"And in part because of me!" a female voice exclaimed behind us.

I swiveled, surprised that a third had managed to sneak up on us. I dropped my jaw as Emblyn came into view.

"Magna fucking *gods* you were hard to catch up to!" she said emphatically, with a big grin on her face as she walked toward me.

I opened and closed my mouth a few times, trying to form words and overcome my shock. "Emblyn!"

"I said for you to clear the path, but I didn't mean blast through it so I couldn't catch up to you!" She reached out her arms and enveloped me in a huge hug.

"I don't understand. How?"

"Lily sent me after you. That is, after I insisted to go. She knew she couldn't be the one to do it in her state. My maeder and Zia wanted to come, but needed to stay with Lily. Same with Maureen and Rachael, they aren't much good in a fight and there's no way they'd not stay with Lily, given her pregnancy."

I cringed a little. "Right. But, what about the Petrafae? Are they hunting us?" I asked, looking over my shoulder to Trachen and Tyrus. I glanced back to Emblyn, who shook her head.

"No, the magistrate ordered a search party, but they were unable to get the city open in time." She motioned with her chin to Tyrus. "He locked the city against Magistrate Zarneh's orders. He messed with the sequence the locks were in."

I spun to Tyrus, my eyebrows shot to my hairline. "You did that? I thought you had said you don't know the code!"

Tyrus smirked triumphantly. "That is true, but I realized I could put them in the wrong order, they would be able to figure it out eventually, but not before you had made a safe escape and we could follow shortly after."

I blinked, truly shocked that Tyrus had thought of that. That he had been willing to take such a risk. Magistrate Zarneh was likely fuming mad at him, it probably meant he was now as culpable as we were. I nodded my appreciation to him. "I had thought I heard the city opening after we jumped, but that wasn't the case I guess."

Tyrus shook his head and smiled. "That sound was me moving the largest blocks to prevent the lock from budging. Studying with you in the biblio helped me learn how to think more about the locking sequences, rather than just moving what they told me to."

I felt Brokk stand a little taller next to me, probably thinking about what *else* happened when I was in the biblio with Tyrus.

"But then ... if the city was locked, how did you get out?" I asked, ignoring the tension.

Emblyn walked past me, then turned and stopped next to Trachen. "We snuck out through the tunnels beneath the city. Trachen guided us, he had guard duty regularly near The Pit, and knew the passage out. As soon as we realized Tyrus had helped close off the city from the usual upper exits, we grabbed him and fled."

Brokk spoke up at last. "No issues with the great beast down there?"

"I asked another guard who was sympathetic to our escape," Trachen answered, "he went and played the drums for the scolopendra, where we had the turba. It called the scolopendra away from the tunnels for long enough for us to get out."

I whistled, processing everything for a moment. Then I remembered what Tyrus had first said when we saw him blocking our path. "You mentioned you have a message from Lily. What is it?"

Emblyn nodded. "We should make camp, then talk about it. You're going to need to sit down for this."

I formally introduced Brokk, which was naturally pretty lukewarm between Tyrus and him. Fortunately Emblyn was the exact opposite, and was very welcoming to him. Everyone then pitched in to find a suitable spot to make our beds. My eyes drifted to Tyrus's bedroll, painfully obvious that he would be sleeping alone, while Trachen and Emblyn had their own, as did Brokk and I. Brokk made us all capuli, though we had to share the cups as we only had the two. They hadn't brought capuli with them, but they had brought something far more important: extra food. Brokk might have bristled at the distinction that I considered food more important than capuli, but he couldn't argue with the sense of relief that we wouldn't have to worry about food for some time. Tyrus, Emblyn, and Trachen had quite a bit more than we had even when Brokk and I had started out our trek.

Brokk handed me a steaming capuli cup, then gave one to Emblyn. I smiled and nodded my thanks to him, that he was considerate enough to let us have ours first. Knowing how much he valued his capuli, it was a noticeable gesture.

"So, we're sitting now, what's the message?" I asked, blowing the steam off of the hot liquid in my cup.

"Yes, well, be prepared. This is upsetting. Right after everything happened: you had jumped with Brokk, the whole city was up in arms … Lily's bonded Faerie, Livi, showed up."

I smiled, thinking of how Livi would leave little sparkling patterns everywhere their feet touched down when giving messages to Lily. "Magna, Livi is wonderful. So, why do I need to be sitting for that news?"

"Because Livi told Lily some disturbing information. She had called Livi well before everything had happened, before she had even told you about the empress. Lily had asked Livi to check out a list of places once she heard Empress Celestine was after you. One such place was Caer Lake. I'm sorry to say, Livi witnessed Empress Celestine there. Celestine has captured the Syrenni, and that includes Neila."

I spit my capuli out. "We need to get there!" My head spun with the terrible news, thinking of how scared Neila must have been. My imagination ran away with me as I thought about what the empress may have already done to the Syrenni.

Emblyn held out a hand and placed it on my shoulder to steady me. "Yes, we do. But first we need to rest. After that, the three of us have already agreed we will go there with you. To fight if necessary. To break the Syrenni free. Whatever we need to do, we are with you."

My lip quivered, the terror I felt was rivaled only by when I had seen Brokk bloodied and battered, captured by the Petrafae. My fear subsided, followed by a surge of anger. I silently vowed I would hunt that empress down and repay whatever she had done to Neila and the Syrenni.

I looked at Brokk, who sat beside me. He had gone white—which I didn't think was possible given how pale he already was. "Brokk?" I said, hoping to garner a look of reassurance, something.

He looked at me finally. "I want to try and convince you not to go. It's definitely a trap, and the empress will do something terrible, I'm sure. You shouldn't go."

"But obviously I'm going to. Of course it's dangerous, or maybe foolish, but I have to go for Neila."

He nodded, resigned. "I am with you also. If you insist on going—even though I think it's not wise—I will go with you and help how I can."

I blew out a relieved breath, but something settled heavily in the pit of my stomach. Something underneath his words left me feeling like he was hesitant about joining me in returning to Caer Lake. I supposed it should be somewhat expected, he was Umorfae after all and she was the ruler over his kind, he must have had some trepidation about directly facing off with her—even if he had indicated in the past he didn't agree with her. I thought back, trying to remember what, exactly, he had said about her. I couldn't clearly recall.

Making an effort to calm myself down, I tried to convince myself that the time for another rest was necessary and would not mean the time lost would equal Syrenni lost. "Okay, we'll get some sleep and head out as soon as we wake." I wanted so badly to believe I could rest, and we would still be successful in spite of the delay. How long had it been already since Livi had told Lily what was happening? I could have punched myself for my mistake. We had pushed so hard to evade who we thought was the Petrafae, but in reality we would have known about the invasion at Caer Lake so much sooner, then all five of us could have set out to rescue the Syrenni.

I brushed it aside, nothing could be done about the lost time now. Our job going forward was to regenerate quickly, then race to the northeast. I handed my cup to Brokk, giving him a slight smile. Had we not had the delay, had the time alone together, Brokk and

I may not have developed what we had between us. I told myself that everything happened for a reason.

The others took turns with the cups, finishing off the capuli and sharing the jerky and dried fruits before we settled down to sleep.

I adjusted in the bed, rolling over to find a comfortable spot. My eyes connected with Tyrus, who looked over just as I had moved. I didn't separate my gaze right away, I looked back at him for a moment, before I turned my head to face Brokk. This might be a long trek with the two of them. I'd probably be well-served to talk things over with Tyrus, at least to clear the air and make sure he knew where I stood … if I even knew.

Later, I would do that later. I had enough on my mind as it was that would make falling asleep difficult. Frankly, my issues between Brokk and Tyrus were so minor compared to what was happening back at Caer Lake. It was my fault, all of it. I needed to fix everything, if it was possible.

CHAPTER 34

We made haste through the forest, heading in the direction Brokk was sure we needed to go. I didn't dispute it, I couldn't be totally sure until we crossed into an area I had been when heading west with Lily. My experience was so limited by comparison.

Tyrus, however, had questioned Brokk for the third time since we had started out after breaking down our camp, challenging his knowledge of the area.

"We are still in the region closest to Adrilan! What makes you so sure? We are not anywhere near Lacausia."

Brokk sighed heavily. "Because, *Tyrus,*" he said with contempt, "I have actually left my borders and traveled far. And I have been to the area surrounding Caer Lake, can you claim the same?"

"All right, that's enough," I said, stopping in my tracks and chopping my hand through the air. "You two, with me, now." *We're going to have it out once and for all.* Emblyn gave me a sympathetic look, then moved down the trail with Trachen. I whirled on Brokk and Tyrus. "You two are bickering like younglings and *I'm godsdamned sick of it.*"

Their eyebrows shot up in unison, leaning back slightly as I admonished them like their maeders might have.

"Well he is always talking like he knows *everything*," Tyrus said, "and he does not want to listen to what I have to say."

"Okay, fair point," I responded, "but frankly, he does know a lot. He's done a lot of studying and traveling. You have done neither."

"So you are on his side," Tyrus shot back, folding his arms. Brokk puffed up his chest, standing a little taller with a smug look on his face.

"A little, yeah. But Brokk, your tone sucks."

"What!" Brokk dropped his jaw and his whole body deflated.

"Well, listen to how you're talking to him, would you want to be talked to that way?"

He looked taken aback, maybe surprised that I had said anything. "No one has ever said something like that to me before."

"Because no one ever dared?" I questioned. The razor-sharp look he gave me confirmed it. I started to wonder why. Why had no one ever said something if he stepped out of line? I certainly had been chastised many times during my growing cycles, always put in my place if I ever said something that the elders didn't like. I found it hard to believe that he simply never said anything as a retort or comeback. He was too quick-witted to not do something like that. I flicked my hand, dismissing the thought and the issue. "My point is, I do think you are the one who knows the most about which direction we should go and what we should do, but that doesn't mean you get to treat him or anyone else poorly. I would guess that you are upset about something else, and are taking it out on him another way."

Brokk looked visibly annoyed. "You know what it is."

"All right, then. So you're mad that I was intimate with Tyrus."

I paused, downright shocked at my ability to just lay it out there, to so easily say what I had done with Tyrus in front of Brokk, to openly talk about it. But it was clearly what needed to be done.

"Yes I'm mad! I'm furious! And now he's here! I have to wonder what he thought he would get if he came after you." His power thrummed, and I felt the push against the volume of liquid in my body as a wave of pressure emanated outward from him.

I didn't respond, I simply shifted my gaze to Tyrus, who had shrunk back a little. At least he was smart enough to recognize that a pissed-off Umorfae was not something to trifle with. I gave Tyrus a look that I clearly wanted him to speak up, and say what his intentions were. I was about to prompt him to do that, because I wasn't sure if he would catch on to my facial expressions to know what I meant, but he cleared his throat to speak.

"I, uh, knew about you, Brokk," Tyrus said. "Emblyn told me. She knew who you were to Sereia once she saw you in the courtyard. When we left Adrilan, Emblyn warned me that I may not find an open-arm welcome. That you are the one Sereia loves, and that I would be left on the outskirts. But, I came to help, not because I wanted to rekindle something with Sereia. I wanted to make sure she was okay. I did not expect anything."

Brokk looked thoughtful, any annoyance visibly settled as he mulled Tyrus's words. I had to admit that my appreciation for Tyrus blossomed, he had made the effort because of his concern for me, and not because he thought he had something to gain. In fact it was probably quite the opposite, he was likely now an outlaw the same as Brokk and I were. I wanted to say something, to try and smooth Brokk over and get him to see reason, but I decided being quiet while he sorted it out for himself was better. Brokk was too smart to be told how to feel. I knew I certainly didn't like when anyone did that to me.

Brokk nodded at last. A slow, almost dejected nod. But one that showed he had come to a decision. "I'm sorry for how I talked to you. I will do better. I appreciate your words, and I know you said you have no expectations for something with Sereia, but I do believe you still have feelings for her."

He didn't wait for Tyrus to answer before he turned and headed down the trail, ready to move on toward our destination. It wasn't quite a resolution, but I figured it was a step forward. Tyrus and I looked at each other, Brokk's words left me wondering if Tyrus *did* feel something for me. I hadn't thought so when we were in Adrilan, he seemed more focused on conquests and didn't seem to be looking for anything serious. Maybe I had been wrong, though. Maybe I made assumptions, then cast him aside. I did have a habit of dismissing him, of not thinking him capable of anything other than shallow relationships. That part mattered little now, because regardless of how Tyrus felt, Brokk was the one I loved. I breathed a sigh, then turned to follow Brokk, and get our party moving toward Caer Lake once again.

Things improved drastically, though there was still the occasional squabble as we continued our long trudge through the forest. At one of our rest points, Brokk led me away to a tree further off, saying he needed some time alone with me. I protested slightly, not feeling like we had the time to be spending hidden in the trees doing something that would undoubtedly shift our focus away from getting to Caer Lake, at least temporarily anyway. I relented easily though, because escaping my tumultuous thoughts sounded pretty appealing. I was sick of thinking over the what-ifs of what might be happening to the Syrenni at any given time.

The trunk of the tree Brokk picked out was sizable, which he used to hoist me against. Part of me wanted to tell him to wait for us to get further from the others before doing anything, but he swept his tongue up my ear and I nearly shattered with pleasure. I looked over his shoulder, making sure no one could see us as he quickly unbuttoned himself, allowing his length to spring free. In moments he pushed into me, and I almost climaxed at his closeness, at the decadent way he plunged into me. A thought flashed through my head, wondering what he had mentioned before might be like, if it were both Brokk *and* Tyrus. Brokk's increased speed pushed the idea from my mind as a climax crashed through me. I was a quivering, heavy-breathing lump as Brokk finished right after.

We settled ourselves to rights, then went for a short walk to calm ourselves down further. I smiled at him, there was no hiding our rosy glow from anyone.

"What?" he asked, kissing my knuckles.

"I noticed how we're both practically glowing. I think it will be hard to hide what we've just done."

"That and our scents."

I stopped walking. "What?"

"Our scents," he answered like it was so obvious. When I gave him a look that I didn't know what he meant, he elaborated. "Our scents have mixed together. We can tell—when someone has done what we did, or even if someone is aroused—the Fae can always tell."

I suddenly felt very bare. "Well that's not fair."

He chuckled, clearly not caring at anyone knowing such information. I, however, became incredibly squeamish at the idea. I started to think back on all the times I had thought about Brokk that way, when he must have known exactly how I was feeling at the time. "So, you knew, before. You knew when I would think about you in a certain way."

He nodded, then laughed.

"That's extra not fair." I felt my cheeks heat and turned away.

He pulled my elbow and cupped my face, not letting me hide myself from him. "Having physical reactions doesn't always mean someone cares about you, so I never let it lead me to an assumption that you felt anything for me. Honestly, a lot of times I try to ignore it because I think you're right, it's information nobody asked to share. I suppose having the sense is good for mating purposes to *know*, but it's an archaic aspect of our physiology. We've evolved, we have better ways of determining interest."

I still couldn't help myself, it was all too much. I crossed my arms over my abdomen, thinking about how we now had to walk back to our companions and it would be so horrendously obvious. Though, it was probably obvious when we had first walked off alone. I shook it off. I couldn't do anything about what they thought, and I had enjoyed myself, so I decided not to care. There were far bigger problems for us to deal with than my discomfort. *Nothing like a looming battle to make my problems meaningless.* I straightened up, remembering how all of them wanted to be here, none of them *had* to join me on this endeavor. So what if I got a little active with Brokk, Emblyn and Trachen were likely doing the same thing. Tyrus though, he was the odd one out. Which would definitely be different from how many partners he was usually able to procure in Adrilan.

"Sereia, I wanted to talk to you again about the plan."

"Oh?"

"I think you should *not* return to the lake."

I opened my mouth to protest, but Brokk held up his hand. "Just listen," he said. "It's likely that Empress Celestine has already killed a number of Syrenni. Neila could be among them. Going back will most likely mean you're handing yourself over to her."

"But we don't know that for sure. I know you're worried, but I have to go if there's even a slim chance I can save Neila, save any of the Syrenni. I couldn't live with myself if I didn't try."

He gulped, looking more and more stricken with worry.

We got back to camp and settled in. Brokk and I had made it back before Trachen and Emblyn, so we sat with Tyrus and started eating. He knew what we had been up to of course, but didn't say anything as he offered us both more food.

I chewed some jerky, thinking about the empress again. "I was wondering, Brokk …"

His eyebrow twitched, that one expression that showed slight suspicion becoming apparent. "Yes?"

"What should I expect when I encounter the empress? What is she like?"

He seemed to counsel himself before speaking. "She is cunning, and ruthless, and always has another angle to play. So even if you think you've worked something out to your favor, it's likely she has something hidden to shift victory into her grasp."

I thought about what that might mean. I hated to admit it, but I was terrified. I then realized what that could mean for Brokk—as an Umorfae himself—with me going head to head with his leader. "Will you be there with me?"

He shook his head. "You don't want me there, I will do everything I can to help you prepare, but it would be better for you if she doesn't know I'm there. She will use me against you. I have no doubt about that."

Tyrus sat through the whole exchange, at first seeming disinterested, or maybe he was just following his usual pattern of not paying attention until it was something that required him to be involved. But then he perked up, curiosity altering his facial expression. "I take it you know the empress?" he asked Brokk.

"Don't you know the leader of the Petrafae?" I countered. "Of course he does."

"My point is, she likely knows Brokk's scent. Given what you two have been doing, his scent is all over you," Tyrus said, motioning to me. "Whether she sees him or not, she will know he is with you."

Oh my gods. I looked at Brokk with round eyes, seeing if he agreed with Tyrus's claim. Brokk cringed, and I knew by his face that Tyrus was right. "What do we do?" I asked no one in particular.

"The easiest way to hide one scent is to mask it with another," Tyrus answered simply.

Brokk clenched his hands into fists so tight they turned white. A muscle in his jaw feathered, and his power once again spiked, surging with anger. "I suppose you are offering yourself," Brokk said through clamped teeth.

Tyrus lifted his shoulders. "I want to protect Sereia. Do you?

If you believe the empress will use you against her, we should hide the fact that you and she are involved. Or am I wrong about that? How else do you suggest hiding what is between you two?"

Brokk let out a frustrated sound, then dropped his head and took a long breath through his nose, finally lifting his gaze to Tyrus. "You are right. I don't like the idea of course, but you're right. It's the only way. If Sereia insists on going back to the lake, we'll have to cover my scent."

Of course Tyrus becomes instantly smart when it involves his cock. I lifted a hand. "Are you two seriously deciding who I am going to be intimate with? I should think that is *my* choice?"

"I am making a suggestion, not deciding for you," Tyrus said quickly.

"And I am agreeing to stand aside while he … well if you decide to join with him again. I'm certainly not going to try to convince you to do it, but it would fix an issue that would undoubtedly crop up when you encounter the empress. She will know otherwise." He hit his leg with his balled fist. "It's my own foolish fault for not thinking about that ahead of time, but we had already engaged in those acts before we found out about her invasion of Caer Lake."

I pursed my lips. I didn't think that me being involved with Brokk would be bad for me if she could sense it, but it would likely be bad for him. But, he did say she was cunning, and maybe I couldn't see now what it would really mean when the time to face her was upon me.

Tyrus leaned closer to me, running his knuckle along my jaw. "It is not so bad, is it? I thought you liked it with me in Adrilan."

Brokk rolled his eyes. "It's not like you were able to make her finish," he muttered.

"I'm not saying I didn't like it," I said without acknowledging Brokk's comment, "but I'm in love with Brokk. I was even back when I was with you, but at the time I thought he and I had no chance together, so I went ahead with you. But now ..."

"Now he is here," Tyrus continued for me. "I get it. But it does not mean you do not love him. You love him still, and can sometimes be with me. I am fine with it, with you not having the same feelings for me as you do for him."

"Real magnanimous of you," Brokk grumbled.

I held up both hands this time, stopping them both from further comments. "We'll decide this later. Right now, we don't have to make a decision because we're still not anywhere near Caer Lake, correct?" I asked, shifting my gaze to Brokk. He nodded once. "Okay, then our focus should be on the trek."

Emblyn and Trachen appeared from the trail. She sat down next to me, and then I noticed what Brokk and then Tyrus had explained, she had a certain smell that was definitely an imprint of Trachen.

Her bright smile lit up her face, and her rosy cheeks appeared dewy. "So, what are we talking about?" Emblyn asked.

Brokk groaned, and I laughed at the ridiculousness of it all.

CHAPTER 35

Brokk grew more agitated the further northeast we went, the closer we got to the lake. He never took it out on me, but he certainly was sharp with everyone else—especially Tyrus. It shouldn't be any surprise, but he was going to have to get a hold of himself because he was the one who had agreed to this whole side quest of getting Tyrus's scent on me—in me—before I even had a chance to balk at it or comment one way or another. I had been more curious about getting with Tyrus *in addition* to Brokk, not without Brokk completely. And that idea had only been because of what Brokk had said about being willing to consider that, I hadn't even thought of it before he brought it up. I then started to wonder if doing just that might be enough, *mixing* the two scents. Would that be discernible? Maybe that would create a result that no one could figure out because that wouldn't belong to one specific individual. *Maybe worth a shot,* I mused.

"Sereia." Brokk's voice cut through the air and through my thoughts.

"What?"

"Whatever you're thinking about, cut it out. It's distracting," he said without turning around.

Emblyn snickered. "Well *I'd* like to hear it!"

I facepalmed myself. "Fucking Fae senses. Screw all of you."

Emblyn only laughed harder.

Camp was now handled differently, and I hated it. Brokk refused to sleep next to me, he said we had to start distancing ourselves. I demanded a deadline, a time when we could return to our sleeping arrangement that I had grown to love. He said simply "Not until after the business with the empress was over." How long would that be? We were still another ten to fifteen rotations from the lake. And then once there, it could be quick, or a long and drawn-out incursion. There was no way to know. I sat on my lonely bedroll, stewing about the back and forth we had about the timing, when Emblyn plopped down next to me.

"I brought two things I thought you would like, one of which I swiped from Maureen before leaving Adrilan."

I raised my eyebrows. "Oh?"

"I think you'll find it *very* educational." She procured a thin book from her bag, the lettering on the outside was worn off, but she flipped it open for me to see the pages.

"Oh my gods, you didn't!" I exclaimed.

She held in her laughter as she bobbed her head.

I looked over her shoulder at the illustrations of the same Fae female with various males in provocative positions, and diary entries near them. She flipped through the book, showing me colorful descriptions for intimate pleasure. "This is what Rachael called the "smut book" right?" I asked.

"It sure is! And ohhhhh does it give some ideas!" Emblyn fanned herself with the pages dramatically, and I burst out laughing.

"I bet Maureen was less than pleased you took it," I commented.

Emblyn shook her head. "Actually, she caught me trying to make off with it, then gave it to me easily to share with you." We giggled quietly to each other, while all the males watched us suspiciously. Brokk seemed the most aware of what we were reading, and eventually smiled and shook his head, despite the crankiness he seemed fully intent on maintaining.

After we spent a solid chunk of time reading and gossiping about who the book might have been about, Brokk interrupted us. "If you two are done with your sex book, I made you capuli." We laughed hysterically as he rolled his eyes, but he couldn't hide the chuckle he let out.

After our capuli, I remembered she said that she had two things that she brought. I asked about it, then Emblyn pulled another book from her bag, this one much thicker and far older.

I covered my mouth to keep from shrieking.

"Tyrus said this was the book you spent most of your time reading. I thought it might be helpful if you didn't get to finish it before leaving the city."

I couldn't believe it. "The Syrenni and the Connexion to the Mist" now sat in my lap. Given what I was about to face when I reached Caer Lake, I could use all the help I could get—if the book had any to offer.

I tucked into a cozy spot on my bedroll, reading while everyone else prepared for bed.

The light had brightened in the forest considerably, we were now about to head into the light rotations. Which meant it had been at least ten rotations since we had left Adrilan. Maybe fourteen. I gulped, it had been that long since the empress had invaded and taken the Syrenni hostage. After twenty cycles of freedom and solitude, she had shown up to repossess them. When we weren't fast-tracking our way through the forest, I was bent over my book studying. Emblyn and Trachen spent their time off with each other, scouting and collecting whatever food could be found to add to our dwindling supply. Tyrus and Brokk did the same, but as I was busy studying, they were forced to either spend time together, or go it alone. We had all decided that foraging or scouting should never be done alone, so, the two begrudgingly would take up a small search radius together.

I scoured the book for details, absorbing all I could whenever I got downtime. My feet were beyond aching from the trek, but I found that my studying time gave my body the rest it needed. I wasn't built quite like the others, my Syrenni half meant that long periods of hiking were harder on me than they were on the full-blooded Fae. But when we found a river again—Tahia be blessed that we managed to cross one—I reminded them all just how agile I was in the water. Everyone had jumped in to take a swim, though Emblyn stayed near the edge as she wasn't a great swimmer. I whipped around Brokk and Tyrus, creating a small whirlpool that spun them briefly and caused them to crash together. Brokk scowled at the fact that they had to steady each other with their powerful arms, holding each other lest they lose their balance and get sucked under. I laughed, pulling away from the funneling force I had created, letting it ebb and then spin off gently down the river.

"Very funny," Brokk griped.

"Sorry," I said, definitely *not* sorry, "it just feels so good being submerged in water again." I sighed and floated on my back, letting my eyes drift up to the misty skies, to my comforting friend that hung over us. The one that always called to me, reminding me of its presence. I basked in the water, listening to the mist, taking the moment to enjoy the calming currents. It wouldn't be long now, we might be at the lake in five rotations or so. It was difficult to know for sure, but I did recognize the river as being the first one we had crossed on our way to Adrilan.

Everyone had finished their washing and got out, but I lounged a little longer. Letting myself feel all of the water surrounding me, my limbs and fins drifting gently, letting every muscle relax. It was my last chance to do this before we arrived. I couldn't stop myself even though I wanted a moment's peace, but I started to think about what I would need to do once I reached the lake. Five rotations would mean I would once again be drying out. I would have to sneak into the lake first, before Celestine knew I was there. Or, we would have to come in from the direction of Brokk's former camp, so I could submerge in the stream there. It wasn't quite enough volume to fully submerge, but it would help. My mind was clearly not resting, so I gave up and got out of the water to help the others.

I used my skill to help everyone dry off, pulling the water from their clothes while Emblyn started a fire for us. She wasn't a Fire Bringer like Lily, but she did have her maeder's Ignisphaera, a small glass bauble on a chain which contained a living flame. Twisting the glass open to give her access to the fire, she drew a filament out and funneled it down to the waiting logs to get the fire started. I had to assume this might be our last fire. At a certain proximity to the lake the smoke would give away our position, and alert the empress that someone was nearby. This was the last one we could safely enjoy. One last respite before the final push to reach the shores of the imprisoned Syrenni. We settled in around the blaze, enjoying the crisp air of the early light rotation as Brokk started a pot for capuli.

I looked at each of my friends, my confidants, my lovers. In a strange twist we had grown into a group which I could rely on. The dynamics of it seemed to have shifted from when we first formed, the tussle between Brokk and Tyrus had subsided, I'd go so far to say they had begun to like each other. Even Brokk and Trachen had developed a rapport. Emblyn had been helpful in that regard, reminding each of the Petrafae not to judge Brokk simply for being born an Umorfae, to judge him on actions instead. I smiled at them, all talking and laughing with each other, not noticing my stares as I soaked in every moment with them.

At last I pulled the great tome from my bag, and began studying once again. I felt Brokk's eyes on me for a moment, before he turned to Tyrus and they started talking. I hid a smile that crept up, my time spent with my nose in the book had been good for the two of them. It had forced them to rely on each other for companionship, and when they had disagreements I tended to stay out of it now. Trachen glanced at Brokk and Tyrus, noticing the in-depth discussion they had launched into, then looked at me. We shared a quick, silent laugh about their new habit of hashing over the finer points of caudex versus domi, once again deliberating whether the Petrafae or the Umorfae had the better game. As caudex needed the skill of moving stone, and domi required control over water, they could never test it out together properly, thus continuing their stalemate over whose game was the most fun to play. Trachen reached over to me, handing me some of the berries he and Emblyn had collected. I popped some in my mouth, giving him a grin before I turned back to my book. I smiled to myself, Trachen had become a good friend, and sometimes he had a knack for interjecting a searing comment at the right moment, which proved to be excellent for comic relief before Tyrus and Brokk had warmed to each other. Trachen's ways may have actually helped facilitate that shift, he always seemed to know when an offhand comment would lighten the mood.

I tossed the last of my handful of berries in my mouth, then wiped my hand to avoid getting any berry stains on the pages. I flipped a page and my heart stopped. There was another etched drawing of a Syrenni holding the sigil, the metal disc clasped in one hand and lifted high overhead, with droves of Syrenni swimming in a circular pattern around her. I shifted my eyes, reading the inscription.

Bravery of the heart is rare, the sigil shares the power when it is there.

I frowned, the words for what was once etched in the surface didn't actually *tell* me what it meant. Did it mean if I had courage the sigil would then do something? And if that was the case, how would it know? How would this ancient metal lump—which seemed to never do anything as far as I could tell—suddenly wake up and do … something. The image didn't even properly illustrate *what* it was doing. Maybe all it really was, all it amounted to, was an icon, an idol. A thing that would help inspire the Syrenni to rise above. To come back to their power and fight. They hadn't fought in over a millennia, they had forgotten. Maybe they just needed to remember. Whether it physically had power or not, I now knew I needed it, and would most likely need help to get it.

"What is it?" Emblyn asked, noting the seriousness of my expression.

I looked at the page again, debating about telling everyone about this possible piece of the puzzle. The sigil had been hidden by the Azal familia all these cycles, and had kept it secret even from other Syrenni. It had been our pact passed down through the generations: keep it secret until the time to rise returns. It had been hidden from the Umorfae, painstakingly protected which sometimes resulted in death. How was I to know if now was the time to rise? There were no clues given, and yet, I had the book. Somehow, through this journey I had ended up with the book that showed the history of the sigil, showing it being used. Thinking I was somehow fated to be the one was complete faex. Me, a half-breed, self-serving opportunist. I wasn't chosen, or prophesied, or even wanted by the Syrenni. But I was *here.* I knew where the sigil was, and I had my friends. Sometimes to survive, we have to be more than what we were born as.

"I have to tell you all something," I said slowly, "and I need you all to listen carefully. There is an item, it was once revered by the Syrenni and supposedly powerful." I turned the book around, showing them the image. I sucked in a breath, praying to Goddess Tahia—or any of the other fucking gods if they were even listening—that I was doing the right thing. "This is the sigil, a metal disc that harnesses power and can lead the Syrenni. This may be what we need to get the Syrenni to rise up and take their freedom back."

Embyln's eyes widened, and everyone leaned closer to the drawing. "How do we find it?" she asked.

I lowered the book, looking at each of them one by one. "I already possess it. It's hidden in my room at Caer Lake."

Brokk dropped his jaw, his fingers going to his chin in thought. "But what if it's already been found? The lake has been under siege for perhaps fifteen rotations already."

I nodded. "I know. But only Neila and I knew about it. It has been passed down only amongst my familia, supposedly entrusted by Queen Sereia herself, the former leader of the Syrenni before they fell. For a thousand cycles we've hidden it."

"Your namesake," Emblyn whispered. "It's meant to be."

"I don't believe in that. How can it be meant to be if I was never meant to exist? Fate or not, it's what might turn the tide. It might be an advantage if we can get our hands on it. We have to get it back." I thought back on Neila's words from so long ago, long before I had left the lake. She said I had been named Sereia to lead the Syrenni to a new era. I had scoffed at her, argued with her, told her she saddled me with expectations I could never live up to. Had she somehow manifested this? The Syrenni now *required* a savior once again. But this time, I didn't want them to simply be free, I wanted them to take back their power, so that they didn't need saving again. They had been formidable once, the book was proof of that. They just needed to find their way back to their source of strength.

"How can we help?" Tyrus asked.

I smiled. "We make a plan."

CHAPTER 36

We sped up our passage through the forest, reducing our number of breaks and quickening our pace wherever we could. Brokk became more agitated the closer we got, and to be fair I couldn't blame him. I hadn't broached the subject, but knowing that we would be fighting his kin must have been eating at him. They were in the wrong, they had invaded the Syrenni territory, but I imagined that wouldn't really make it that much easier for Brokk. Add on top of that my impending joining with Tyrus in order to keep Brokk's involvement a secret, it all must have been chewing a hole through him.

He had taken to spending more time by himself, not really talking to any of us when it was time to rest. I frowned as I watched him lay down in the moss alone, removed from the rest of the group once we had stopped to make camp. We only had the four bedrolls, so he had started finding as comfortable a spot as he could. Every rotation he had tried to convince me not to go to the lake, that I would be offering myself as a sacrifice to the empress even if I didn't intend to. He told me how she is treacherous and manipulative, and also bent on revenge against the Syrenni and Lily. If the empress found out that I was important to Lily, Celestine would torture me that much faster. Brokk told me how much Celestine hated Lily, how the empress blamed Lily for completely changing the lives of the Umorfae. But, regardless of how many times he warned me of the dangers, I still needed to try and save them, at the core of my being I needed to make the effort. I couldn't slink off to live in a hovel in the forest with Brokk.

Tyrus rubbed my shoulder as I looked at Brokk's back, his face turned away so that we couldn't even lock eyes. "He is trying for you, you know. Holding you at an arm's distance is not what he wants."

I covered Tyrus's hand with mine, not looking away from Brokk. My heart hurt, he was even sleeping on the ground. I knew that out of all of us, he was the most sensitive to where he slept. But he had refused any of the bedrolls and insisted I sleep on ours, that my fin could too easily get damaged if I slept on the dry ground. Tyrus had tried to offer his as well, but Brokk declined.

I awoke to Tyrus gently nudging me.

Sitting up and rubbing my eyes, I looked around to see the others had already put away their bedding and were off scouting or making preparations. I looked back at Tyrus, who knelt near me and waited, watching me.

"What is it?" I asked.

"It is time, if you are ready and still want to."

The blood drained from my face. "To face the empress?"

He smiled softly. "No, for us to go into the forest, alone. For you and I to join again."

"But, Brokk." I gulped.

"He was the one that told me to ask you now. He said we should not put it off any longer if we are to do this. We are close enough to the lake that it is time to cover his scent." Tyrus reached down, taking my hand. "I promise to make it easy for you. Or if you want it over quickly, it can be."

I looked at his hand in mine. His broad palm was so unlike Brokk's. His skin coppery and fingers shorter, not dexterous and nimble like Brokk's which helped his ability to draw the things he finds beautiful. No, Tyrus's were strong, made for lifting things and for exerting his skill over rock. The two of them couldn't be more different from each other. I loved Brokk fiercely. Tyrus's comment when we had first discussed this possibility cropped up in my mind. That doing this doesn't mean I love Brokk any less. This was an agreed upon covenant, there was no secret about it, no wrong-doing if we proceeded. It would even protect Brokk, we could shield him from the empress and his kind by doing this. I nodded to Tyrus. I couldn't form the word yes, but I agreed nonetheless.

He helped me up, then guided me along a pathway further into the Praegra Forest. We walked until we reached a beautiful glen. Softly glowing flowers bordered the area, their lavender hue casting a haze on the lush green ferns that unfurled beneath them. He led me to a spot that the flowers encircled, framing the mossy ground like a bed. Tyrus started to kneel, to get down on the ground and tugged my hand to have me join him, but I stayed standing.

"Not on the ground," I said, looking at the area. It was too pretty, too intimate. It was like a dreamscape. If I got on the ground with him, it would be softer, and romantic. I didn't want romance from him, that was reserved for Brokk. That was for making love. No, I wanted something visceral, something of the body, not the spirit.

I walked over to one of the massive trees that bordered the area instead. Thinking back to some of the drawings the book from Maureen had detailed, I decided on staying standing, He stood, then followed. Facing away from him, I slipped off my shirt, then dropped my pants. I looked over my shoulder at Tyrus, inviting him to come up behind me. He whipped his shirt off, then shucked off his pants in moments, stepping up to me to press his muscular body against me from behind. His arm reached around me, cupping my breasts as the other hand braced us against the tree. I felt his considerable shaft pulse against me, hardening in anticipation. My mouth dried out and I closed my eyes. As he touched me, my body heated, warming to him, wanting him. I propped up one leg on a tree root, and he angled himself up inside me. I gasped as he filled me, stretched me, the feeling making me arch my back. I leaned forward a little as he started plunging in and out.

This was not like when we had joined in Adrilan at all. When we had before, he seemed only focused on himself, doing what would feel good to him, what would bring him to completion. It was only after further experience with Brokk that I really understood that. This time Tyrus seemed considerate, careful, and yet at the same time hitting all the right spots while he sped up. His hand released my breast and reached down, his fingers gliding over the center nub between my legs. For the first time with him, I climaxed in one breathless shockwave. He came shortly after, his sudden thrust and garbled sound telling me he had finished. He stayed inside me for a few moments, catching his breath and slowing his system down.

Tyrus pulled himself free, and the warm rush of fluid slid out of me. The very thing that would undo Brokk's imprint on me and protect him. Our little ruse, hopefully once was enough to cover him. It was physical only, because if the empress could somehow see the mark Brokk left on my heart, she would know. Nothing Tyrus could do could mask that part. Brokk was an indelible score that I would forever bear, a line etched that I had begged for, ached for. I wanted him to draw that line on my heart like he sketched his drawings. For him to put his mark on me and claim me.

I turned around and faced Tyrus. For someone who had just had a massive physical release, he looked a little sad. Maybe it wasn't as easy for him to have a physical-only joining, in spite of his prior claims. In truth, I did have feelings for him. I cared about him, cared about his safety, and had grown to appreciate him in many ways. I leaned forward and brushed a kiss to his cheek, then wrapped my arms around him in a gentle hug.

The gesture seemed to surprise him, he went rigid for a moment. But it wasn't long before he lowered his head and hugged me back. The embrace was strangely platonic, given what we had just done. We stood there, hugging in silence and just being for a time. I supposed we were each processing everything in our own way. It was a strange thing, to join with another to protect the one that I love. The idea seemed contradictory, so much so, that guilt welled up in me. It was a natural reaction, because despite repeated requests from Brokk to not proceed to the lake, I was unwilling to give up on Neila. I couldn't put aside the fact that Neila needed me. And because we were going to the lake, we *had* to cover Brokk's scent. If we didn't go, maybe we wouldn't have needed to do that.

We dressed, then walked back to where our camp had been. Everyone was packed and ready to go, but Brokk was nowhere to be seen. Emblyn held out some food for me, and a water skin to replenish myself. I finished eating then slung on my pack, just as Brokk appeared from around the bend on the trail ahead. His eyes shifted from me to Tyrus, seemingly gathering all he needed to know with just one glance. He nodded his head, bobbing with understanding. I blinked in surprise, he was shockingly okay with what had obviously transpired. He must have steeled himself for the eventuality, and the truth was, the moment we were clear of this whole mess I was going to make sure *his* scent was all over me again.

This would be the last leg of our journey, we would reach the lake and then we would see what I was really made of. See if I could swing the habits I had—which I had previously tried to change— into something we could use to our advantage, if bold-faced lying might prove to be a weapon for me.

Everything started to look familiar, to *feel* familiar. We were nearing the area of the forest I had known most of my life. I shuddered, thinking of the fearsome empress striding confidently through the trees, just before she swooped in and snatched away the Syrenni's freedom *again.* I wondered if any had died, and if so, how many. What had been the toll? I let my power spool inside of me, building up in intensity, letting it fuel me, fuel my rage. When the time came, I would unleash it.

The difficulty, or part of it, would be maintaining the element of surprise. Brokk had warned that there was likely a perimeter established, a system in place to alert the empress of our arrival. He detailed how they usually planned them. His extensive knowledge of how far her Umorfae guards, the Praetors, would be from her, and how quickly they could communicate, was a critical factor in us realizing how much earlier we needed to split off from each other. A series of arrows would likely be used to deliver messages, relaying them quickly with my location. Since I was the one the empress wanted, I was going in alone.

As bait.

CHAPTER 37

The irony was not lost on me, being the bait and playing a lure to free the Syrenni, who were essentially part fish. But the idea was that Celestine wouldn't know how many others were with me, and her designs were to capture me. At least, that was what we could determine based on what Lily had told us, just before I had fled Adrilan. The empress was searching for *me* after she had learned of my existence, so we were going to use that to our advantage.

The others veered off the path, spreading out to make their way to the lake from different directions, while I stayed on the main worn path which wound its way through the forest to Adrilan. It served as a natural funnel, and where she might expect me to come from if I were returning to my homeland. Just as expected, I felt the bodies hiding behind trees, I sensed their water as they tried to shield themselves. They didn't know I could essentially see them all, even if they tried to obscure themselves with leaves. I walked onward, not slowing in the slightest even though their numbers steadily increased the closer I got. I felt movement from one, I could tell by the changing position of the water in their body that they shot an arrow. I had to hand it to them, I didn't even hear it.

That was the point, I supposed.

Another twenty paces closer, another arrow launched. They were tracking my pace and my direction. Praetors moved in closer, abandoning their perches as they sought to encircle me.

Fifteen paces further, more of them lined the perimeter around me, still silently moving and invisible to the eye, but I could see them. The moisture in their bodies was like a beacon to me, all of their fluid suspended in space, giving me the ability to gauge how many and how far they were from me, from each other. I couldn't see weapons, but I could sense if they carried any based on their poses. I could tell when someone held a sword, or nocked an arrow. I could tell which ones I would be able to use, to force *them* to use their weapons against their brethren.

I saw a sliver of the lake through the trees, and all was deathly quietly. Umorfae converged behind me now, stacking up in rows just beyond sight in the tree line, preparing to encircle me so I couldn't retreat. Brokk had told me they would do that. The more of them that did, the better. That would mean less Praetors to guard outlying areas where my friends approached from.

Something was up in the trees ahead of me, but it was hard to tell what it was. Various shapes were scattered high over the trail at the rim of the last line of trees before entering the lake proper, near the common area the Syrenni had always shared. The shapes were somewhat large, but there was little to no water in them for me to make out what they were. I had to rely on my vision alone. It finally clarified once I got close enough.

Bodies. A line of dead Syrenni spread across and over my path ahead.

I choked back tears. I couldn't see who it was from this distance, but now I knew why I couldn't tell what they were using my water ability. I counted twenty that had been dried out, husks of former lives hoisted in the air, as a warning and a promise. There wasn't enough water left in them to discern them from drying wood. My fists balled involuntarily, had these Syrenni been denied submerging before they died? Most likely, it was torture to a Syrenni. What could be greater torture than to be so near their water source, a plentiful lake depth if only they were allowed to dip into it.

Brokk had told me something like this might happen, that she might kill some as an example and use their carcasses to invoke fear. He had used it as another reason why I shouldn't come back here. I had still insisted on pressing on and steeled myself for the possibility instead, but nothing could have prepared me for it properly. The Syrenni were docile, and poorly equipped to defend themselves against such a foe. Their stricken cadavers formed an archway I was forced to enter underneath if I wanted to make it to the lake. As I walked steadily onward, pretending like I was *not* absolutely shaking, I tried to avert my eyes from them, from their gaunt and twisted faces. But I couldn't help myself. And as I neared, I started to recognize who she had selected to die.

Nearly unrecognizable now, I saw the face of a male I had once loved. Prant was one of them, trussed and caught like a fish on a line, his fin tattered, his body bruised and damaged. He had likely tried to fight back, or knowing him, come to someone's defense. He wasn't skilled at fighting or naturally agile, but he was kind and honorable. He would have done something like that. I fought back tears for him, for everyone. The Syrenni as a whole had been unkind to me, but I never wanted them to die. I wanted them to live their lives in peace, with me well away from them. But just as Neila had wished, I had been called back, a clandestine and ill-fated mestisius to carry the weight of the injustice that had been wrought here. The empress had done this to get to me. Though I had wanted to be free of the responsibility which Neila hoped I would honor, it was neither wants or hopes that brought me here. It was Celestine who had truly forced my hand.

I shifted my gaze to the lake, and something in me clicked. Something in *the world* clicked, like the rotating of some unseen dial. For as wrong as the bodies of the Syrenni felt, heading toward the center of the lake felt *right*. Maybe it was my swirling emotions, the anger bubbling inside me, but I could have sworn I felt an additional force, something that quietly nodded to me that, yes, this was where I was supposed to be. To do what, I wasn't sure. Kill all the Umorfae who served under the empress? Maybe. Release whatever Syrenni still live? Definitely.

I walked onward, past the desiccated bodies, toward the common area. Everything was deathly still, and too quiet. I spun, looking through the trees to the Umorfae that I knew lurked nearby. Not one of them were visible, but I could feel they had only gotten closer. What were they waiting for? I turned again, looking out toward the lake, then walked to the shore. Not a single living Syrenni was visible, no signs of life anywhere aside from the encroaching Umorfae. Dread welled in me that they had killed all of them, but only displayed a few.

As my toes touched the water a rumble came from the center of the lake, and a massive bubble formed on the surface, rising up from below. The ground shook and a series of ripples radiated outwards in the water. The bubble dome lifted higher, water streaming off of the sides and rushing into the lake, obscuring what was inside. Then the bubble popped, and there she was, sitting on a throne of waves which churned upward. It held her aloft with the vertical momentum which was remarkably steady, the water cresting then fanning out in a graceful arc around her. The only sound in the whole area was the constant cascade of water from her unconventional throne.

Empress Celestine was *stunning*. More like terrifyingly beautiful, her cold expression frozen on her unflinching face. Her crystal blue eyes, much like Brokk's, barely shifted as she stared back at me. I couldn't manage the same, I took in everything on her and was incapable of hiding it. Her long, opal-white hair with lustrous tight curls shimmered over her slim shoulders and spilled down to her lap, framing her delicate hands which rested with the palms facing up. Her pale aqua embroidered gown was perfectly smooth, aside from the edges of it fluttering from the seat made of rushing water. Her skin, her hair, her dress, it was all a perfectly coordinated color palate with the water that supported her. The only unexpected pop of color was the mismatched large amber jewel that hung from her neck. Her look exuded serenity, aside from her fingers which were the only aspect of her that looked rigid as she sat, her digits pointed upward from where they pressed on her thighs. I realized then she made the throne from her own power, by controlling the water into an upward plume.

My eyes drifted back up to her face, to a scar which ran up along one side of her jaw. The lumpy and webbed skin looked to be an old burn. Celestine's lip curled in a sneer as she noticed me staring at the uneven tissue there. Scar or no, she was gorgeous. The gorgeous face of a ruthless murderer. Looking at her, I didn't for one moment forget what she had done here, what she had done to those Syrenni hanging over the walkway. Her beauty was a mask hiding true treachery.

The rush of water lifted higher, helping her stand. She shifted the position of her hands, now holding them out in front of her to create stepping stones on the water, controlling the surface to hold her body weight as she stood. My breath quickened as she took several steps toward me, appearing to walk on water.

"So, the elusive mestisius has returned at last," her eerie, silky voice slithered out of her like liquid.

I looked around, seeing that the Umorfae Praetors now visibly encircled me, drawing in closer to prevent me from going back the way I came. It was toward the empress or nothing at this point. There was no backing down now.

"Where are the rest of the Syrenni?" I demanded.

She flicked her hand in a careless gesture behind her, toward the center of the lake. "They are being held below. Depending on how this goes, they will either live, or die. That outcome is up to you. The time of the Syrenni's freedom has ended. You will assist in guiding them back to Lacausia where they belong."

I clenched my fists, my jaw, *everything*. If I could have burned her with my eyes, I would have, and added to that scar that snaked the side of her face. "What do you mean?" I wanted to scream at her, so it was incredibly reserved of me to merely bite out the words at her instead.

She scoffed, making a show of glancing around the lake. "Would you say they are thriving here? Look at this, living in the mud, eating *fungus*. Is this what freedom means for them? It has been over twenty cycles and they have done *nothing*."

I kept my face still, though hiding the wince that I felt throughout my whole body was difficult. I had said nearly the same thing, had looked down on how little they had done since escaping the palace. I had espoused similar thoughts that now aligned with a brutal killer. Neila flashed in my mind, the times I had argued with her, lied to her, said disparaging things about the Syrenni to her.

"In Lacausia they were fed," she continued. "Fed fish, not this muck they have been eating here. Well dressed, and housed in proper rooms."

"They were also slaves that were often tortured or beaten, sometimes killed. Don't make it sound like it was some kind of charity case where you were their benevolent ruler. You brutalized them. And it's not like you've somehow changed." I motioned to the dead Syrenni still hanging, rotting.

She lifted a shoulder. "Sometimes a display is needed. Something to convey the gravity of the situation. It was merely a way to send a message."

The use of the word "merely" to describe what she had done to them caused my chest to heave. I was ready to burn this bitch *down.*

Empress Celestine took the last three steps toward me, closing the distance. Her eyes drifted over my face, taking in my features up close. Her nostrils flared, her eyes snapping back to mine. "Interesting. Tell me, where are your Petrafae friends?"

I kept my face still, not letting any emotion flicker that she might read. I didn't want her to see my relief that I knew what she had just scented on me. And what she *didn't* sense as well. "What Petrafae friends? I'm alone here," I lied easily.

A wicked smile grew on her face. "Why, you are good, are you not? That shall come in handy for me, when the time is right. But, that is for the future. For now, I will also take the Ignisfae female and unleash upon her what Queen Deniza did to me." She motioned to that burn on her face, a muscle in her jaw feathering with the intent to exact her revenge.

This time I couldn't hide the flush of worry. I opened my mouth to try and backpedal, or make up something. Anything to shield Emblyn.

"Do not bother," the empress said, lifting her hand to caress my jaw with her knuckles. "I know of your companions." She pulled her hand away and started to turn, heading toward the lake. She spun back, backhanding me in the cheek so suddenly I saw flashes in my vision. I stumbled, falling down into the mud. I landed with a squelch, blinking in surprise at the hit I didn't see coming. Straightening up, she adjusted her dress and squared her shoulders. "Now, where is my spymaster?" She turned, looking into the forest to the east. "Join us, Cymbrokk," Celestine called out.

Spymaster? Cymbrokk? I tried to process what she was saying, trying to unravel what she meant. There wasn't a single sound or movement from the trees, but I could see the form of a Fae right where she had directed her attention, I could see the volume of water in their body. The leaves rustled, then Brokk stepped forward to the shoreline.

"Ah, Cymbrokk, my filio. I am so pleased to see you, and pleased with how effective you have been. Come, join me at my side."

I glanced back and forth between the empress and Brokk, his steely gaze avoided connecting with mine. "Filio?" I whispered.

"Why, yes," Celestine said as she turned back to me, glancing down with a patronizing smirk. "I am Cymbrokk's maeder, did you not know?" She let the words hang there, watched my face as it sunk in, as my heart split and the breath went out of me. Watched as devastation took hold of me that he had withheld the fact that he was *her* child.

CHAPTER 38

Brokk walked the shoreline toward Empress Celestine, *his maeder.* I couldn't believe what I was seeing, what had just happened. I didn't bother trying to hide my shock, I was too overwhelmed to possibly feign anything. The pain struck harder than anything I could have imagined, to be so betrayed by him. Everything played back in a rush, all the things he had said and done. So much of it I had thought was sincere, but now I saw how he had skirted the truth, how he had avoided telling me of his familia, of why he had really left Lacausia. The truth was now horrendously evident, he had left under orders. He had left to spy for her and gather information. Then I remembered the book, and how it had even detailed the different ranks of Umorfae: Praetors, Generalises, and Spies. I was such a fool.

A wild sound unleashed from beyond the shore, and the foliage split as a streak of color rushed toward him. Tan, brown, and a trailing black braid raced to him. Emblyn was a blur of fury as she pumped her legs to reach him.

"I'll kill you!" Emblyn screamed. I saw it before she did, the Umorfae converging to head her off. They reached her, spears raised before she got to Brokk, grabbing her and pulling her down into the mud, stepping on her chest to hold her down. She wrestled them, then managed to sit up for one moment, thrusting her finger at Brokk. "I'll *end* you for this betrayal, Brokk!" I winced as another foot shoved her back down, immobilizing her in the silty shore.

I looked back at Brokk, whose face finally faltered, showing some semblance of guilt. His eyes met mine, but he only allowed the connection for a moment. His glance didn't seem like the hardened gaze of someone indifferent to what they had done. There was something unreadable, but then, it was only for a moment, and my desperate and wailing heart still wanted to believe that this wasn't happening.

But it *was* happening. I was at Empress Celestine's mercy, Emblyn now lay pinned down by countless Praetors, and Brokk walked steadily onward toward his maeder. His *maeder* for gods' sake, how stupid was I?

The empress looked at her nails as the scene calmed down, as if none of what had happened so far was even the slightest bit of a threat. "Well, as I was saying, the Ignisfae female is *not* free to leave. Praetors, retrieve the Petrafae." She flicked a hand to the main group of visible Umorfae, several of whom separated from the group and disappeared into the woods. I breathed heavily, wanting to leap up from my position below Celestine and throttle her horrible, wretched throat. Before I could, Praetors returned, holding Trachen and Tyrus by the arms. Tears welled at my waterline, nearly spilling as I looked at them. None of our plans had worked, we had utterly failed. My idea to free the Syrenni had only resulted in us all being captured. How could we have prevailed with someone like Brokk in our midst? Able to help orchestrate from the inside, to guide us to where Empress Celestine could easily take her victory. But, he had tried so many times to divert me from the lake, from returning to try to save the Syrenni. Were those tests? Was it meant to only spur me on faster? The pieces of my broken heart withered and hardened into angry little shards as I looked at Trachen and Tyrus, watched as Trachen tried to reach Emblyn. Tyrus looked back at me, sadness filled his eyes. I had failed him, too. He had left his people, his safety, all for a female who ended up only using him. I was a villain nearly as bad as Celestine.

"The Petrafae may go," the Empress announced.

I dropped my jaw and snapped my eyes back to her. "Go?" I repeated. Even Brokk faltered as he had nearly reached her. He couldn't hide his look of surprise.

"They may return to Adrilan without injury," she went on. "Praetors, guide them away from the lake, and make sure they do not return." Six guards started hauling them away.

"Take eight extra Praetors," Brokk ordered. Celestine raised her eyebrows. "I traveled with them, they are powerful. Twelve total are needed, I believe. That is, if you agree, Maeder," he added with a flourish.

She gave him a single shrug of her shoulders like she didn't care one way or the other. He motioned with a hand to other Umorfae waiting nearby, who then joined the group hauling off the Petrafae. I frowned, Tyrus and Trachen could have done *something*, used their skill to open the ground, or lifted themselves out of reach on a rock. But they were apprehended and restrained too quickly.

"Is there a reason they are being allowed to return to Adrilan, Maeder?"

Celestine arched her eyebrows and a subtle smirk grew on her lips as she toyed with her necklace. "An agreement I made with Magistrate Zarneh. In addition to the vast food supplies we delivered, no Petrafae were to be harmed by Umorfae hands, weapons, or skill."

He rubbed his chin, nodding with understanding. "The fish they had, the bread. They did not have enough food to feed their people, so you made a deal. They gave you information in exchange, that was their trade. They told you of Sereia's existence."

Celestine looked all too pleased with herself. "Among other things. The fine jewel was gifted by the magistrate herself, from her private collection." She made a show of turning the necklace, causing it to sparkle. "But, of course, I value information most of all. They told me about the fact that you had been found. I knew then that you must have found the half-breed for me, and were probably en route to deliver her."

"Quite cunning indeed, Maeder." He paused, seeming to mull something over. "But, they had caught me in Adrilan and were going to punish me."

She shook her head. "It was all for show. The magistrate would have quietly released you without further incident after the display, when no one was watching. You did not need to escape over the edge with that filthy female."

The information was enough to snap me out of the downward spiral I had fallen into. My anger stirred at hearing Brokk call her "maeder," and the revelation of the Petrafae leader's involvement. It woke up a beast in me. I was not going to submit, to allow this *empress* to simply walk in here and take what she wanted. I cast my senses out, let my power well in me until it was churning for a release. I closed my eyes, feeling everything around me. I sensed the Syrenni, all of them far below the surface and swimming slowly in a mindless circle. There was some sort of barrier above them, a layer of water cycled in a downward current, keeping them at the bottom of the lake. Umorfae still hovered close behind me, but the way to the east was now mostly clear since the group had taken Tyrus and Trachen. Only the two that held Emblyn down remained. And depending on how pissed off Emblyn became, two was nowhere near enough to contain her. She had stopped fighting them for the moment. I opened my eyes and looked over to where she sat, her gaze connected with mine. Though she looked calm, I knew she was far from it. I could almost feel her rising energy simmering below her skin, that pent-up fire looking for a way out. If I could break away from this ridiculous one-sided standoff that I was on the losing side of, we might have a chance. But what to do, where to go? I closed my eyes again, sending my senses outward.

The mist pinged back, a reminder of that ever-present friend, always hovering, waiting for the time to be called. It felt sentient in a way, like it had been watching the whole series of events unfold, and waited for the moment where I would connect with it. I felt all those familiar threads link to me, the same ones that had slowed our fall when we jumped from Adrilan. Apparently it had been a fool's mission, as I unwittingly saved the enemy, but I had learned the capabilities of the mist then. Now, I felt those threads go taut, ready to pull me *up* this time. Not slowing a descent, but being the cause of an ascent. Another thread connected, one that ran from my fingertips to the surface of the water, and down. Under the surface, and into my room. I plucked that cord, feeling where it went.

To the sigil. The mist led me to the sigil. Somehow, the sigil was what I needed.

I felt eyes on me, and glanced at where it came from. Brokk had watched me as I tested the waters near me, watched me evaluate the mist and what else was in close range. I gulped, suddenly feeling vulnerable because he would know *exactly* what I was doing, he was the only one who understood my capabilities. My eyes rounded as I realized I may have made a terrible mistake.

Celestine noticed as well a moment later, perhaps it was my locked gaze with Brokk, or the steeled resolve I had mustered within myself as I tried to discern a path out of this mess. She turned to look at me over her shoulder.

"Do not bother with any ideas, mestisius," she said. "Any wrong move and I will start killing Syrenni."

"You mean *more* Syrenni?" I spat back at her.

Brokk had reached the empress's side at last. "Maeder, perhaps we should—

The powerful strike from Brokk's fist to Empress Celestine's gut came at the same time that I wrapped my hands around those threads to the mist and pulled. She doubled over, then Brokk yanked her by the hair, pulling her back up.

"Sereia, run!" he shouted.

I didn't have time to be surprised at Brokk's sudden maneuver, I was already sailing through the air toward her, tethered to the threads which pulled me rapidly up. I unleashed the hardest kick I could, catching her square in the jaw before I cleared over her head. I heard her splash down a moment later, toppling over from the force of the impact.

I flipped in midair, changing my direction so I was pointed head first toward the water. Releasing the threads, I dove in, propelling myself down, engaging my fin to swim faster along the front of the Syrenni dwelling. My room was on the far side at the top of the stacks, but I decided skirting the bottom before rising would be a small tactic to avoid the Umorfae who had no doubt already descended upon my last location, to their empress's defense.

I slowed only a little to prevent cresting the surface, then slipped into my room. The sigil was exactly where I had left it, using it as nothing more than a weight to hold down a few hand-woven items I had made, preventing them from floating away. Snatching it from its resting place, I felt the weight in my palm. I shook it slightly, feeling the inner workings shift, but nothing happened. I didn't know what I expected, if I thought it would finally activate after all these cycles. It had never done anything before, I half suspected it would only be good for throwing at an enemy's head. I took it anyway, heading back out of my room.

I looked both ways before exiting completely. A brilliant flash lit up the sky from the east. I smiled to myself, realizing it was a river of flame. I rose higher, letting my eyes rise above the surface. Sure enough, I spotted Emblyn funneling a torrent of fire at the guards that had kicked her and held her down. More Praetors lined up at the treeline, lifting their bows to unleash a volley of arrows in her direction. Thrusting my hand out, I felt for the water in their bodies, and pulled. I didn't have time to think, I had mere moments before they were going to loose their arrows and take her down.

Some were already in process of firing, which caused them to shoot wide to the west. I followed their trajectory, realizing some were heading right to where I had last seen Brokk. He was in the midst of a fight with several Umorfae.

I made a decision without deliberating. Reaching to feel his blood, I wrapped my hand around that invisible yet tangible cord and yanked him toward me. Brokk lurched backward, falling with a splash in the knee-high water.

The arrows arrived at nearly the same time that he fell, some of them finding marks in Umorfae chests or limbs. Blue blood burst from those impacts. I cringed at seeing the same blood that I had. But I was not like them. They were here to brutalize, to control, and to reestablish their dominance. I was having none of that faex, if their blood had to run to prevent them from taking over, so be it.

My eyes shifted to Brokk, who stared at me. I nodded to him once. I knew now that he had done what he had to do. Like he had said, Empress Celestine always had another angle to play. She had found out he was with us long before we arrived at the lake. He had come up with another ruse to make his maeder think he was serving her orders. Of course, there was still a chance that he was still aligned with her—he had lied to us after all—but in that moment, with that one chance I had to decide his possible fate, I couldn't let him be killed or injured. I had been prepared to fight on my own, but there was no honor in letting him die.

The sigil moved in my hand. It was a subtle motion, just enough to get my attention. Somehow, it had woken up. Something inside of it started to spin, causing it to rock in my hand. It began to heat up, becoming unbearably hot, but I couldn't uncurl my fingers from it. A strange sensation took over, like a straw had been tapped into my power, siphoning it off. It funneled into the sigil. I felt my magical well diminish, and panic set in as I sensed it was *taking* my power. I desperately tried to pry it out of my palm with my other fingers to no avail. My power dwindled to a point that was exhausting me. My legs shook, struggling to hold me up. I looked at Brokk for help, who scrambled to reach me.

"Sereia, what's happening?" He held my shoulders as we both stood in the thigh-high water.

"The … sigil," I managed to say with gasping breaths. "It's taking everything."

He grabbed my wrist, trying to use his might to wrench it free from my grip. I looked down, my fingers had turned white-hot. He ripped his hands away, unable to handle the heat any longer as steam rose from his palms and fingertips. "I'm sorry, I couldn't …"

I crushed my eyes shut, a tear working out from them. "You tried." The heat traveled up my arm, my skin felt like living fire as neared my shoulder. My power was nearly depleted, and the sigil only spun faster. Perhaps this was the way, the sigil could only be activated when someone was brave enough to sacrifice themselves to it. Once I was empty, maybe then the sigil would be full and ready to break the Syrenni free. Finally awakened to do whatever it was designed to do.

For a moment, the pain abated as the worn off inscription flashed in my mind. The book had said "Bravery of the heart is rare." It was that word which I had said to myself that brought the memory back. Bravery. But the book also had the rest of the inscription which was supposedly etched on the surface so many cycles ago, "the sigil shares the power when it is there."

Shares.

Another straw tapped itself into me, this one funneling the power back in, amplifying everything it had absorbed. It completed a circuit, a loop, where my power went in, then returned to me stronger and stronger. The brilliant heat traveled along my collarbone, searing its way up my neck, eclipsing my jaw, then finally encompassing my head.

Every nerve in my body burned, but after a moment, I mastered the feeling, then opened my eyes. Everything was rimmed in a white haze, which must have been the brightness of my superheated skin giving off a blinding light. Brokk stared at me in wonder, but the moment didn't last. My eyes shifted to over his shoulder, where Empress Celestine charged at him from the shoreline. Whatever Brokk had done to disable her had only lasted a short time.

I held up my hand, gripping the liquid in his body, then moved him with a simple motion of my wrist, sending him carefully far to the west edge at the treeline. She couldn't reach him now without diverting her forces. I looked back at her, face muddy and tear-streaked, and absolutely enraged as she now charged toward me instead. With Brokk out of the way, I became her prime target.

It was funny in a way, her seething anger. She heaved comically and her whole demeanor was almost a caricature. I cocked my head at her, finally seeing her for what she was.

Small, and insignificant.

Her heart was as black as could be, her ill intent unmatched, and she certainly lacked any semblance of good within her. She had done terrible things which deserved justice to be served. But really, Celestine was a mockery of a ruler. She ruled by fear but had little to back that up, if her Praetors didn't do as she commanded she would have no recourse. She had her power of course, but I had mine tenfold now.

I turned toward the center of the lake, deciding not to engage someone so useless. I didn't have to close my eyes to sense the shifting waters below the surface which kept the Syrenni submerged. It was something Celestine must have set in place, a whirlpool cycling forever down, keeping them from swimming up past it. I heard Celestine slam the water in frustration, trying to get it to hold me in place so she could attempt to exert her will upon me.

I was having none of it. I didn't even bother looking at her as I flicked my hand behind me, a wave burst toward her. I felt it crest directly in her face. I smirked, then jumped into the heart of the whirlpool to find my people.

CHAPTER 39

The now brightened sky offered little light as I dove down to the dark blue depths of the lake. It didn't matter, my body emitted a steady glow from the surface of my skin. It cast a soft umbra of white around me. There was nothing for the light to cast onto yet, I hadn't reached the lake floor.

The sandy base came into view. I flipped around, landing with my feet and used my fin to steady me. My light picked up far-off shapes swimming in a circle, the Syrenni seemed in a trance as I spun, watching them. So far none of them had noticed that I had arrived.

The sigil whirred, like it was trying to get my attention. I had no idea what to do, how to even get this enchanted device to do what I desperately needed. I needed to slap them out of this semi-conscious state. I wished I could connect to them, get them to hear me. But we were underwater anyway, even a scream would be indistinct.

If only I could connect to them like I did to the mist. I thought back to that drawing, the one showing a Syrenni at the center and a swimming cyclone of Sisters around her. She had the sigil raised high, and little lines etched in a circular array out of the disc. I clenched a fist to my heart, steadying myself, reminding myself of who I was. I was a godssdamned Syrenni. Imperfect or not, mestisius or not, it didn't matter. I was here to lead them away from the misery Celestine would force them back into. I was here to give them their identity back.

I was *brave* enough to do it.

Lifting the sigil high, I focused on all the bodies rotating around me. I sent my power through that loop again, funneling it through the sigil to intensify it.

My power grew, but it was like a sphere cast wide. A sphere with no direct connection to anyone, merely a volume they swam through. The whirlpool pushed down, increasing its force. I looked up, seeing Celestine's distorted shape high above.

I shook my head, not letting her appearance annoy me. She was trying to exert her power to maintain control. Closing my eyes, I focused on the sphere again. It wasn't working for the Syrenni, but it was butting against the power Celestine funneled downward. I flexed my arms, and sent a jolt while stamping my foot as I unleashed a blast outward. The sphere pressed against the whirlpool, then erupted upward, causing a massive bubble to burst through the surface.

The empress was nowhere in sight. Whatever force had come up to the top had sent her backward, at least for now.

I refocused my effort on reaching the Syrenni. Instead of a wide glowing sphere, I shifted tactics, thinking of how I used tethers with the mist. I couldn't catch anyone circling me if I sent them all out, so instead I tried a single one.

One at a time, if that was what I had to do. Multiple threads missed their mark, but finally, I connected with one. I couldn't feel or tell who it was, but I could feel the connection, feel their awareness starting to filter back in. I sent out another thread, then another, getting faster at hitting the mark, until finally I had all Syrenni that kept the flow of Celestine's whirlpool going.

But now it was no longer her whirlpool, it was *mine*. Faster we turned, the sigil held aloft with hundreds of threads connecting me to the frenzy of Syrenni. The current picked up, and now twisted away from the lake floor. We had reversed the direction of the force, sending it skyward.

As one connected unit, we lifted. I spun at the center, guiding us higher. Celestine came into view as we nearly crested the water, her twisted face surprised by the onslaught of writhing Syrenni. Umorfae had encircled the space behind her, probably preparing to use force to squash the literal uprising. I tugged on those threads, checking our connection all at once. As the threads tightened, it pulled away something long-since embedded below the surface of each Syrenni. I realized the sigil had done more than connect me to them, and allow me to instruct them on what to do, it had also ripped down that film which had blocked their senses and their motivation all this time. The very thing that Celestine had relied on to keep the Syrenni in check while they were locked in servitude, and the thing that had most likely prevented them from advancing once they had moved the Caer Lake.

The Taming. And now, after a thousand cycles, it had finally ended.

Through those cords I felt the rising fury of the horde, the dawning of a new era for them. They now *knew* of how they had been manipulated, blocked and redirected to be placid and subservient. It was at the point where it had been bred into them,

a spell so powerful it had been passed along through the generations. Many Syrenni had lived and died, only knowing life as a
Tamed Syrenni. It now added to their mounting anger. It hadn't
been Celestine who had created it, of course, that had been done
by Vitus Augustus. But Celestine, and almost all Umorfae, had
certainly taken advantage of it. They had used this generational
trauma to their advantage.

We burst forth from the lake surface, the top now a frothing
mess as Syrenni scattered, latching onto any Umorfae necks their
teeth could find. They were brutal, swift, as they ripped throat
after throat from any Praetors nearby, letting that blue blood flow
bright. I snapped my connection to them, now that they were
untethered from the Taming, they were able to unleash themselves
upon their enemy without me dictating their actions. There were
still a considerable number of Praetors left, but the Syrenni were
moving through them at a surprising rate. Emblyn battled more
Umorfae further off, and now Trachen and Tyrus had broken free
from the ones that held them to come fight with her.

The empress shrieked and tried to run, but I lifted my hand
and gripped her blood with my power, halting her escape. She
attempted to thrash against me, but I only squeezed tighter, slowing
her pulse. Celestine's eyes bulged as she stared at me in fear.

The look made me drop my hold on her for a moment, seeing
her afraid had surprised me. I never thought I would be capable
of switching our roles. Perhaps that was why the sigil found me
worthy, because even though I had decided to fight and to do what
I could to free the Syrenni, I didn't actually believe that I would be
strong enough to go head to head with the empress and succeed.
For whatever my faults added up to, this virtue defined a side of

me that was greater than I had previously known, a side that I was proud of.

Celestine tightened her fists. "Fight me, you coward."

I narrowed my eyes at her, evaluating her. Her words didn't nearly hit the mark. I may have been a lot of things, but a coward I was not. "I'll fight you, but I think you've already lost. And if you choose to fight, I won't be gentle."

She rose on a bubbling platform of water, arcing high overhead in an instant, not bothering with a response.

Fine, request granted. I shot a quick glance to the Syrenni, who were finishing ending the last of the Umorfae. The sigil whirred, engaging the loop faster, the thread of it glowing brighter as it funneled power into me. I gathered my hands, drawing in water to make my own platform, causing it to rise to meet her. It lifted higher, leveling out and merging with hers to make a massive disc.

She stood at the center, her lip curled as she spat at me. "For turning my filio against me, I will mount your head on my wall. And the Syrenni? They no longer have a place with me, they will all die for this offense."

I scoffed, she hadn't quite realized what the Syrenni had become. "Act ignorant, and you'll become enlightened." If I didn't beat her in this match, the Syrenni surely wouldn't let her leave.

But then I thought better of it. Celestine was unpredictable— at least according to Brokk—and the Syrenni were coming out of a thousand cycle stupor. I probably couldn't expect them to be able to handle her when she might have any number of tactics she could be merely shielding, biding her time. The others were all busy fighting the Praetors. No, this was up to me.

Empress Celestine screamed as she lunged toward me. It was a futile attempt. I stopped her blood with one hand, then unleashed a powerful kick which caused her head to snap to the side. She nearly lost her balance, but managed to stay on her feet, readying herself for another bout.

It was a fool's play. Had she not seen that I could stop her? I could grip her blood and prevent her from even getting close to me. At this point, what was even the end goal? The Syrenni were no longer the docile creatures she remembered, they were now mentally freed and seemed to have a hunger for Umorfae flesh. It was shocking how blue the waters had turned from the Syrenni's wrath, the entire shoreline bloomed with cerulean blood and was littered with bodies.

Nevertheless, Celestine tried again, lunging at me from across her disc, trying desperately to reach me on mine. I pivoted on one foot and delivered another kick, which sent her reeling, this time squarely in her ribs. Still, she managed to stay mostly upright, attempting again and again to charge at me, each time being met with my upraised hand stopping her cold before she was within swinging distance, until my foot connected with her.

Blinding light pierced my vision, everything around me whiting out as something slammed me forward so hard that I landed on Celestine's side of the platform. The pain was so intense my breath went out of me. Far off, I heard screaming.

It was Emblyn, I realized. Then Brokk filtered in. And Neila. They were yelling my name. I blinked, getting my legs back under me. My vision resolved in time to see Celestine stalking toward me, a triumphant smirk on her face. She put a foot to my shoulder, then pushed me back down again. Searing pain ripped through me again as I fell back, the water that flowed upward and created the platform we were upon pressed against something that was wedged into my back. I looked down, then did a double take at the metal tip of an arrow, glistening with blue blood.

My blood.

I dropped my jaw. I had been fucking *shot*. One of her archers must have skirted the fray, then taken me down from a distance while she distracted me. Everything went sideways as the realization settled in, my ears rang with a strange sound as all other noises were blotted out. It all went far away, the sounds, the blood, my opponent. I was off somewhere, ready to leave it all behind. Maybe this was it. I distantly felt my hands open and close, my arms trying to move, but there wasn't much left to control. Was it blood loss? Was it my inner self leaving this mestisius body, the one that should never have been?

I had gotten to experience love in this life, friendship, to learn about myself, my faults, and my virtues. I had released the Syrenni, I had *done* it, activated the sigil which had lain dormant for so many cycles and used it to change their fate. Perhaps that meant that *I* was done, that I could leave at peace. I had been ready to commit myself to this end, even if I didn't know what it meant.

Euphoria washed over me, and I didn't care if I died. Celestine could hate me with whatever ferocity she had within her, could take pleasure in watching me fade away. I closed my eyes and savored the sweet release, sagging down. It was not a bad way to go, in spite of the wound. But the wound no longer hurt, and my hearing had come back, I could hear the water rushing below me, lifting me slightly as it burbled along my body. To die surrounded by water was a gift.

"The Syrenni will fall," a voice sounded next to my ear. I

opened my eyes to slits and could see the form of Empress Celestine bending down to speak to me. "Now that I have the book in my possession, I will reenact the Taming. They will be mine."

I blinked slowly. "The book?" I whispered.

"The one you took from Adrilan. The one that useless Magistrate Zarneh was supposed to deliver to me. My Praetors found your gear, and now I have it. The Syrenni's newfound clarity will be *gone*." The laugh that oozed out of her, it was like poison, like liquid putrescence. It was everything vile that I had ever encountered in one sound.

Life flooded back into me, awakening every nerve, every limb and digit. With that came the resurgence of pain, all of it slapping me alive with a burst of gritty, awful truth. Of what it meant to be a creature in this world, to live, to die. And if I died now, she would win. She would undo what I had wrenched free. Which meant I still had to fight if I cared about the outcome.

The mist called to me, sang to me in a harmonic voice that insisted I connect, that I use it to get myself up. My own body lacked the strength, and the sigil was gone, it had skittered out of my hand at some point. Celestine smiled at me with a rictus grin, her face now contorted in a way that showed her as the demon she was. Lunging toward me, she brandished a blade that she had pulled from somewhere hidden, sailing down in an arcing motion. Had the attack come before she mentioned the book, before I knew that she would enslave the Syrenni again, I wouldn't have bothered to fight back. I was already dying from the arrow, a finishing blow would simply make the inevitable arrive sooner.

The mass of connections to the mist happened almost without my doing, her attack on me made my power wake up in a way I hadn't felt before, almost like it acted of its own will. The thousands upon thousands of threads to the mist tightened, and I pulled not with my muscles—those were basically useless—but instead I pulled with my burgeoning power to lift me. I realized with her sailing down toward me, she would collide straight into my chest. I gritted my teeth, straining to pull my knees up to cover my injury.

She collided with my shins, her body crumpling around mine as she lost hold of her blade. The impact made us both recoil downward for a moment, the connection to the mist going unbearably taut. Threads were almost snapping, and I felt the pressure build. We were about to spring up the other direction, I could sense it before it happened. The pull on the mist was more than it could handle. Though my connection remained strong, the mist was somehow losing its cohesion, its stability weakened. All of the individual millions of particles came down as she and I went up.

We both shot toward the sky, the speed flattening out the planes of my face and body. She screamed as it flung her high, faster and farther than I had thought possible. Her shrieks became far away, swallowed by the distance. The connection tightened momentarily, holding me at the peak while Celestine rocketed further away.

Then, I was falling. Everything was falling. My threads went slack, and it felt like the whole world melted. The water below me dropped, what had previously been the platform of water came crashing to the lake below in a thunderous roar. The whole area became impossibly bright, searing my eyes as intense light streamed in. This was beyond any brightness I had ever experienced during a light rotation.

My eyes started to adjust, the churning water began to calm as I floated face up, and the noise of everything abated. I looked up, squinting my eyes to see Empress Celestine disappear in the bright blue sky, only a shrinking far-off speck until I couldn't see her anymore. She was *gone*.

And so was the mist.

That comforting presence that I had grown to appreciate, that silent friend which surrounded our world in a shield had dissipated. I cried out as I realized I had pulled it down, removed that barrier which had been erected a thousand cycles before. It had saved me several times, and now I was the one to obliterate it.

Emblyn ran toward me, sloshing through the water to reach me as she used one arm to try and block the light from her eyes. Brokk headed toward me a moment after her, running across the water as he pulled up the water to form a bridge. They reached me at the same time. Neila's voice sounded in my ear as her arms came up from below, sliding in to support my weakened body.

"My filia, you are so brave. Stay strong, stay with us," her voice wavered as her hands found mine.

"The arrow," I said, crushing my eyes shut. "We have to take it out."

"No, Sereia," Brokk said, "if we take it out now you'll bleed out."

I opened my eyes to look at him, then looked at Emblyn, who nodded.

"We can't take it out," she agreed.

"I'll die either way, I'd rather die without this in me. Just end it now."

"You are not going to fucking die!" Emblyn shouted as she cried. "We are going to fix this. You have to *hang on*."

I heard water splashing near us, then saw Tyrus and Trachen

appear. Tyrus moved in next to Brokk, putting one arm around him and his other hand over mine. "We are here," Tyrus said. "Just hold on, Sereia."

"We have to get her to the Well," Brokk said to them. "It's the only way."

"We'll have to hurry," Emblyn responded. It was the last thing I heard before that impossible brightness faded to black.

CHAPTER 40

I awoke periodically to the surroundings rushing by. Trees and foliage blurred and the jostling was more than I could bear. I laid on something, a litter of some kind, which was being carried and raced along a path. I drifted in and out of consciousness, each time was the same. I could hear the sound of heaving breaths, of footfalls, of a relentless pace through the forest. I couldn't sense the water of the lake, we were somewhere far away. A hand would sometimes caress my forehead, someone would give me water. Then I would be out again. I vaguely felt a tickle across my cheeks, like tiny feet running over the bridge of my nose. I swatted ineffectively at whatever it had been, trying to shoo away the small insect or flying pest.

Something reached through into my subconscious, a voice that called to me. At first it was indiscernible, I couldn't make out the words or even who might be saying it. Then I heard more clearly, it was a song. A lilting melody of a female broke through with sudden clarity. It sounded like everything peaceful, every comfort I had ever known. It was love and acceptance and reassurance as she sang my name over and over. I tried to sit up, looking around to see who it had been.

"Sereia!" Emblyn said. "You have been unconscious for so

long, we're almost there. Just hang on for a little longer." She tightened her grip on the front corner of the narrow platform they carried me on.

"I can hear her," I said. "She's calling my name."

Emblyn looked at Brokk in confusion. He nodded to her as he held the other corner near my feet. "Sometimes she calls out, beckoning when we are near."

Emblyn bobbed her head. "I've never visited the Maeder Tree, this will be my first time."

We crested a rise, and as my litter angled down when they began to descend the hill it allowed me to see The Well far below, with a stunning, ethereal tree at the center. The luminous liquid surrounding it gave off a glow which cast a teal blue on the nearby plants and rocks, even in the overly bright light from the sky it was brilliant enough to shine.

"What is it?" I asked no one in particular.

"Our creator," Brokk answered.

They walked me down the hill toward the shore, then carefully set the platform down. Helping me up, all four of my friends lifted me, getting me ready to enter the water.

"Before we go in," Brokk said as he brushed my hair behind my ear, "we have to remove the arrow."

The arrow. I had somehow forgotten. In the haze of our journey to this place, I had forgotten about my grave injury. I knew I was in pain but couldn't recall why. Perhaps it was a blessing that we could make this trek and I was spared the knowledge of my current state. I looked down and saw the bandage on my chest, soaked in my blood and poking up from the obvious protrusion below the fabric. "I didn't die," I whispered as it all came back to me.

"By some fucking miracle!" Emblyn exclaimed. "But Brokk did manage to help with that, he used a lot of his skill to keep your blood in your body."

"I did all I could, I wish I could have healed you completely," he added.

"I was ready to kill him for what he had done, for lying to us all," Emblyn cut in, "but to his credit, he did everything he could to help get you here. And the Syrenni did something as well before we left, something that prevented an infection."

"Neila?" I asked.

"She's magna," Emblyn said and reached forward to squeeze my hand. "She and the other Syrenni are still at Caer Lake, starting over again."

Tyrus's broad palm wrapped over my shoulder. "We have to cut the shaft free now, it can't stay in any longer. We shortened it for travel, but the part inside you had to be left until we arrived."

Emblyn cringed, squeezing my hands again as they got me onto my knees. "This is really going to hurt," she said, "but it will be temporary. As soon as the arrow is free, we'll all go into the Well. It's up to the Maeder Tree after that."

I blinked at her, not entirely sure what she meant. I opened my mouth to ask a question, when a piercing, horrendous pain radiated from my back. Tyrus had cut the arrow away from my skin near my spine. I gasped and fell forward, as Brokk wrapped his hand around the arrowhead and pulled. While he wriggled it out, he slipped a knife along the opening, cutting where my blood and flesh had congealed to the wooden surface. My vision whited out as a pain so strong and unreal took over every sense I had. I heard nothing except a high pitched drone, saw nothing except a brilliant circle of light overhead. The pressure in my chest built, pulling me forward, then a rush of fluid sprang from my center.

I felt Brokk's hand cover the gaping wound, pushing my blood back inside me again. Everyone's hands were all over me, dragging me, then we all toppled over the lip of the lake edge, splashing into the thick-feeling water. I free floated, completely submerged in a liquid suspension, with no sense of up or down.

It all went quiet again. There were no hands on me, no others surrounding me. A cocoon slipped around my body, encasing me. The female's voice returned, echoing in my head.

"Sereia. You have grown well, my filia."

I had no words to answer the voice in my head. I wanted to respond, but I couldn't think straight. I felt dried out patches of my skin heal shut, the crackling webbing between my fingers turned supple. I hadn't noticed how tight and scaly my skin had become. I swished my limbs through the fluid, whatever the Well was made of wasn't water. It was thicker, and slipped over my skin like a glove. The wound at the center of my chest warmed, and a glow the same color as the liquid I was suspended in emanated from within. My world narrowed down to that spot, to where the glow now forced the tissue to grow toward itself, stitching in the middle.

As the hole sealed, I remembered Lily telling me about this place, about the Maeder—the great maeder. The one that presided over everything in our world. Lily had promised long ago to eventually take me here. To show me what she claimed all in this world should see before they Fade, so that they can know their origin. Lily had told me that even if we were born to different races, we were all created by the Maeder Tree, she provided the spark of life that made the Fae, the Faeries, the Vale Born, and others possible. I closed my eyes, savoring the feeling. It was like my real maeder held me in her arms, like she had never been killed by the Umorfae and had been allowed to live, allowed to care for me. Her embrace filled my heart with such light, brighter even than the light the great disc in the sky bathed the land in.

I felt the power ebb, she took her arms away and lifted me, raising my head out of the Well. I looked up and saw her at last, a beautiful female with flowing, golden hair. Her transparent image blended in with the tree, her arms the branches, her body the trunk. She smiled at me, nodding in approval, like I was exactly as I was meant to be, as she had intended. I wasn't a mistake, wasn't some half-breed that escaped destruction and shouldn't have lived. She had *wanted* me this way. I was the best of both in her eyes. We were all her creations. I felt her love, her pain that we sometimes killed each other, that we were incapable of living peacefully. But she also understood. Sometimes it was the actions of a few, and the rest of us were left to either defend ourselves, or allow violence against us. It was a terrible, sad truth of the world, all she could do was give us her best, and hope that we make good decisions.

So much knowledge and understanding flooded my mind, all I could do was look up at her and receive it. For those moments, I was connected to her like I had been to the mist, through threads that allowed the transfer of something greater than power. She caressed my mind at the thought of the mist, that I had been responsible for its removal. With that one touch, I knew the mist was not gone, only transmuted into something else. There, waiting to be called upon again, the mist would rise once more. I gulped and held back tears, hoping that was truly possible.

I looked around and saw my companions apparently receiving

their own knowledge, enrapt in communion with her. I smiled, watching them bask in whatever truths they were being granted. I hoped they were being given similar intangible gifts, knowing that they were who they were meant to be, and that she loved them.

The glow in the area dimmed, and I felt her presence waning. I glanced back at the Maeder to see her form retreating into the tree, and the connection diminished to a slowing pulse.

I blinked, returning completely to myself, then turned to face Brokk, Emblyn, Tyrus, and Trachen. We swam toward each other, the five of us clasping hands. Brokk's eyes drifted down to my chest. I looked as well, seeing a star-like pattern of blue-tinted, glowing skin. Healed completely closed, the smooth skin retained a subtle radiance. I let go of their hands, then threw my arms around Brokk, grabbing Emblyn and Tyrus, too. Trachen put his muscular arms around all of us as we laughed. I didn't know what else to do besides laugh.

CHAPTER 41

The bright disc in the sky was nearing the horizon, and the light had started to dim. I found out we had traveled for twelve rotations to get to the Well. That was almost the entire light rotation, and we were now steadily approaching the dark. I sat by the bank of the Well, alone while I watched the tree. Pulling some grass from the ground, I wove the strands like I used to when I needed to do something with my hands. It had been so long since I had done that by the shore of Caer Lake, everything about my life had flipped on its head and changed since then. I searched for signs of the Maeder while I braided. I hadn't seen her again since she healed me, I had hoped I would, but it seemed she had done what was needed and then retreated to whatever spirit realm she inhabited. I wondered if she knew Goddess Tahia, if she was also a real goddess like the Syrenni claimed.

It then dawned on me that I had little knowledge about Umorfae beliefs, did they have any gods or goddesses? I supposed now that I had survived, I could spend some time learning about that half of my heritage. Or move somewhere new and figure out what to do with myself. It was a strange prospect, to finally be at the point where I *could* make a decision like that.

I looked away from the Maeder Tree and saw Brokk walking toward me. I rolled my lips together, thinking about the plans that we had made. So much of it had been under false pretenses, I didn't know if any of it was real.

He walked over, then sat beside me. Brokk said nothing, did nothing at first, he merely sat and waited, watching the view next to me.

"I suppose you're here to give me the chance to question you," I said.

"Yes. I figured I would make it easy for you. I knew you would want to, so here I am. I will be honest."

"Even though you weren't before?"

He sighed. "Yes. I'm sorry I wasn't before. I have no good excuse. I thought I could hide it, I thought I could move on and pretend I wasn't her filio. I wanted to be someone new entirely."

"But when we all knew who was lying in wait at the lake, why didn't you tell me then? That knowledge could have changed things. Maybe I wouldn't have nearly died from being shot! Did you think about that?"

He winced. "You're right. It could have possibly changed things had I told you the truth before we arrived. I tried instead to get you to not go there, but you wouldn't let me deter you. So instead I had decided to hide and wait it out, helping in secret as I could. I intended to stay hidden. I should have told you instead of going with my foolish plan, but it was a lie that I was then too scared to admit to. I had kept it up for so long, it felt like I couldn't get away from it. I convinced myself that you would leave me if you knew the truth. I don't think I would have blamed you if you did leave me for that, but I also knew I wouldn't recover. Everything I did to hide the truth was selfish and dangerous. I can never say I'm sorry enough, but I will try. I am so sorry, Sereia. I was wrong, and I wronged all of you by lying about who I really was."

"She said you were her spymaster, that you were her best! That's beyond being her child, that's being her operative as well. I hope you can see how that is like a double betrayal."

He nodded. "I wasn't a good Generalis, I didn't want to lead Praetors into battle. I had leaned towards being a Spy when I was much younger, because it gave me the most opportunity to study. As her filio, I had to pick one of the two. And it was how I was able to leave Lacausia. I couldn't simply walk out of there, she would have sent Praetors after me. I wasn't *free*. There were a lot of things she wanted information on, she hoarded information—which is why she eventually made a bargain with Magistrate Zarneh. I convinced my maeder to let me leave to gather intel for her. She had no idea that I had no intention of ever going back. I had no other way out of Lacausia, it was the only way to get out from under her control. When I met you, I did tell you a version of the truth, I was looking for a different life. I didn't want to go back there. I was ashamed to be an Umorfae and wanted to carve a different path for myself."

I watched him pull pieces of grass out of the ground like I had, but instead of weaving them, he tossed them blade by blade to float on top of the Well. I didn't say anything, I simply watched his demeanor, his expressions as he talked.

"When she saw me at the lake, she thought I planned it all," he continued. "The truth was, I realized quickly that I had to act like I had planned it so that I could catch her off guard. Before we arrived at Caer Lake, I didn't know that she knew I was with you, and I thought we had all done a good job covering that you and I had been together." His eyes fixed on the Maeder Tree, his mouth turned down in a frown.

I nodded. I had seen that during the heat of the confrontation. In spite of the earlier lies, I believed him now. I could certainly relate to getting in too deep with falsehoods. But this lie was so much bigger than any lie I had ever told. I wasn't sure if that made me feel better, or worse.

"So, now what?" I asked. "Where do we go from here? How am I supposed to trust you? And how do you feel about me? I killed your maeder, what does that mean for us?"

He looked away from the tree and into my eyes, taking a long moment before responding. "It's complicated. I wish I could say I'm sad that she's gone. I didn't want to kill her myself, but I did think for a long time that she needed to be out of the way for a lot of others to be able to live their lives. She wasn't a good maeder and she definitely wasn't a good leader. With her, it was always about her, whatever her needs and wants were. She was vain and cruel. It was never about what the Umorfae needed, or what her children needed. I knew she was problematic from an early age. Yet, I was her filio. I could never voice those thoughts. In a way you've done me a terrible favor. What I'm more sorry about is that it was you who finished it and so you now carry the burden of killing her, even if the mist was instrumental in making it happen. For myself, I barely knew her until I was older, others took the role of caring for me. So in many ways, I really only knew her as my empress, and not as my maeder. As far as what you killing her means for us, I think that is up for you to decide. I harbor no blame and only wish to rebuild what has been shaken."

I saw Emblyn peeking over from across the Well, checking on

me and Brokk. I gave her a single nod of my head, trying to let her know from a distance that I was okay. "What did the others say? I'm sure Emblyn had it out with you."

"Oh she sure did," Brokk said in all seriousness. "She wasn't joking when she said that she wanted to kill me. And the logical part of me understood completely. But also, I wasn't about to simply let her do that. I managed to have a meaningful conversation with her after she stopped yelling. Eventually she relented and agreed that I had made a huge mistake, but that I was not being malicious or that I set out with the intent to mislead you. All of them, Tyrus, Trachen, and Emblyn, decided that you would get to have final say in what happens with me."

I blew out a breath, kneading my thighs as I shifted my gaze back to the Maeder Tree. Thinking about what I had experienced when I saw her, hearing her made me realize how much I had learned in this world, and how much more there was to learn. I would probably always be finding my path, sometimes making decisions that might lead me astray or might take missteps that cause issues in one way or another. I had certainly done that plenty of times. Brokk had taken missteps, but he was also handed a set of hurdles when he came into this world. He was born an Umorfae, and was the child of a ruthless leader. He had functioned and sought a path as best he could, and of course made mistakes. Sometimes all we can do is manage with what we're given.

"It's not going to be easy moving forward," I said. "My trust *is* shaken. And I have to remind myself how I felt when I thought you had betrayed me. I was crushed and heartbroken. But those feelings were intense because of how I feel for you. I'm in love with you, the fact that you didn't tell me the truth didn't erase my feelings. So I think that means that we *can* move forward, but I have to give you this warning: I don't know how much space I have in my heart for more sleights against it. There is a breaking point, and I don't know exactly what that is. But I don't want to test it."

"That's fair," he said. "I have to admit I'm relieved. I know it won't be easy, and I'll have to rebuild trust with each of you. But I'm ready to work for it."

I twitched a smile at him. Part of me wanted to lean forward and kiss him, but another part wasn't ready for that yet. He put his arm around my shoulders, and angled his head down to rest against mine as we looked at the Maeder Tree again. I reached over to Brokk's lap, then domed my hand over his as it rested on his bent knee. I didn't know where we would go, what we would do, but it felt like a new beginning in spite of having a rocky bump in our path.

I wondered what it might mean for all of us, if we would stay together or go our separate ways. Glancing over to where Emblyn had been, I searched out the others in our group. None of them were there, but I saw the leaves rustle near where Emblyn had been last, then someone started to emerge from the forest.

CHAPTER 42

For half a moment I had thought it was Emblyn who poked her head out of the trees, but quickly noticed the only thing she had in common was the black hair with ruby highlights. Zia cast her gaze around the perimeter of the Well, then spotted Brokk and me from across the way. "They are here!" she shouted over her shoulder.

The foliage parted, then Kerenza and Queen Deniza stepped through into view, followed by Lily, Maureen, and Rachael. Brokk recoiled at seeing Lily. I squeezed my hand that rested over his to reassure him, though I was as surprised as he was to see them. Lily started making her way toward me, more visibly pregnant now and walking with a slight waddle. I stood, then walked to meet her halfway. Brokk stood also, hovering awkwardly behind me.

Lily held out her hands and enveloped me in a hug. "Sereia! I'm so glad you're okay!" Kerenza, Queen Deniza, Zia, Maureen, and Rachael crowded around us, commenting on their relief at seeing me.

"Maeder!" Emblyn dashed out of the tree line from the far side of the Well. Within moments, both groups huddled together, swapping greetings. Thankfully it wasn't tense as I introduced Brokk, I knew it could have easily been. I thought about when

I had last seen them, when I jumped with Brokk over the side of the high wall surrounding Adrilan. I cringed thinking about that moment, but Lily didn't seem like she was about to rehash that whole incident.

"We must talk," Lily said, her voice rising above the others in that authoritative way she sometimes employed when she stepped into her princess mode. Everyone hushed. "Something has happened that may have changed the course of this world. I don't know what it means for any of us, but with the mist gone, there may be new threats around the corner."

I gulped, feelings of guilt once again surged at the thought of what I had done. "I didn't mean to pull it down," I said.

Lily's eyebrows shot up. "You, Sereia? You mean you pulled down the mist?"

I nodded. "In the fight with Empress Celestine, she had imprisoned the Syrenni, so we returned to Caer Lake to fight her. I killed her, apparently, and destroyed the mist in the process."

"After all this time, she is finally dead," Queen Deniza said. She and Lily shared a long look, then reached out to hold each others' hands. "She tried Lily for treason, and had kept me imprisoned in Lacausia for many cycles. When I fought her during my escape I let her live, so that she might raise her children, and make better choices."

"Neither of which she ever did," Brokk commented.

Lily frowned. "How did battling her pull the mist down?"

"In the battle, I threw her …*somewhere*, and the mist came down. I was connected to the mist by these threads, and could anchor myself with it for more strength. The power it took to launch her into the sky caused an equal reaction of bringing down the mist. I didn't realize it until it was too late."

"I see. The Faeries weren't sure how the mist disappeared, but as soon as it did, they sought us out and delivered messages. They are frightened, they said that the borders of the realm are unguarded, and far off to the northeast there is a vast body of water, with a land mass visible off in the distance. Aside from that, there will be environmental impacts."

"What does that mean? What sort of environmental impacts?" Brokk asked suddenly.

I lifted my brows in surprise at him, that he had actually decided to speak to Lily after all. The corner of my mouth quirked up at his expression, he looked like he might have realized at the same moment how he had blurted out his question. His interest in the sciences and studying nature probably made him momentarily forget about his negative feelings toward Lily.

"I think it will take time to know the full extent of what it means for the world," Lily answered. "The flora has had around a thousand cycles to adjust to having the mist shield the sun. This is what it's like where I'm from, the sun provides direct light many days—that's what humans call them instead of rotations—and there is no ever-present mist covering the sky. I don't know if this means plants will start dying, the sun can burn plants that didn't grow to handle direct sunlight. If plants burn, animals will die without food, and so on. But, the mist was artificially enacted, which means a thousand cycles ago or so, this was actually how it was. So maybe the world will adjust. Time will tell."

"You mean it's going to be this bright all of the time?" Emblyn griped, rubbing her temples dramatically.

Lily bobbed her head. "Probably most of the time. It's not

all annoyances and concerns though, wait until you see the dark rotations. I know you've been to Starcrest, Emblyn, but many haven't seen what lies beyond the mist. The stars, the Moon, and other planets are breathtaking. It was one thing that was hard for me to lose when I first came here, that I couldn't ever see the night sky, until I visited Starcrest." Lily turned to Brokk, Tyrus, Trachen, and me. "It was previously the only place you could go to see what was beyond the mist, it's on the far side of TerraIgni and high up on top of a spire. A great contraption was built that could pierce the shield."

Brokk dropped his jaw. "There are things above us?" He didn't even bother to hide his shock.

I was stunned as well, the mist had been there for so long that I never thought there was anything beyond it. I was starting to realize that the combination of my lack of knowledge and me taking this world for what I saw resulted in my own limited understanding. But, if no one ever taught me otherwise, how would I know? I could easily say shame on Lily, she did know, and never told me. But, it wasn't fair to heap all responsibility on her to teach me everything there was to know. I only saw her twice a cycle, that wasn't a lot of time to educate me on every aspect of Alternis. Maybe that blame should be on Neila, for never letting me leave to go learn in TerraIgni. But, there again, it was hard to place the blame on Neila, she probably didn't know how much there was to learn. The blame was on circumstance, and all of the decisions that had been made by generations before us.

"Space is vast," Lily said, breaking me out of my thought storm. "When there is no light from the sun in the sky, we can see past our own world to the space beyond."

Brokk stared up at the blue sky, marveling at what he couldn't yet see beyond it. "Could someone reach what is up there? Is there some other place where someone might land if they were flung out into this "space?" Like a piece of earth there?"

Lily shook her head. "Humans have done it, with a lot of technology and engineering, but even with those technological advances it isn't easy to reach those vast distances."

I suddenly understood why he was asking. "You're worried that your maeder could be somewhere up there."

He nodded. "I wanted to be sure she didn't get catapulted out of this world only to land on something else, then be able to somehow make her way back here. She's cunning and also weirdly lucky, if that could happen to anyone, it would be her."

Based on the confused glances from everyone in Lily's group, I gathered she and the others didn't know the truth regarding Brokk. All she had heard in this moment was that Brokk was worried his maeder was alive, most would want the opposite to be true. "Brokk is Empress Celestine's filio. It, uh, complicated things, but rest assured he is on our side." I gave him an apologetic look. I figured it was best to let her know that important piece of information before we went further, though I knew it would not be comfortable for him. His face stilled, perhaps waiting to see how Lily reacted to the news, but subtly shrugged toward me in silent agreement.

"Aside from how far away things actually are up in space," Lily said smoothly, not addressing the massive beast of information I had blurted out, "there's no air up there. Anyone would die as soon as they were out of our atmosphere."

I blew out a relieved breath, both at the way she handled the news *and* how she confirmed Celestine must be dead. Perhaps that was her way of moving toward acceptance with Brokk, of not being overly judgmental of Brokk's true lineage.

"I did have bigger things to talk to all of you about that pertain to the mist, or lack thereof," Lily continued. "The Faeries delivered word that when the mist fell, they sensed something far off to the northeast. The landmass I mentioned. The Faeries sensed activity there, but it's too far for them to travel."

Emblyn looked at me, Brokk, Trachen, and Tyrus, then turned back to Lily. "So, what does that mean for us?"

Queen Deniza stepped forward, addressing Emblyn. "My filia, I think it is time for you to take up the mantle, and perform your first mission for TerraIgni. Your Queen commands it. We want you to go and investigate it. Then return to TerraIgni to report back to us."

"And I want you to join her, Sereia," Lily added.

I looked back and forth between them. "To the northeast?" I didn't even know what that might entail, but I knew that if Emblyn was going, there was no way I'd let her go alone.

Kerenza cleared her throat. "It would mean so much to us if you would go with her. You and Emblyn have formed a special friendship. Lily and I started our sisterhood this way, with an adventure, and we watched out for each other."

It wasn't even a question in my mind. "Of course I will go!"

Queen Deniza nodded with a serene smile. "I am glad. Kerenza, Lily, Zia, Rachael, Maureen, and I must return to TerraIgni. Lily is not able to make this journey to see what is at the northeast border, and the rest of us are sworn to guide her back home right away. You will be on your own from here on out. However, we have supplies we can send you with."

"Since I'll be leaving from here, can someone send a Faerie to Neila and tell her I'm not dead?" I asked. "The last time she saw me I was on my way to the Fading, I want to reassure her before I disappear to the edge of the world."

Lily smiled and nodded, then turned away from the group and opened her mouth. I couldn't hear anything, but I could feel a pulse emanate from her, a rhythmic blast to went off into the trees. It wasn't long until Livi arrived, greeting Lily first, then they ran across my cheeks to say hello. I laughed as their feet left dustings of glittery prints on me. My smile faded as their tinkling sound echoed in my ear, delivering messages.

Emblyn noticed my expression. "What's happened?"

I put my hand to my mouth, unsure of how to explain what Livi told me. Livi had been trying to deliver the message earlier, before we had arrived at the Maeder Tree, but I had been unconscious. "It's Prant," I whispered. "The Syrenni male I was involved with a long time ago. Celestine killed him. Before he died, Livi found him. He told Livi to tell me that he was okay, no matter what happened to him, and that it wasn't my fault. That he was honored to have been with me, and that the Syrenni had been blessed to have me as part of their community. He said no matter what the empress said or did, the Syrenni were on my side. He said the Syrenni held strong and didn't sell me out. Even when she offered a false promise of protection, no one told her anything." I gulped, fighting the tears. I had assumed they would tell Celestine if they knew something, I wouldn't have blamed them if they did. But hearing that they didn't, that they stood their ground even when showed how ruthless she was, it bolstered my faith in them.

Emblyn looked like she might cry as well, she nodded and

placed her hand on her heart, clearly touched by the sentiment.

The sound of tiny bells rang in my ear again as Livi delivered more messages. I smiled this time. "Livi says they were sending messages back and forth as we traveled here, letting Neila know the updates. Neila knows I made it through and told Livi to spread blessings to all of you for racing me through the Praegra Forest to get me to The Well. She's proud of us all, and thankful we have each other."

Emblyn reached out and slung her arm around my shoulders. "I couldn't agree more."

Lily smiled and nodded. "And now that Emblyn and Sereia will go to the north, it's time for you two to decide what happens next for you both," she said to Tyrus and Trachen. "You will both be welcomed back to Adrilan, as far as I know, if you would like to return now."

"Well I am not going back! You heard Livi, we all have *each other*." Trachen declared. "I will go wherever Emblyn goes. I will go to help protect her, and Sereia."

"And I will go as well!" Tyrus added. "I will pledge to help however I can. I would not want Sereia to make this journey without my protection."

I smiled and reached over to give Tyrus's hand a quick squeeze. I wasn't surprised at this point, he had more than proven that he would continually show up.

There was a short pause, before Brokk spoke up. "I know that my company might be ... problematic," Brokk said, "but I want to go with you, to earn your trust and help how I can." He said it not only to me, but to Emblyn as well.

I appreciated that he wanted to earn Emblyn's trust, I tried to not let it show, but it softened my heart toward him. I yearned to reach forward and wrap my arms around him. Things weren't easy, in fact they were pretty damn confusing, but I knew I couldn't deny my heart even if he had momentarily shaken my faith. I loved him, there was no simpler truth than that, and this convoluted world wasn't going to diminish that.

"You don't think I'd let you get away with not joining us, do you?" Emblyn gave him a hard glare, but then smiled at him, pushing his shoulder lightly in a playful gesture as she nodded in agreement. He laughed finally, giving in at last to her infectious ways. Emblyn turned to me, reaching forward to clasp my hands. "We have a new path to clear, isn't that right, Sereia?"

I beamed at her. "Absolutely. Clear the path, Emblyn!"

Her huge, radiant smile spread across her face. "Clear the path, Sereia."

THE END

ACKNOWLEDGMENTS

I have a lot of thanks to give, as always, as this book was years in the making, not to mention the longest one I've written (so far!) Naturally, that means there are a lot of people that helped me or inspired me along the way. First off, I must acknowledge you, the reader. Song of Blood and Mist is a spin off book, and that means it couldn't have happened without support of the Vale Born series. Whether you read the whole series (yet!) or not, you're reading the acknowledgments now, which means you invested your time to read this book, and that is hugely appreciated. Without you, these books couldn't happen.

To my husband Kirt, and our three kids, you all mean the world to me. Thanks for being my family and for being the light of my life. I love you all with my whole heart!

To Laura, very few people can have a best friend that they can not only rely on, but also write with. In truth, it's only a fraction of our friendship, but one I really appreciate. There's no one like you in the whole wide world! You're the absolute best!

Fatebound Books, thank you for the support in getting this book out into the world!

To That Bitch Robyn, Whaben the Bobbin, the OG sister of my heart. I love you.

To all of my friends, Meg, Jackie, Alison, Nikie, Nina, Liza, Chris, Darian, Patrick, Jeff, Dev, and so many more supportive friends, I am so thankful for all of you. I appreciate each of you!

To my aunt, Mitzi Zilka, who is a talented and accomplished writer. It has been incredible connecting on an author level, and I am so proud of the work that you've accomplished. And for anyone reading this acknowledgment, go read her historical fiction books!

To my beta team: You are all the absolute best!! Thank you all for your feedback and excitement, it's so wonderful having your support and hearing all of your comments!

Raina Sveinson, you had such helpful feedback and I loved hearing your reactions to different parts of the book! As always your input and help were so valuable, and I truly appreciate your time and careful catches! The story is richer because of your input.

Natasha Pritchard, thank you for once again joining the beta team and proving how good you are as a beta reader. Hearing I got you on the edge of your seat was so fun! And I always appreciate how you can comment on what might need more depth, what areas of the story left you wanting more. The book is that much better thanks to your comments.

Brandy Rogers, thanks for providing your feedback, I loved hearing how you loved Tyrus as well, he is clearly shaping up to be a favorite. Your comments helped him grow a little more, and we'll definitely be seeing more of that with the next book as well!

Kyla Streeter, your careful and considerate feedback was instrumental in developing a few things further, thank you for taking the time to give such a great perspective. It's a testament to the beta process, several things were improved because of you!

Nichole Lattimer, Valerie Smith, and Shannon Hahn, thank you for joining the beta team and for lending your support!

TO MY BOOKTOK BESTIES: Who knows what's in store for us for 2025, but I'm so glad to have connected with you all. What an incredible community, and I'm so grateful to be a part of it. You all lift each other up, send the alert when there's something to watch out for, start engaging and thoughtful discourse, and have the best book recs ANYWHERE.

To all my industry friends, whether we worked together at Nickelode-
on, Dreamworks, or at FuseFX, I miss you all so much. We'll all live
to die another day soon and trauma bond on the next big production
intent on killing us. (But we live through it because we're damn scrappy
artists.) Side note: these studios are amazing to work at, and I loved my
time working on the many productions we pushed out into the world.

I am NOT ACKNOWLEDGING the evil overlords who started this
whole downturn in the entertainment industry because of their greed,
who decided to starve out the writers, actors, and artists of the industry.
But, you have done this to writers, who will no doubt eviscerate you in
fiction.

To my fellow Animation Guild members, and our guild leaders, keep
up the good fight!

Thank you to all of my family, by blood and by marriage, thank you for
all of your support! Most of all to my parents, Jay and Carla. Also to my
family: please tell me you did not just read this Why-Choose romance
that came out of my brain …

ABOUT THE AUTHOR

Raised in a rural town called Elfin Forest, magic and inspiration surrounded Lorin throughout her childhood. Fantastical stories permeated her life, and eventually she started writing her own. An award-winning fantasy and science fiction author, Lorin loves weaving epic tales that retain human-relatable experiences with a kernel of truth. She believes the vastness of the human spirit can be explored through fiction, and through character-driven fantasy we can discover more about ourselves. Lorin can always be found with a book nearby, absorbing stories or crafting her own. She lives in Southern California with her husband and three kids, loves the outdoors, and is always doing something creative.

Thank you for reading! If you enjoyed this book I'd be very grateful if you posted a short review. Your support really makes a difference, leaving a review is one of the most impactful things you can do for an author. Thank you for your support!

Get updates on release information, exclusive giveaways, and insider info by signing up for my newsletter at
www.lorinpetrazilka.com

Stay tuned for news on the next book in the series, as we join Sereia and the others on an adventure where their story will reach exciting new heights.

Other Books by Lorin:
Vale Born
Plight of the Syrenni
Pull of the Vale
Yoke of the Vale
Vale Born: The Complete Series

Samhain Eve Masquerade

The Zenith Decoy
co-written by Lorin Petrazilka and Laura L. Hohman
Not So Silent Nights: A Collection of 3 Holiday Novellas
co-written by Lorin Petrazilka and Laura. L. Hohman